PRAISE FOR

THE OTHER SIDE OF EVERYTHING

"Owens sets up a wicked premise—someone is murdering elderly women in a Florida town—then transcends the serial-killer genre, digging deep into the lives of the victims' neighbors: a widower, a painter, and a teenager, all broken in some way. The result is a compelling tale of survival and hope."

—*People*

"Intriguing and expertly paced, *The Other Side of Everything* is a tantalizing literary thriller you'll want to finish in one sitting."

—*Bustle*

"[A] tense, rich debut. . . . Owens impressively captures the emotional landscape of three generations and the varying compromises required of women in each. Fans of crime fiction wanting literary flair and emotional depth will gladly follow this trio of complicated characters."

—*Publishers Weekly* (starred review)

"A literary thriller with everything book groups are looking for: fine writing, a flawlessly constructed story, and relatable characters providing plenty of questionable decisions rife for discussion."

—*Booklist* (starred review)

"A slow-burning thriller that explores the cost of love turned askew."

—*Kirkus Reviews*

"Each character's reaction to the murders, as well as how the invasion of violence galvanizes the neighborhood, creates a solid plot. Each realizes a strength, as well as a vulnerability, they didn't know they had. Owens delivers a quiet mystery in *The Other Side of Everything* that expertly uncovers the emotional depth of each character . . . A terrific debut."

—*Sun-Sentinel*

"Lauren Doyle Owens . . . is someone to watch. Her stunning literary murder mystery debut is at once a nail-biter and a brilliantly nuanced evocation of how communities work and don't work. . . . Ms. Owens builds a vibrantly realized world spreading across three generations. She traces the ebbs and flows of individual and collective destinies, her narrative charged by a lyricism that is constantly evocative and revealing. A large cast of well-drawn supporting characters reinforces the themes of connectedness and renewal. This is a remarkable debut by a distinctive talent of great promise."

—*Florida Weekly*

"Someone is killing the widows in Seven Springs, Florida. And there are plenty of suspects. *The Other Side of Everything* is a dazzling, and often unsettling, debut novel full of honesty, charm, and insight, and it is much more than a murder mystery. It will remind you of just why you started reading stories in the first place—to be transported to a world more vivid and compelling than the one you're living in. Lauren Doyle Owens has an expansive heart, a keen eye, and a lyrical voice. This story of loneliness, loss, compassion, and renewal will carry you away."

—John Dufresne, author of
I Don't Like Where This Is Going

"Lauren Doyle Owens's illuminating novel shows us the power of community to both bind and separate. Its multigenerational characters shift between internal demons and a real-world killer, looking for connection. The beauty of the story lies in its ability to find hope in tragedy. A wonderful read!"

—Janis Cooke Newman, author of
A Master Plan for Rescue

"*The Other Side of Everything* is a riveting murder mystery that also, amid all the fabulous mayhem, offers a tender, empathetic exploration of what it's like to stand at life's two great precipices: adolescence and old age. You won't be able to put it down, and after you turn the last page you won't forget its characters, young and old, who struggle to find the seeds of renewal in the shadow of tragedy. This is a fantastic debut."

—Heather Young, author of *The Lost Girls*

THE OTHER SIDE OF SIDE OF EVERYTHING

A NOVEL

LAUREN DOYLE OWENS

TOUCHSTONE

NEW YORK   LONDON   TORONTO   SYDNEY   NEW DELHI

Touchstone
An Imprint of Simon & Schuster, Inc.
1230 Avenue of the Americas
New York, NY 10020

First Touchstone trade paperback edition October 2018

For information about special discounts for bulk purchases,
please contact Simon & Schuster Special Sales at 1-866-506-1949 or
business@simonandschuster.com.

The Simon & Schuster Speakers Bureau can bring authors to your live event.
For more information or to book an event, contact the Simon & Schuster Speakers Bureau
at 1-866-248-3049 or visit our website at www.simonspeakers.com.

Interior design by Michelle Marchese

Manufactured in the United States of America

1 3 5 7 9 10 8 6 4 2

Library of Congress Cataloging-in-Publication Data
Names: Owens, Lauren Doyle, 1978– author.
Title: The other side of everything : a novel / Lauren Doyle Owens.
Description: First Touchstone hardcover edition. | New York : Touchstone, 2018.
Identifiers: LCCN 2017024766 | ISBN 9781501167799 (hardcover)
Subjects: LCSH: Interpersonal relations—Fiction. | Serial murderers—Fiction. | BISAC:
FICTION / Suspense. | FICTION / Literary. | GSAFD: Suspense fiction. | Mystery fiction.
Classification: LCC PS3616.W4694 O84 2018 | DDC 813/.6—dc23
LC record available at https://lccn.loc.gov/2017024766

ISBN 978-1-5011-6779-9
ISBN 978-1-5011-6780-5 (pbk)
ISBN 978-1-5011-6781-2 (ebook)

For Chris

There is a crack in everything, that's how the light gets in.

LEONARD COHEN, "ANTHEM"

THE OTHER SIDE OF EVERYTHING

ADEL

HER SHOES HAD COME OFF DURING the struggle. One lay next to her head, near its crown, where her hair had become matted with blood the color and texture of crushed cherries. The other was gone. A clock ticked out the time in rhythmic staccatos, filling the house with bored urgency. In the kitchen, an egg timer went off, calling for her with its certain and persistent buzz.

She was not a young woman. The skin on her face was loose, the folds around her eye deep. Her eye itself was brown and open and staring, it seemed, at the hemline of her living room curtains. The other eye had taken the blow that killed her, and was no longer intact. Its vitreous humor oozed onto the floor, pooling with blood and broken tissue; the eye itself—the yellowed sclera, detached retina, puffy iris, and perfect lens—was now lodged in the cavity behind her nose.

The house was not particularly bright. The curtains were drawn and the furniture dark, the appliances brown. Pictures in equally dark frames lined the walls and covered tabletops and shelves. Her favorite, the one from her wedding, had overturned during the struggle and fallen to the floor. So her husband, handsome in his military blues, had not seen her get struck with the heavy cast iron kettle he'd given her for their sixth wedding anniversary. But the others could see her just fine. Her sisters and brothers, children and grandchildren, parents and friends, could all see her now—her mouth agape, her blood staining the cold terrazzo floor.

An hour after the egg timer began to buzz, the oven started to smoke. Smoke streamed from the oven and drifted from room to room, touring the three-bedroom ranch the way a guest might. The smoke found the house's corners, its closets, its secret places, but did not trigger any of its five smoke detectors, which watched the smoke without warning of its arrival. When the house was nearly black with it, smoke exited slowly through the cracked mechanics of the house's old, jalousie-style windows. It poured from the house in thin, steady streams, appearing to lift it from its foundation, as if on strings.

Then, it began to rain.

The rain was soft at first—tapping politely on the flat white roofs; dribbling down blades of grass; collecting in droplets on large, saucer-like leaves. Then, the rain began to drive, battering the large, bushy fronds of cabbage palms, disturbing delicate bougainvillea blossoms, and hammering the ground, causing mud to rise among perfect blades of St. Augustine grass, creating puddles where the driveways met the streets of Seven Springs, Florida. A ribbon of lightning split the sky, its thunderous sound causing the geckos, anoles, and skinks, which had been jumping to and fro in the soft rain, to scurry beneath shrubbery, into drain spouts, under doorways, and into houses.

The rain grew harder, denser, louder. It pounded against windows, drummed against streets, flooded garages. Curtains of it rained down on the golf courses, swimming pools, and highways in and around Seven Springs, causing whiteout conditions and minor traffic accidents. Another thread of lightning shocked the dark gray sky, causing a boom so loud it rattled the windows of houses and tripped the alarm sensors on a half dozen parked cars. Still, smoke poured through the broken seals of the little yellow house where the old woman had lived and died, darker now.

Several blocks away, a man stood in his backyard with a shovel, sweating, though the rain had made it cool. He began to dig a hole.

AMY

FROM THE HEIGHT AND DISTANCE OF the highway overpass, Amy saw the smoke as a trick of the eye—a string of thermals reaching down to lick the rooftops, a brushfire that appeared closer than it was. That it was something else entirely occurred to her only as she exited the highway and drove north. The closer she got to home, the larger the plume appeared—dark and thick and dangerous-looking. She kept expecting to turn and realize it was down some other street, that it had arranged itself over some other house. But she made a left, and it was closer. A right, and it was closer still. Amy felt her arms and legs grow heavy. She made her final right and drove toward it.

At the lip of her driveway, Amy stopped and watched the smoke rise steadily over her house. "Fuck," she said and threw her car into park. Amy ran toward the house, thinking of her cat, who would have burrowed deep into the bedcovers, and of her husband, who would blame her no matter what. She touched the doorknob cautiously, afraid that it would be hot. When it wasn't, Amy swung open the door, prepared for a shock. But the house was just as she'd left it—breakfast dishes in the sink, a basket of laundry by the door. No smoke.

"I'm going crazy," she whispered, and believed it until she walked through the house and out the back door. There, she saw it—smoke, gray as lead—coming from every hole and seam and crack of her neighbor's tiny, perfect, yellow house. Briefly, Amy was dazzled by it—the dreamscape of color, the weightlessness of smoke. She imagined the plume as a hot air balloon that would carry the house away, and nearly closed her eyes to wish that it—that something extraordinary—would happen. Then there were sirens, deep and mournful. She let out a breath.

Back inside, Amy thought briefly about getting her camera or sketchpad to capture the scene—some version of her would have. But this version, the woman who lived alone on SW Eighth, opened a screw-top bottle of wine and carried a cigarette outside. There, she took in details of the evening calamity: the dark gray of smoke against the deeply bruised purple horizon, the deep-orange blossoms of her royal poinciana standing in for flames. Amy thought of the difference between the true gray of smoke verses the blue-gray of the evening sky. Then of the woman who lived there, whose hair was gray and skin sometimes too.

She had once given Amy an armload of mangoes from her tree, and Amy had eaten them all in a single sitting, unable to stop after one. She'd stood at the kitchen sink and eaten one mango after another, letting the juice run over her hands and face, the front of her T-shirt, the kitchen floor. By the time Pete arrived home, she was sick from sugar and covered in sticky pink syrup. He stood in the doorway staring at her, his white oxford and loosened tie in stark contrast to her concert T-shirt made sticky by the binge.

"What the hell did you do?" he asked.

"I . . . mangoes," she said finally, not sure what else to say.

"Jesus, Amy," he said, downshifting into exasperation. "Clean it up."

Just thinking of it, Amy could feel the heady ringing of sugar against her cheeks, the sting of her husband in the afternoons. She swished the last of her wine around in her mouth and went inside to make a sandwich.

AMY USUALLY LIKED how quiet the house was in the evenings, she and Pete having settled things more or less for good, but tonight it would have been nice to talk to somebody—to share the experience of driving home and seeing the plume; the relief of seeing her house perfectly intact. She thought about walking around the corner to see what had happened, and talk to some neighbors, but she didn't want to be one of those people who gawked at tragedy. So she continued with her nightly ritual, washing that day's dishes, folding yesterday's laundry, and taking a shower.

She had gotten a tattoo recently, a quarter-size phoenix on the inside of her wrist, and she took care with it in the shower, careful not to break the scab that had formed along the edge of the wing. Out of the shower, she covered it with ointment, as she had been instructed, and rubbed cocoa butter over the thin smile of her hysterectomy scar and the zigzagging train tracks that ran across her chest, a result of the double mastectomy she'd had two years before. She covered her face with the expensive night cream her sister had sent her for her birthday, and pulled on the robe Pete had given her before she went into the hospital that first time. It was red and silk and long. "Like something a woman in a soap opera might wear," she had said when he'd given it to her. And, when she saw that her reaction hurt him, "I mean, I love it."

Amy was just about to make a pot of tea when someone knocked on her door, a rare occurrence if there ever was one. She thought of her neighbor, gray-on-gray, and tightened the sash of her robe.

On her stoop stood the man she and Pete had always referred to as Angry Dad. She was pretty sure she had never spoken to him, but had once seen him tear down his mailbox with a baseball bat, and often heard him ripping around the neighborhood on his Harley, after, she always assumed, a bitter argument with his wife.

"The old lady that lives behind you was murdered today," he said. "I just thought you should know." The words came easily, as if he had rehearsed them, or perhaps repeated them over and over as he walked down the street, knocking on doors. He said that I-just-thought-you-should-know but stood there, a beer in his hand, staring at her.

Amy thought of the fire—the smoke. "Are you sure?"

"Buddy'a mine's a cop. Said he saw the body. Someone beat her up pretty bad, is what he said."

"Who?"

"That'd be nice to know, wouldn't it?" He smiled at her and Amy took an involuntary step back.

"OK. Well. Thanks." She started to shake, and put a hand on the door to steady herself.

"You OK here? Your husband been out of town or something?"

"No. He's here."

"OK, you have a good night. Be sure to lock up."

Amy was shaking as she walked through the small, ranch-style house, turning on lights. In each room she checked the windows, which did not lock but shut with a crank. She tightened the crank on each, doing what she could. Back in the kitchen, she stood on a stool to reach above the refrigerator for the bottle of brandy she sometimes sipped from. Once she had poured a drink, Amy lit a cigarette and watched the light fade from the picture windows.

AN HOUR LATER she could hear the phone ringing in the other room but was too drunk to answer, so she let the machine do it. It was her father, who frequently read the *Miami Herald* online, wanting to know what life was like for his daughter here, in the dense suburban sprawl between Miami and Fort Lauderdale. "Call me back and let me know you're OK," he said, short and sweet and typical of him. Ten minutes later her sister called: "Amy—Dad's worried. Come on, pick up." Sometime after that—Amy couldn't be sure when, but it was fully dark—Pete called.

"Hey," he said, "my mom called me. She wanted to call you, but . . . she doesn't know how to deal with you. I don't mean that in a bad way, I just . . . Let me know you're OK, all right? Call whenever."

Amy knew that she should call someone, but she realized that, at this point, she'd likely slur her words and cry into the phone. Instead, she made a cup of tea and carried her laptop to bed.

She turned on the television to put some noise in the room, and navigated to the adoption website, to look at the kids.

There were 105 tonight, more than there were the last time she'd checked. Each had a photo listed alongside his or her height, weight, ethnic background, and eye color. There were more teens than toddlers, and of the toddlers listed, most had a developmental disability, or an older sibling, some impediment to an easy, happy ending. Still, Amy found comfort in their presence, in the hope that they held. She liked to imagine that, when she was ready, she would place a phone call or click a link and little José or Janie would be hers.

She hovered over the photo of a three-year-old girl, and lingered for a bit, noting the girl's tired eyes and crooked smile. Amy imagined making breakfast for her, and making up songs about tying shoes, teaching her how to paint, and walking her to school. She imagined a life in an instant, and, just as fast, it was gone.

The phone rang again, and Amy clapped the laptop closed, embarrassed.

It was Pete. He hardly called at all, much less twice in the same night.

She took a breath, answered.

"Hey," he said, and she felt her eyes well with tears.

"Hi," she said, almost inaudibly, afraid her voice might crack.

"Are you OK?"

"Yes."

"Do you know what happened?"

"No more than you do."

"Are you scared?"

Amy waited a beat before answering. "Yes."

"I'm sorry I'm not there."

"No you're not."

"I mean . . . I'm sorry that this happened and that you're there by yourself."

"I'm sorry that this happened," she repeated. "I'll put it on your tombstone."

"Oh, Amy . . ." he said, exasperated.

"How's San Juan?" she asked.

"It's great, actually. The work is going well."

"I'm happy for you."

"No you're not."

"OK then, Pete." Amy sighed. "Thanks for calling."

"Make sure you lock the doors," he said.

"The doors are locked."

"And Prissy Girl?"

"Your cat is fine."

"Call me tomorrow, OK? Or . . . call my mom tomorrow."

"I don't want to talk to your mom, Pete."

"Fine. Well . . . I'm glad you're OK."

"I'm glad I am too," she said, and hung up.

Agitated, Amy went into the kitchen to pour a glass of water and swallow a preventative ibuprofen. She walked through the house and turned off the lights, stopping at the back door to look out at the old woman's house. It was too dark to see anything, so she tightened the sash on her robe, went outside, and walked barefoot through the grass to where her yard met her neighbor's.

There was hardly any sign of damage—just a small black hole in the back, near the kitchen window. It looked like a cigarette burn. It reminded Amy of a ruined garment—a small thing, a disappointment. She thought about what had happened inside that house not twenty-four hours before; the sheer and sudden violence of it. Amy watched a pair of gauzy clouds pass over the moon, amazed by how cruel the world could be, going on as it did.

BERNARD

BERNARD STARTED TO SMELL SMOKE JUST as the five o'clock news was coming on. He went into the kitchen to check his coffeepot and toaster. When he found them unplugged, he assumed that lightning from the storm had ignited some brush in the Everglades. He sat back down in front of the television, returning his attention to the news of the day.

The storm had delivered four inches of rain in an hour, the weatherman said, and Bernard whistled, remarking to no one. Then there was something about a police shooting in Miami, something about a hit-and-run. It was the same stories every day. They were tragic, but boring. Fifteen minutes into the news, Bernard sighed, turned down the volume, and leaned his head back, allowing himself to doze.

An hour later, he woke with a start. The smell of smoke was so strong that he was sure his house was on fire. He checked each room and went outside. When he saw the smoke rising over Adel's house, he ran back in, called 9-1-1, and hurried over to her house.

Bernard tried to get inside, but the doors were locked.

"Adel!" he called, banging on the doors. "Adel!"

He lifted a large piece of coral from her garden and threw it through a window, but the pane was too narrow to fit him and the smoke too strong, besides. Nothing else he could do, Bernard paced the street in front of her house, certain that she was dead as the result of his complacency.

It felt like an achingly long time, but it was only a few minutes before the fire department's hook and ladder truck came roaring down the street, the police and paramedics in quick succession. A group of firefighters broke through the front door and quickly put out what had, it seemed, only been a small fire.

Bernard watched as the paramedics and police rushed in, waiting helplessly in the street, his arms folded across his chest. Neighbors gathered alongside him, also waiting. But the paramedics and police did not rush out. They did not lead Adel outside to cough the smoke from her lungs. They did not give the all clear. Instead, they carried equipment inside—cameras and plastic cases of God knows what—and soon, they carried Adel out too, a slight lump under a white sheet.

By then, a good crowd of neighbors had gathered in the street, coming out of their cars and houses to gawk and gasp and gossip with one another, trading stories about what they had seen and heard. When the police carried Adel outside, someone said, "She's been there forever." Another said, "Not anymore."

Then a policeman approached the crowd and motioned for Bernard to join him. Bernard followed the policeman until they were some distance away from the crowd.

"Do you know if your neighbor had any enemies?" he asked.

"Enemies?" Bernard asked, nonplussed.

"Anyone who might want her dead?"

"No, God no. Who would want to kill a—?"

"What about medications? Do you know if she was taking anything someone might want to get their hands on?"

"I suppose we all are . . ."

"Just to be clear, you didn't hear or see anything suspicious this afternoon?"

"No."

"What about recently? Anyone walking around the neighborhood that you don't recognize?"

"I don't recognize most of these people," he said, gesturing to the crowd that had gathered in the street. "They're all strangers to me."

◆　　◆　　◆

AFTER BEING QUESTIONED by the police, Bernard went home and vomited into the toilet. He rinsed his mouth, washed his face, and sat on the edge of the bathtub, not sure what to do. Ordinarily, he'd be asleep already. He'd have eaten dinner, watched his television programs, and turned in, exhausted from nothing in particular. But he was too agitated for sleep. His mind would not go quiet; his hands would not stop shaking. He twisted his beard between his fingers, and smoothed his hands down his pant legs, comforted by his own touch. Finally, he pressed his fingers into his eye sockets and cried.

When his sobs receded, and his breath returned to normal, he heard his wife's voice, strong and clear, as though she were in the room. "What are you crying for? She was *my* friend. You hated her."

"I didn't . . ." he started, and then raised his arms in a huff. It was just like Irene to goad him into an argument from the grave.

His nerves got the better of him once again, and he made his way back to the toilet.

AN HOUR LATER, and still unable to calm his nerves, Bernard rummaged through the freezer, looking for the Ziploc bag that contained the left-over marijuana Irene had smoked, illicitly, during her chemotherapy treatments. He remembered hiding the marijuana inside a box of Popsicles, but there were no Popsicles in his freezer, only a Costco-size bag of burritos and a couple of empty ice trays. Then he remembered: the marijuana wasn't in the freezer—it was in a box of stick margarine in the door of his refrigerator. His daughter had put it there after chiding him for hiding marijuana next to the one food item in the house that the kids might actually want. "Here, Dad," she'd said, holding up the box of stick margarine with an air of condescension, "*margarine.* Your drugs are in the margarine." Sure enough, he opened the refrigerator, found the box inside, and found the marijuana.

He put his nose in the bag and smelled it, but it smelled nothing like good marijuana should; this, if anything, smelled like something left too long in a plastic bag. Still, he pulled a plate from the cupboard and began to untangle a bud, separating the delicate threads from their stems. He sprinkled the weed into a V of delicate white paper, which had been stored alongside the marijuana, and rolled it tightly in place, licking the edge of the paper to seal the cigarette. He then found a book of matches inside an old German beer stein that sat, forever, on the counter. Feeling vaguely criminal, Bernard drew the draperies in the living room closed before easing into his Barcalounger and turning on the television. He struck a match to light the cigarette, pulling hard to encourage the flame, and smoked while the ten o'clock news colored the room blue and white and red.

WHEN HE WOKE, it wasn't quite dawn. Aside from the television, which went on and on in animated loop, the room was still. Bernard switched off the television and watched as it sucked the last bit of light out of the room. He sat for a moment in the dark stillness, wondering if this was what it was like to be dead.

He thought back to the evening newscast, which had offered nothing in the way of news, and then to what must have been Adel's last moments. When Irene died, her body more or less surrendered; she stopped pushing against the inevitable and allowed the cancer to take her. For Adel, of course, things had been different—someone had entered her home and, for whatever reason, beat the crap out of her. Bernard wondered which would be best—to die slowly and in agony, but to know at least that it's happening; or to be surprised by death, the way someone comes behind you and covers your eyes.

In the kitchen, Bernard brewed a pot of coffee and slipped the last two slices from a loaf of Wonder into the toaster. He prepared his coffee with a heaping spoonful of powdered creamer and carried his meal to the dining room table, which was set with a single place mat and a single cloth napkin, a holdover from his life with Irene, who liked things to be nice even when they weren't.

He listened, for the next few minutes, to the sound of his own chewing. It wasn't always this quiet. Sometimes, Irene or Vera, or both of them, joined him—their individual voices strong and clear in his head, as indelible as permanent marker. Sometimes, they each nagged him, Irene commenting on his diet, and Vera telling him that he really should sit up straight. Other times, they'd comment on the news of the day, or the weather, or on how drab things were looking around the house. Mostly, they just kept him company. But today they were silent. Irene, he suspected, would be with Adel—the two of them finally on the other side together, or wherever you go when you die. He didn't know where Vera was. Maybe he had been imagining her all along, and his imagination had simply run out.

When Bernard was finished eating, he slipped his arm into the electronic blood pressure monitor that sat, always, on the dining room table, and took his blood pressure. It was 130/90, lower than it had been in years.

"Well look at that," he said. "Must have been the marijuana."

Given the positive results, Bernard thought about using more, but he didn't want to be stoned, so he took his Sectral, Aldactone, and Lipitor as usual, taking a pill from each of the bottles that sat in a cluster at the center of the table, and swallowing them with the last of his coffee. He sat back in his chair and watched as the day's first light crept in through the space between his curtains. He thought: *Adel is dead*, and added her to his mental tally that separated the living from the dead. The list of dead had grown long these past few years, taking his wife and most of their friends. Taking even, and suddenly, one of their grandchildren, who went surfing the day before Hurricane Frances swept across the state, and drowned.

Bernard sighed, and stood with great effort. It was Wednesday. Errand day. His favorite day of the week.

WHEN IRENE GOT sick, his daughter taught him how to separate the darks from lights, how to operate the washer and dryer, how to iron a button-down shirt. But Bernard didn't have patience for any of it, so he took a load to the dry cleaners each week and had his clothes laundered. It was his favorite errand of the week. He loved the vaguely chemical scent, the efficiency of the turnstile, and the woman behind the counter, who always asked him how he was.

Today, though, she seemed to know.

"Mista," she said, "I saw you on da news."

"Oh," he said wearily, "my neighbor . . ."

"Poor *woman*! I called my son and told him to put extra lock on my door."

"That's a good idea."

"You should too!"

"I think I'm OK . . ."

"They said on da news! Nobody safe. They said extra vi-gil-ance," she said carefully, sounding out the word.

He agreed for the sake of agreeing and took his clothes, which were neatly folded and wrapped in paper, just as they were every week. Then, he drove across the plaza to the supermarket.

Bernard moved slowly down the aisles, alarmed, as always, by the prices. It was four dollars for a gallon of milk, three for a dozen eggs. In the frozen aisle, he loaded up on the burritos he liked to eat for dinner and the ice cream sandwiches he ate in the afternoon after his nap. While there, he picked up a square container of rainbow sherbet, because he had craved some the night before, and a bag of fish sticks, because they were on sale. He was rounding the corner from Frozen Foods into Paper Goods, muttering, "Toilet paper, paper towels, toilet paper, paper towels, toilet paper—" when he ran into an old friend.

"Well if it isn't!" Danny said, smiling broadly and extending his hand. "My old friend!" He took Bernard's hand and pumped it vigorously.

"Well hiya, Danny," Bernard said, knowing him almost immediately.

"Terrible thing, isn't it? Terrible thing."

Bernard agreed that it was.

"Who do you think did it? Anyone we know?"

"Anyone *we* know? Of course not."

"I think it was one of those drug addicts, myself. Got so caught up with killing her that he forgot to steal anything."

"Could be," Bernard said.

"So where've you been? I thought you might've died!"

Bernard wanted to say that he might as well have died—he hardly left the house anymore but for his weekly errands—but he didn't want to be morose. Instead, he said: "Down the road, same as always. Just forget to leave the house sometimes. You know how it is."

"I do! But these are the best years, aren't they? This is what we did all that other stuff for."

Bernard was taken aback. These were hardly the best years. They were more like purgatory.

"Think about it," Danny continued, a finger in the air, "our *wives* are gone, we can do whatever we want, with *whom*ever we want. We can have whiskey sours for breakfast! We can look at Internet porn! *In–ter–net* porn!"

"I don't have the—"

"Listen, what are you doing later?"

"Later?" He thought for a second—what *was* he doing later? "Nothing," he said finally.

"Then come by for a drink! It'll be like old times."

BERNARD DID NOT think it would be like old times. But that didn't stop him from leaving his house promptly at 2:55 and walking the side streets down to Danny's, crossing the street every now and again to stay in the shade. It was May in Florida and hot as Hades. As he walked, Bernard sweat through his shirt. He was forty pounds overweight and held it all in his stomach. He had the frame, his son John had told him recently, of a woman pregnant with triplets. "A *tall* woman pregnant with triplets," Bernard had said, "an Amazonian."

"Sure, Dad," John had said, "whatever you say."

God, how his kids could condescend.

Halfway to Danny's, Bernard stopped and looked around. He hadn't forgotten the way, but the neighborhood seemed so different, changed as much by time as he was, that he questioned himself for a second. Danny's was just a few blocks from here, wasn't it? He looked up at the houses and tried to remember which house had belonged to whom, but so many of them were unrecognizable. The lawns were overgrown, the houses badly in need of paint and repair—symptoms, Bernard thought, of the foreclosure crisis, now in its second year. On one house, a vine had forced its way into a window and overtaken it, weaving a tapestry between the jalousie panes. In front of another, a mailbox had grown so heavy with bills and flyers and magazines that it had fallen forward, its contents spilling out onto the street. In another lifetime, these houses were vibrant, filled with a sort of 1960s-era optimism. Now, it seemed, they hung heavy with regret. What was once pink was now beige. What was once manicured was now returning to the earth. The midday sun only exaggerated the blight, drawing attention to the neighborhood's failed promise, its absurdity.

And then there's Danny's, Bernard thought, coming upon the house as though from out of a dream. Here was a house that never changed. It was forever white with blue trim, painted every few years by one of Danny's sons who did that now for a living. A couple of palms stood in the front yard, neither stately nor uncomely.

"How you doing there, old friend," Danny said, opening his door before Bernard even reached it. "You OK?"

"Course I'm OK," Bernard said, irritated by the question. "You see the weather girl on Channel Two? She said we shouldn't even go out today."

"And yet here we are," Danny said, putting a hand on Bernard's back and leading him in.

Once inside, Bernard frowned at Danny. "Don't you have air-conditioning?"

"I never turn it on. Waste of money! Besides, I love the heat. Makes you sweat! It's like exercise without the work." He opened his refrigerator. "What do you like to drink?"

Bernard couldn't remember the last time he'd even had a drink. Drinks seemed extravagant now, wasteful. And the way they made him feel—woozy and unattached—he felt now constantly. Still, he said: "Whatever you're having."

Within minutes, Bernard had a whiskey sour in his hand and Danny was ushering him out to the sunporch with the directive to "take a load off."

The drink was strong, but cold. Bernard, who figured he needed the ice more than the whiskey, held an ice cube in his mouth and sucked on it.

"So, who do you think did it? Anyone we know?"

"You asked me already. And no, no one we know," Bernard said.

"I think it was one of those drug addicts, myself."

"You mentioned that."

"Terrible thing, addiction," Danny said. "Makes ya nuts." He stuck a finger into his whiskey sour and sucked on it for a bit, quieting down.

Bernard looked around the sunporch, hunting for familiar objects. They used to play canasta out on the porch on hot summer nights in the days before air-conditioning. They would smoke cigarettes and laugh and drink. He could feel the ghosts of them all in that room, he could almost see them, almost hear their lighthearted chatter, almost smell the cigarettes and beer.

"Danny . . ." Bernard started. "What happened to us?"

"Same thing that happens to everyone," Danny said. "If you're *lucky*."

"If you're lucky," Bernard mused, shaking his head. "You sure do have a funny way of seeing things, Danny."

"What about you? What happened to you? You used to be the life of the party."

"*Me?* No . . ."

"There was a time, there was a time . . ." Danny mused.

"Do you think any of the others will be at the funeral?"

"I imagine so . . . Not anyone *you'd* care about, though. All the lookers are gone. Either dead or moved or both. Vera's dead, of course."

"I know," Bernard said. "I mean, obviously I know."

"Of course. I'm sorry."

THE FIRST TIME he saw her was at the counter of The Smiling Pig, a barbecue shack within walking distance of the neighborhood. Bernard often took the kids there for dinner on warm summer nights when Irene complained it was too hot to cook. Vera looked exceedingly out of place with her shock of red hair in a high French twist, gingham dress, and movie-star sunglasses. "You must be lost," Bernard quipped. "You need directions somewhere?"

"What makes you think I'm lost?" she said, her southern drawl thick as molasses.

"You're not from here, I can tell that much."

"*Nobody* is from here."

"True enough," he said, shrugging.

The kids were dancing around him—Pam, John, and little Daniel—asking for *pork 'n' beans, Daddy,* and *fries, Daddy,* and *Coke, Daddy,* and *Daddy can I have a sangwich?*

"*Sangwich?*" Vera said, looking down at Pam. "Do you mean sandwich?"

"No," Pam said, crossing her arms, emphatic and pouty.

"So, where you from?" Bernard asked.

"Atlanta." She sighed.

"I take it you miss it?"

"Not really."

"Can't say I blame you."

"Oh?"

"Well, it's hotter there in the summertime than it is here, I know that much."

"And where are you from?"

"Baltimore. Interstate went in right where our house used to be. Eminent domain. We took the money and ran."

"Oh." She yawned. "Does *everyone* here have a boring story about how they arrived?"

Bernard shrugged, smiled. "What's yours?"

"Let me tell you something about southern gentility, mister . . ."

"It's Bernard." He held out his hand to her but she did not take it.

She accepted the paper bag the woman behind the counter handed her and said, over her shoulder as she walked away, "We keep our stories to ourselves."

He thought about her the entire night, and then the night after that too—the smooth white of her neck, the way her dress moved as she walked.

On the third night, she was standing at his door.

"I'm sorry for the way I behaved the other night," she said. "I was exhausted."

"It's OK," he said, alarmed because Irene was in the other room and would want to know *who* this woman was and *what* other night she was referring to. "How did you know I lived here?" he asked, looking over his shoulder.

"I watched you walk home. I live just over there," she said, pointing to the house on the corner. "Just moved in."

"Oh," Bernard said, frowning. He wanted to charm her but didn't know how.

"Can you help me with something? My husband's out of town all week and that stupid air-conditioning box stopped working."

"Um, sure," Bernard, who made his living as an accountant, said. "I can *try.*"

They walked back to her house together, Bernard nervously stuffing his hands in his pockets, and Vera moving in that way of hers—slow and sure and swanlike.

"Feels great in here," he said, once they were in the house. "What did you say was wrong with the AC?"

"Shhhhh," she whispered. "The kids are asleep."

"Sorry," Bernard said, looking around. "Where's the, um—?"

"How about a drink?" she asked, gliding over to the kitchen, the skirt of her dress swinging.

"Sure."

"Gin and tonic?"

"OK."

Then, there was the sound of ice cubes cracking beneath the gin. And then she was in front of him again, and he noticed more of her— her lips, her eyes, the subtle flush of her cheeks. She looked like she had just heard a joke, or was about to tell one.

"Why don't we sit on the sunporch?" she said. "It's private."

"So, then, the AC?" Bernard asked, following her.

Vera turned to him, smiling. "Must've fixed itself."

Outside, there was a wicker sofa-and-chair set with thick outdoor cushions a color Irene might call Sun Kissed, or Burnt Orange. There were cardboard boxes pushed into corners, and a basket of unfolded laundry.

"We haven't finished unpacking yet," she said, settling on the sofa.

"Where's, um, where's your husband?" Bernard asked, sitting tentatively in the chair.

"He works the night shift at the hospital."

"Oh," Bernard said, "which, um . . ."—he cleared his throat—"which hospital?"

She shrugged. "Does it matter?"

"No," he said, taking a nervous sip, "not to me."

There was a silence, an unbearable gulf Bernard wished he could jump over, or sink into.

When she finished her drink, Vera put her glass down and looked at him. "Why don't you come over here?"

He frowned at her. "I should really . . . I should go."

"You should *stay*," she said, and sat up just enough to tug at his wrist. There was something in her touch that he was simply powerless over; she pulled at him and he came willingly, a loose thread from a sweater.

MADDIE

MADDIE WATCHED FROM BEHIND THE COUNTER as the first customers of the night walked in, took their seats, and looked at the menu. Last night it was cops, fat in their blue uniforms; tonight it was men in dress shirts and sport coats that didn't quite hide their shoulder holsters. Detectives, Maddie assumed. They were the next step in a process she didn't understand but would nonetheless watch, characters in a television drama that had come to her door.

She waited until one of them stuck a finger in the air and walked over to him.

"What can I get you?" she asked.

"Pulled pork. With coleslaw."

"Sandwich or platter?"

"Platter. No, sandwich. Make sure they put the coleslaw on the sandwich and not on the side."

"And for you?" she asked his partner.

"I'll have the same."

"And to drink?"

"Coffee," they said in unison.

Once the cops had their food, the regulars started filing in. The afternoon and early evening were always dominated by the geriatric crowd, who loved to tell her stories but hated to leave her tips. Then it was the single men from the trailer park across the street. Then it was

Charlie, the man who begged all day at the intersection of Highway 7 and Seminole Road, and spent his earnings on forty ounces of beer and a plate of brisket. If he had a good day, Charlie would be in before sunset. If not, he'd stand at the intersection until long after rush hour. Maddie would watch him as she worked, catching glimpses of him beyond the neon sign shaped to resemble the head of a smiling pig. Sometimes, it seemed that his bad days mirrored hers.

Tonight, he was in early.

"Hi, Charlie," she said, walking up to him, a slight bounce in her step.

"How's the brisket look today?"

"It looks really, um, *brown*," she said. Just the other day she had told him that she didn't know how it looked and he'd yelled at her. *Oh, come on, Maddie!* he'd said. *You've got to give me something!* So, she was giving him something.

He winked at her. "Just the way I like it! I'll have the brisket with a side of greens."

"And to drink?" she asked, out of habit.

"I'm set," he said, tapping on the paper-covered bottle between his legs.

"Lot'a cops today?" he asked her.

"Yeah."

"Everybody's talking about it, the murder."

"What're they saying?" she asked.

"Pointing fingers at each other, you know how it is."

She didn't know how it was, but she appreciated that Charlie thought she might.

"The desperate do desperate things," he said, looking down into his bottle. It was one of his favorite refrains.

"Well, I'm going to put in your order now."

"Go!" He raised his arm, excusing her.

There was a lull after the initial burst of tables, and Maddie was able to stand behind the counter and pull the paperback from her apron. She had to have the first ten chapters of *The Awakening* read by the next day. She was on chapter three, reading about Mrs. Pontellier's "habitual neglect of her children," when a man came in and sat at the counter.

"Hi," she said, holding the book by her side. "What can I get you?"

"I don't know," he said with a shrug. "What's good here?"

"Pretty much everything. Just steer clear of the frank 'n' beans. They suck."

"Maybe I like food that sucks."

Maddie shrugged. "Maybe you do."

"You serve beer here?"

"No. You can get some at the gas station across the street."

He looked at the menu. "I think I'll have the ribs," he said, not looking up.

"Half or full rack?"

"Half."

"Wet or dry?"

He looked at her a moment before answering. "Wet."

"You want anything with them?"

"Like what?"

"Greens, potato salad, coleslaw . . ."

"Potato salad."

"OK, coming right up," she sang.

She put in his order but did not return to her spot behind the counter, deciding instead to get a head start on her side-work for the evening, refilling the barbecue sauce and ketchup containers.

A couple came in and she waited on them. Then a family whose children engaged in a mini food fight—throwing French fries and crayons across the table and onto the floor. Then one of her neighbors came in. She wasn't sure if he would recognize her because she hadn't seen him in years, but he did.

"Little Maddie Lowe!" he exclaimed. "How about that!"

"Hi, Mr. White," she said, doing a slight dip with her head.

"Call me Bernard! Imagine you old enough to work here . . . Where has the time gone?"

"I don't know," she said sheepishly. "Can I, um, get you something?"

"I haven't been here in . . . probably twenty years."

"Food's all pretty much the same."

"How's the pulled pork today?"

"It's good."

"I'll have a platter with corn bread and greens and . . . Oh, just bring me a little of everything. I've had one hell of a day."

"I saw you on the news last night."

"You did? What channel?"

"I don't remember."

"Say, where's your mother been? I never see her anymore."

"Can I, um . . ." Maddie shook her head, looked down at her pad. The letters started to blur. "Do you want a Coke or something?"

He looked at her as though he was lost. Finally, he said, "I'm sorry. I forgot."

She shook her head.

"A Coke would be great."

Maddie brought Bernard a Coke and put his order in, her hands shaking the entire time. She had seen a therapist briefly after her mother left. He taught her how to calm her thoughts and slow her breathing; taught her how to, as her brother said, "get a fucking grip." She tried to hear her therapist's voice now, but all she heard was *I never see her anymore, I never see her anymore, I never see her anymore.*

The moment she could get away, she grabbed her backpack and disappeared into the bathroom. There, she held on to the ancient, iron, Pepto-pink sink, looking down at a rust stain to focus her thoughts. She pictured her mother driving out of Florida and into some unknown future. *I never see her anymore.* She pictured her mother waking up in a motel. *I never see her anymore.* She pictured her mother paddling a kayak over a steep waterfall. She squeezed her eyes shut to get rid of the image, and opened them when it was still there.

She dug into her backpack for the Swiss Army knife she carried alongside the first aid kit she'd taken from her father's hurricane supply shelf in the garage, and took her jeans down so that the tops of her thighs were exposed. Because her upper thighs were the only things she cut, Maddie's left thigh featured a three-inch line of scars and scabs, like notches carved into a doorframe. When she ran out of space in that row, she would start another one next to it, just as she had on her right thigh, the space on which was mostly used up now, mostly ruined with tough pink scar tissue arranged in neat, one-inch lines.

Maddie peeled the largest blade from the Swiss Army knife and cleaned it with an alcohol pad. She positioned the blade a centimeter or so below the most recent cut, bit her lower lip, and pressed the blade firmly into the tough flesh of her upper thigh. The skin broke and blood welled around the blade, fresh and red and beautiful. The blade was still wet with alcohol and the cut stung worse than usual, but she stayed with it, wadding tissue underneath the opening and pushing the blade in deeper when the pain started to wear. She wanted to cry out, but swallowed the urge and pushed the blade in even farther, bracing herself against the sink.

Soon, all she felt was the pain radiating from her thigh, up through her pelvis and down to her foot. It was amazing how one little gash could do so much to change her focus. At one moment, she was caught in the undertow of unbearable grief, the next, her leg throbbed so badly that none of it mattered.

When she was finished, Maddie cleaned the blade, returned it to her backpack, and walked back into the dining room just in time to bring Bernard his order.

TEN MINUTES BEFORE closing, Maddie switched off the neon signs and locked the door. She cleared the last few tables, wiped down the booths, and swept and mopped the floors. She counted her tip money and squared it with the earnings for the night, counting the cash and credit card receipts inside the register. She had made forty-five dollars, not bad for a Wednesday. She traded in her smaller bills for larger ones, and carried the drawer to the back, past the kitchen, where the staff was cleaning to the beat of a reggaeton song.

"We're all set," she said to her boss, poking her head into the doorway of the room that housed the smoker.

"How'd we do?" he asked, not looking up from the smoker.

"Pretty good for a Wednesday."

"Good girl."

"Can I hand this to you?"

"Yeah. Give me a sec."

She watched as he piled a few logs of mesquite into the oven and closed the firebox. He clapped his hands together and wiped them on the front of his pants; he was covered in soot, as he was most nights by this time.

"Lot'a cops out there tonight?"

"Some," she said.

"Heard anything?"

"No."

"My parents knew her, you know. They knew Adel."

"Oh," she said.

"Did you?"

"She lived near me."

"So you must be pretty scared."

"No."

He raised an eyebrow. "It'd help you to get a little scared sometimes. Can't be too careful."

"OK," Maddie said, agreeing for the sake of agreeing. She had had a similar conversation with her father that morning, and had promised him that she would ask for a ride home from work, rather than walking. But now, as she listened to the stilted sounds of reggaeton and the kitchen staff erupt in laughter over some unheard joke, she didn't want to have to be there any longer than necessary. She thought of her father, miles away on a tarmac at the international airport, his face in a turbine, and decided that what he didn't know wouldn't hurt him.

◆ ◆ ◆

MADDIE HAD WALKED this route four nights a week for the past six months. It was a short walk, just a couple of blocks past the gas station and the drive-thru liquor store, and then another three once she was in the neighborhood itself. The neighborhood stretch of the walk used to seem like the safest part. But no one had been killed at the gas station or liquor store. It was funny, she thought. The things you think to be afraid of are never the things you should be.

But it turned out she was fine, walking home. It was the same place it had always been. Same streets, same sidewalks, same cars in the driveways. She didn't know why everyone assumed that just because one person had been killed that another would be. It didn't make sense, statistically speaking. You had a much better chance of being struck by lightning. It was true—she had looked it up on her phone that day during lunch. The chance of being struck by lightning over the course of the average lifetime was one in six thousand–something. The chance of being murdered was one in a million-something.

Still, she walked quickly, even jogging past the bank-owned house with the overgrown lawn that her dad said was probably full of snakes and rats. When she got home, she raced up the front walk and fumbled too long with her keys.

Inside, the house was dark. Her brother was in his room, watching television and talking on the phone—she could hear both going at full clips—the TV broadcasting some inane wrestling program and her brother going on about his algebra teacher (her tits, her skirt, the way her bra showed through her blouse). He had the door closed, but she knew that there were soda cans and dirty dishes and clothes piled up on the floor.

When she got into her room, Maddie closed and locked the door. She went to her closet and took a large shoe box from a high shelf, standing on her toes and grazing the box with her fingertips to maneuver it down off the shelf. Once she had it, Maddie opened the shoe box, took a long leather boot from it, and reached deep into the boot, pulling out a wad of cash. She counted the money and then added that night's earnings, putting the twenties with the twenties, the five with the fives. She had a bank account, but was only able to get to the bank whenever she ran errands with her dad. The boot thing was relatively new. She had been keeping her cash in her top dresser drawer, but it kept disappearing—a crime she blamed on her brother. She was saving for a car, and she'd never get there if he kept stealing from her.

Maddie took off her soiled clothes and got in the shower. After a night at The Smiling Pig, she sweat barbecue, her hair smelled like mesquite, and her fingernails were rimmed with dark, sticky sauce. In the shower, Maddie scrubbed her nails with a nailbrush and scrubbed her body with a plastic mesh loofah, taking care not to reopen her fresh cut. She scrubbed the heels and soles of her feet with a pumice stone, and scrubbed her face with an apricot exfoliant. When she was finished scrubbing, she stood in the steam and let the hot water hit her like bullets.

When she was out of the shower, Maddie pulled on an old Pretenders T-shirt that had belonged to her mother, and switched on the lamp beside her bed. When she went to close her blinds, she noticed that the man who lived in the house behind hers was standing at his fence, watching her. She could see him in the glow of the safety light her father had installed on the shed. He was short, balding. He reminded Maddie of a teacher she had once, who was eventually fired because of the way he treated the younger girls. It wasn't him, she was sure of that, but he gave her the same uneasy feeling, like she better cover up, hide herself.

Maddie lowered her blinds, and pulled the tab on her curtains to put an extra layer between them.

AMY

FOR THREE NIGHTS, AMY DREAMED THAT someone was breaking into her house. In the first dream, she was sleeping and woke to the sound of breaking glass; she lay still as death, listening, as the intruder walked from room to room. In the second, Amy was taking a bath when she saw a figure walk past the bathroom. She sat in the tub until the water went cold. In the third, she had returned home from work to find her front door kicked in, all her mother's jewelry gone; when she called the police, they suggested she get an alarm system and new windows.

"But they kicked in the door," she said.

"Then get a new door," they told her.

Really, what she needed were new locks. When Pete bought the house, smitten with the midcentury architecture and open layout, he scoured area thrift stores for original fixtures, including original doorknobs and locks. Once, when they had accidentally locked themselves out of the house, Pete got past the lock easily with a credit card. "Should probably replace that," he said, once they were back in the house, but it slipped their minds almost immediately afterward. There was always something else to fix, something else to attend to. It was the same since the murder—Amy thought about it, then forgot about it, then thought about it again, but never actually got around to calling a locksmith. Plus, she didn't like the idea of Pete not having a key to the house. It felt almost like a betrayal. And so she took to keeping various weapons by her bed—a beach umbrella, a golf putter, a Maglite—just in case someone broke in.

Some nights, when the noises came, as they inevitably did—the AC compressor whirring; the refrigerator humming; the house settling into the soft earth—she'd lie in bed, too exhausted to get up, and think: *Do it, kill me, I don't care.* More often, she'd think: *Maybe it's Pete*, and her heart would quicken in anticipation. She'd listen for keys at the door, wait for the house to quickly inhale, registering its surprise. Sometimes, she'd imagine it all so clearly, she'd fall asleep with the notion in her head that he had returned. She'd wake hours later, disappointed all over again.

THEIRS HAD BEEN a slow unraveling.

At the center of it was her cancer diagnosis, which took them, at thirty and thirty-three respectively, by complete surprise. They had been married a year. At one moment, they were at the beginning of what felt like everything—their entire lives stretching out before them in luminous possibility. The next, they were at the edge of a cliff, holding on to each other for fear of what might happen if they let go.

Her gynecologist sat them both down early one Thursday and said: "cancer . . . hysterectomy . . . death."

Amy, whose mother had died of ovarian cancer fifteen years before, said simply, "No."

She got up and walked out of the office.

"We're going to do everything," Pete said in the doctor's office, on the street outside the office, and in the car on the way home. He said it again on the phone to their friends and family, reassuring her father and sister, "We're going to do everything. Hysterectomy, radiation, chemotherapy, whatever it takes."

But Amy, whose hands were shaking and throat was raw, said simply, "No."

She got a second opinion and then a third. She researched alternative therapies, and started drinking wheatgrass and eating exotic mushrooms. She handed her savings over to a Reiki practitioner who laid his hands on her pelvis three times a week in an effort to dispel the tumors. None of it worked. And three months after her diagnosis, Amy acquiesced. She submitted herself to the hysterectomy, chemotherapy, and radiation, a passive but willing participant. When it was over, Amy was changed. If Pete was still standing on the cliff, Amy had fallen off.

The only thing that made her happy was smoking the marijuana a friend had given her during chemotherapy. She had been ashamed to use it once she no longer needed it, so she would wait until Pete went to bed before going into the den and smoking from the small wooden bowl her friend had given her. There, she would live out her favorite moments of the day, curled up under a blanket, watching the late-night talk shows, feeling doped and happy and light.

When the pot was gone, Amy was too embarrassed to ask for more, so she bought a bottle of brandy and hid it under the couch in the den. She knew she wasn't supposed to be drinking it. Not after the two glasses of wine she frequently had at dinner. And not after being treated for cancer. Plus, it wrecked her sleep and made her feel spacey and uncomfortable during the day. But at night, under the warmth of her blanket and in the blue glow of the television, it made her feel safe, salved, content.

When Pete found the bottle, they had their first of many fights about, what he called, their "disintegrating lives."

"You walk around here like a ghost," he had said. "You're all . . . blurry around the edges."

Amy, who felt like a trapped animal, said simply: "I don't want to be."

"Then stop. Just stop. It's a *choice*."

"It doesn't feel like a choice, Pete."

"Tell me," he said, reaching out for her. "Tell me how I can help you."

Amy shook her head. "I don't know."

"What about seeing my mom's doctor? She can help you with the hot flashes, the depression . . ."

"I don't want to see your mom's doctor, Pete. I don't want to go on hormones."

"What about your work? Can you get back to what you were doing . . . before?"

Amy, who had left Antioch halfway through their graduate art program to move to Florida to be with him, had been painting a series of blue-green abstracts before she was diagnosed, but that work no longer felt relevant.

"I'll try," she said.

For a week, she drank nothing but water and chose her sketchpad over the television. She drew fantastical versions of what had happened to her—the cancerous blooms spiraling outward from her ovaries; her sleeping body on the surgical table, the doctors playing Operation on her, removing the plastic limbs of a toy baby rather than her womb; the humiliating experience of internal radiation—the doctor fumbling to insert the medieval device inside of her while others stood and watched.

But the work only took her to darker places. She put her sketchpad away, bought another bottle of brandy, and hid it better.

A year later, they found tumors in both her breasts and an aggressive but isolated cancer. And so Amy underwent the mastectomy, resigned to it, at that point, that she would have parts removed until there was nothing left. She drew funny little pictures of herself, comic strip images of her breasts walking away while Amy clutched her chest, calling after them, "Are you sure there's nothing else I can do?"

Her sister visited, as did a friend from Antioch. But when they were gone, and her life was meant to resume, Amy couldn't get her bearings. She left the house every day and drove to Miami, where she worked as a graphic designer for an ad agency, but she couldn't get close with anyone—all her coworkers were young, their lives and bodies unblemished, whereas she felt ruined. So she kept to herself and faced her screen all day, designing ads for the tourism bureau and a local cruise line, escaping into idealized images of the tropics until it was time to drive back up I-95 and into her life. Two years passed like this. The cancer didn't return, but she was always sure it would, showing up in some obscure region of her body—presenting in organs she didn't know she had.

Then, Pete left for San Juan.

HE TOLD HER about it over dinner. It was February and raining, and they were eating at the bar in their kitchen, not looking at each other but into the kitchen, which was messy from the preparation of their meal. He mentioned it as though it was a small thing, something he'd heard on the radio or something he might do that weekend. It was between bites, between sips, between breaths. His firm was awarded a big contract—a hotel planned for a vacant lot in Old San Juan. He'd have to go down to oversee the construction.

"Wait. What big contract?" Amy asked.

"It's a hotel," he said coolly. "For Hilton."

"How long have you been working on this?"

"Six months," he admitted, exhaling slowly.

"Six months!"

"Well, yeah, Amy. I submitted initial designs. And then they wanted to see more, so I sent them a few more sketches from different perspectives. They flew down here to check out our operations, we flew out there to check out the site, and then . . ."

"Wait—you flew *out* there? *When?*"

"In October. You were in Ohio for your mom's memorial thing. I knew you were preoccupied with that so . . ."

"You just kept it to yourself this whole time."

"I didn't want you to get your hopes up. This is really big for me—it's really big for us."

"And you've known now how long?"

He pushed food around his plate with his fork. He was looking down at this plate when he said, "Four months."

"And in that time you've been?"

"Creating models, hiring staff, getting permits from the city . . . It's a huge operation."

"And you've kept it all from me," she said, more to herself than to him.

"I . . . I didn't think you'd be happy for me," he said finally.

Amy looked into the messy kitchen; even that was too much. There were two pots on the stove along with a roasting pan dirtied with bits of beef that had been cooked into oblivion. On the counter was a salad spinner and a cutting board; on the cutting board were discarded bits of vegetables—the ends of carrots, some onion skin, and four broad white celery nubs. She noticed that she had left the milk out and wondered how long.

Amy drained her wineglass. She wanted to pour another, but she knew that Pete had been watching her, so she just sat there, wanting more than ever to set fire to it all and run away.

"I'm going to have to be in San Juan for quite a while," he said.

"How long is quite a while?"

"Close to a year."

"A *year*?"

He didn't say anything further, and Amy got up and went into the kitchen. She poured herself a healthy glass of wine and started to clean.

"What am I supposed to do here without you for a year?"

"Do what you're doing now. Work. *Live*."

She turned to him, put her hands on the counter, and narrowed her eyes. "*Live?* I don't live, Pete. I—"

"Destroy yourself," he said.

"Is that what you want me to do?"

"What do you think?"

"What do I think? *I don't know.* I don't fucking know, Pete. For all I know you've already written me off. How is it that you've been working toward something for *six months* and not told me about it? It's like we're not even married anymore. It's like we just *live* here together, and eat meals together and sleep in the same bed together. And now you don't even want to do that." She started to cry. "You don't love me anymore."

"That's not true."

"How am I to know what's true and what's not? Where is the *evidence*?"

"You want evidence?" He leapt from the barstool and pushed the glass from her hand just as she was about to take a sip. Wine streaked across the kitchen, the glass breaking against the backsplash in a spray of burgundy.

"Why do you take *everything* from me?" she screamed, pushing him aside and storming out of the kitchen. She slipped on her flip-flops, grabbed her keys, and left the house, slamming the door behind her. He didn't run after her, and the next morning, he didn't ask her where she had gone.

IT WAS AMY who suggested they end it. A threat she never thought he'd take seriously.

"If that's what you want," he said, leaning back in his chair. They were at a restaurant in Fort Lauderdale, sharing a plate of spaghetti carbonara. He was due to leave for San Juan the next day. It was her last-ditch effort to get him to stay.

"It's not what I want!" she said in a high whisper. "I want to live with you! I want to feel better, to adopt a baby, to paint and work and . . ."

She watched his eyes, hoping for a trace of love or tenderness but saw only resignation.

"Maybe it's better that we separate. That we take this time to . . . see where the dust settles."

"Am I the dust?"

"No," he said, dismissing her. He signaled for the waitress and that was that.

The next day, he left. Amy stood in the street, watching until his taxi was just a yellow blur among the trees.

AND NOW THERE was this: coming home every night after work to an empty house. Since the murder, at least, she'd had something to focus on besides the silence, the loneliness that sometimes felt like a boot pressed against her chest. Every night she'd fix dinner, pour a glass of wine, and carry it outside so that she could watch Adel's house for signs of activity. She had read every article she could find about the murder, and often watched the news at night before bed, sure that there would be some new information about what had happened. A week later, though, there was nothing. The police knew what they knew and nothing else: there was no forced entry and no robbery. The person who killed Adel walked in, selected a weapon at random, and bludgeoned her, they said, striking her once with a heavy cast iron teakettle, and walked out.

From these scraps Amy started to form pictures in her mind of what had happened, breaking the scene into frames. She saw the fear in Adel's eyes, the surprise in the murderer's, the impact of the kettle against Adel's soft, old-lady face. The images scared and overwhelmed her. Once they started coming they would not stop, so she took out her sketchpad and drew frame after frame, a pencil in her right hand, a cigarette often in her left. She sketched Adel over and over, her face changing as she moved from shock to fear to horror. She drew a man's face, sallow cheeks and narrow, angry eyes. She drew a man's hand wrapped around the handle of a kettle, and the kettle itself, slamming against Adel's face.

Spooked, Amy ripped the final drawing out of her pad and balled it up.

She lit a cigarette and watched Adel's house, noticing how high the grass was already, how wild the yard had become, as if overnight. There were usually hummingbirds buzzing around a large red feeder that hung off the back of the house, but they were gone. In their place was a pair of blue jays, battling over territory, and a blacksnake, slithering up a drainpipe.

Amy picked up her pencil again. This time she sketched the back of the house, darkening the kitchen window and the small cigarette-burn hole, leaving everything else so faint that it was as if the house wasn't there. On another page, she drew the fire as she had seen it, the smoke rising from the house in thick black party streamers. On a third, she drew the house as it was before the fire, well maintained and manicured, but with a single, cartoonish, dark cloud directly over it. Satisfied with her work, Amy turned the page and started a fourth drawing. This time, she drew Adel handing mangoes over the fence, her concerned look as she told Amy to "Eat them soon! They're very ripe!"

When she finished the last one, Amy ran her pencil furiously over the page, scratching out her work. Then, she tore the page from her sketchpad and set fire to it with her cigarette lighter, but immediately regretted it—the curl of fire that enveloped Adel's face.

She pushed her sketchpad away and stared at the house. The snake was gone, the birds too. Mosquitoes and no-see-ums had started to rise from the grass and hover, tiny helicopters with invisible wings. It was mango season once again, and Adel's tree hung heavy with them. Amy watched as one broke free with a snap and fell to the ground. She thought about climbing the fence and picking it up before the bugs ate it clean. Instead, she went inside to pour a drink and draw a bath.

Amy brought her brandy and cigarettes into the tub with her and soaked, thinking of Adel, and the mangoes, the murder. As she soaked, she looked up at the ceiling so she wouldn't have to see her scarred and grotesque body. She felt sometimes that cancer had been a mistake she had made—that she'd chosen the wrong way at a fork in the road, or gotten the blooper gift on a TV game show. Thinking this, Amy wondered if Adel had been saved from some other, more monstrous future—one where she is neutered and disfigured in the name of survival; where she suffers an aneurysm and lives like a dangling tooth.

The light in the room was changing, the trees outside throwing shadows across the ceiling, the water, her body. She looked at it now, plainly in the waning light. She said, "My boobs were never that great anyway," starting the joke that usually ended: my womb was never that great anyway. Ovaries, cervix, fallopian tubes—what have you done for me lately? As if on cue, a wave of panicked warmth washed over her and she leaned her head back against the tile, waiting for the hot flash to pass. Drinking brought them on, so did hot baths, so did sugar. Just about everything she enjoyed made her body's faulty thermostat go haywire. She remembered a friend of her mother's telling her years ago that a hot flash felt like being trapped in a hot car. To her, though, they just felt wrong. They were reminders that she was doing the wrong things with her body and that her body itself was wrong. She had been dissected, neutered. There was a violence to it, a brutality she couldn't get her head around.

Amy took her last sip of brandy and held it in her mouth for a few seconds, a pill she wasn't sure she needed. She then spit it into the bathwater, said, *"No mas,"* and rose from the tub. She dried herself, covered her scars with cocoa butter, and carried herself to bed.

HOURS LATER AMY sprung awake, terrified. Her skin was wet and cold, her heart was racing. She must have dreamed something, but she couldn't remember what. All she had was an image, an idea. In it, two figures stood across from each other, separated by a thin band of light. Amy felt compelled to get it down. She took her sketchpad into the kitchen and furiously sketched the scene—the figures, one small and one tall, the light coming in from a nearby window, separating them. Dissatisfied with this, she dressed, putting on the old denim shirt she used for painting and a pair of gym shorts. Her heart was racing as she slipped on her flip-flops and went outside and into the garage, which Pete had turned into a studio for her when she traded her life at Antioch for a life with him.

She turned on the high, bright lights and rummaged through drawers of paints and brushes, looking for something to use. But her paints had all hardened in their tubes. Her canvases were covered with cobwebs, mold, and lizard excrement. Undeterred, she selected a piece of prestretched canvas and cleaned it as best she could, dusting the cobwebs and excrement off with her hand, and anchored it to her easel.

Her brushes, at least, had been kept nice. They were clean and dry and in the drawer where she had left them the day before she experienced the sharp abdominal pains that led to her diagnosis. She selected a #12 flat brush and a #10 filbert and set them by her easel. Her palette was another story; it was caked with dust, oil, and oxidized paint. It would take hours to scrub. She set it aside and ripped off the top of a cardboard box that stored CDs they'd long ago digitized. She would use that instead.

The only paints that hadn't dried were Burnt Sienna, Medium Cadmium Yellow, French Ultramarine Blue, and Flemish White. She squirted a bit of each onto her cardboard palette, took a knife, and mixed the yellow and blue together until she had a deep, mean, chromium green. She then mixed the yellow with the white, creating hues of daylight, and mixed the blue, sienna, and white to create shades of gray. She stepped in front of her canvas and took a breath. It had been three years since she stood there—three years since she'd painted anything. Her hand was shaking as she picked up the flat-tip brush, dipped it into the darkest gray, and touched it to the edge of the canvas.

BERNARD

THE CHURCH WAS FULL OF FACES Bernard hadn't seen in decades. Faces that once belonged to younger, more attractive people; faces he barely recognized. It seemed to him that there was something missing, and as he looked around the church, he tried to figure out what it was. Finally, it came to him—the church was filled with *halves*. There was a husband here, a wife there, but there were few couples, few pairs among his peers. It reminded Bernard of seeing a half-moon in the night sky—you knew something else was there, but you couldn't see it.

He did a mental roll call before the service started, going around the room, checking off names. Maryanne Wilkerson, present; husband Gerald, not. Harry Trawlers, present; wife Elaine, also present. Susan Boon, present; husband Felix, not. He went on like this, isolating the familiar faces until he had a long and uneven list. There were more wives than husbands, more women than men. It was true that women lived longer, but Bernard never understood why. It always seemed to him that they had a heavier burden to carry.

"Nice flowers," Danny, who was sitting next to him, said.

"What's that?"

"The flowers. They're nice."

"Oh," Bernard said, noticing them for the first time. There were huge sprays of lilies on the altar and beneath the large, stained glass windows. Bernard never understood the use of flowers at funerals. They always seemed a waste.

When the procession started, he rose with the rest of the congregation and started singing along to the hymnal: *The day Thou gavest, Lord, is ended / The darkness falls at Thy behest / To Thee our morning hymns ascend / Thy praise shall sanctify our rest.* But Danny's voice quickly drowned him out, and Bernard stopped singing, unable to hear himself. Instead, he stood awkwardly, the hymnal by his side, and swayed to the music made by the heavy organ.

As the casket was wheeled down the aisle, Bernard couldn't help but wonder about Adel's body. He knew from watching TV crime shows that it would have been part of the investigation. He couldn't help picturing the pretty girl from *CSI Miami* standing over Adel's broken body, looking for clues. Now that she was being buried, he figured, that part of the investigation must be over. He wondered if the police had gotten what they needed. Maybe, he thought, they were arresting the murderer right now.

The priest said, "Let us pray," and Bernard hung his head along with the rest of the congregation. He tried to focus on what the priest was saying, but the words meant nothing to him; he was never one for religion or ceremony, and so he let the words go past him. Soon the room was filled with prayer, and music, and silence, each in its own time. Bernard thought about a way to quantify sadness, a meter or unit of measurement. His own sadness was off the charts. It was worse than when Irene died; worse even than when his granddaughter died. It was as if each death magnified the pain from the deaths that came before.

Each of Adel's grandchildren read a passage from the Bible, and Bernard watched as Danny wiped a tear from his eye. Bernard wished that he could cry too. He wanted to lie down and hold his belly and bawl. Instead, he coughed and closed his eyes and waited. Finally, the priest stood and delivered the homily. He told a story that Bernard did not listen to, and then said: "Resist the urge to ask 'why.' Because if you ask *why, why, why,* you will find that nothing satisfies. A question that cannot be answered is like a hunger that cannot be sated. So do not ask the Lord 'why.' Just accept. Just tell yourself *it is. It. Just. Is.*"

At that, Bernard felt a tightness in his chest. He put a hand on his heart and tried to catch his breath, which had been knocked out of him. Finally, he hung his head, covered his face, and wept into his hands.

AFTER THE SERVICE Danny rounded up a few of their old friends from the neighborhood and made plans to meet in a half hour at Tropical Acres, an aging steak house by the airport. Bernard, who wanted nothing more than to crawl into bed and sleep for the rest of the day, grudgingly agreed to go along.

There were eight of them altogether—Roberta Flarety, whose husband, Dominick, was dead; Leslie Nelson, whose husband, Avery, was dead; Harry and Elaine Trawlers; and Cal Hendricks, whose wife, Mary, was forever by his side. There was talk of investments and politics and golf scores, of grandchildren, vacations, and real estate. Finally, when their steak lunches were all but decimated, Cal pushed his plate away, cleared his throat, and asked the question on everyone's mind:

"How in the hell does someone break into an old woman's house and beat her senseless?"

And, when no one responded:

"What is *wrong* with the world today?"

"Don't get me started on the world," Harry Trawlers said. "Inflation, gambling, war . . ."

"Yes, but the *murder*," Cal continued.

"I think we should just forget it," his wife said, taking his hand in her lap. "These things happen." She shook her head. "There will *always* be lunatics."

"But we don't know it was a lunatic who did it." Cal pulled out a cigar and looked around. "Can I still smoke in here?"

"I'd rather you didn't," Elaine Trawlers said.

"Fine," Cal said, and tucked the cigar behind his ear.

"What about you, White?" Cal asked after a beat. "You never liked Adel, maybe you did it."

"Oh, Cal, *really*," Mary said.

"What?" he shot back. "She did publicly out his affair with Vera."

"That was a *thousand* years ago!" Mary countered.

Bernard cleared his throat and with a shaky hand, tossed his napkin onto his plate. "I . . ." he started, but could not find the words to say the thing he wanted to say, which was that Cal was an ass and had always been an ass, and that people in glass houses . . .

"Look, the one thing we shouldn't do is point fingers at one another—or anyone else, for that matter," Harry said.

"How can you not?" Cal asked.

"It may be a fun parlor game, but it's not exactly helpful," Harry said.

"Thank you," Bernard managed. "And for the record," he said, "I'm the one who called the police."

"Doesn't make you any more innocent in my book!" Cal said.

"I don't give a damn about your book," Bernard managed.

"YOU WERE A real help back there," Bernard said as he and Danny drove back to the neighborhood.

"I don't like to argue," Danny said. "I never get involved in those things."

"Yeah, but the guy all but accused me of murder."

"What do you think of Roberta?"

"What do you mean, what do I think of her?" Bernard asked.

"I kind of like her."

"What are you in *high school*?"

"What's age got to do with it? I'm still *alive*, aren't I?"

"Not where it counts," Bernard said, glancing at Danny's lap.

"Speak for yourself!"

"OK," Bernard said, holding up his hands in surrender. "But if you ask me, impotence is the greatest gift of old age. When I think about all those years and all that time I spent thinking about sex—what a waste! Just think of what I could have done . . ."

"Like you're doing anything now!"

"Now is different. Now I'm . . . *old*."

"You let yourself get old, is what I think," Danny said, and after a beat, "So what are you doing now?"

"Now? I'm stuffed full of steak and potatoes. I'm going home to take a nap."

"See? That's exactly what I'm talking about. Why don't you come over instead? We'll play cards."

"Some other time," Bernard said. He pulled up in front of Danny's house and kept the car running.

"You sure you don't want to come in?" Danny asked. "I feel so . . . restless."

"I feel like bricks," Bernard said. "If you're so restless why don't you call Roberta?"

"Maybe I will," Danny said, raising his eyebrows.

Danny shut the heavy door of Bernard's Taurus wagon, and Bernard watched him meander, in his funny old-man way, to the house. Bernard wondered if he looked like an old man when he walked, and decided that he probably did.

ONCE AT HOME, Bernard stripped down to his underwear and washed his face and hands. He felt sick from lunch—the heavy New York strip and bad conversation. He wished he had made an excuse and come home right after the funeral. He could have taken a bath and smoked some marijuana and forgotten the dead, at least for a little while. He could have taken himself out to lunch—a solitary lunch with a pretty waitress and delicious food. He could have . . . Wait—who *is* that?

Bernard stood in front of the mirror, horrified by the sight of himself. The man staring back was oddly familiar, but it wasn't *him*. *He* didn't have liver spots; *he* didn't have an explosion of blood vessels stretching out from either side of his nose. This face looked more alien than human, more like his father's than his own. Bernard touched the mirror and then touched his face. It was him.

Bernard sighed deeply, went into the bedroom, and eased himself into bed. He slept. It was a long, deep, dreamless sleep. When he woke, the light was different, like a watered-down cocktail. Bernard took note of the shadows on the wall and ceiling and decided that it must be around seven. He'd missed the entire afternoon, including *Oprah* and the evening news. He wouldn't know what had happened, if anything, until ten o'clock. He told himself that it didn't matter. Adel would still be dead no matter what news they found.

He sighed heavily and closed his eyes. "Get up," he heard his wife say. "Get up! Get up! Get up!"

Bernard sighed again and rose slowly, thinking of the wasted daylight. He then thought of his father, who had driven a truck for a stint before buying a farm on Maryland's eastern shore and raising chickens. "Boy," he would always say, extending out the vowel in the manner of eastern shore chicken farmers, "don't waste the daylight."

"You're wasting time!" he heard Irene say.

And then came Vera's laugh.

Bernard walked out into the empty living room. The dust swelled in the slanted light. His mind was crowded, but the house was empty.

WHEN IRENE WAS upset about something, she would clean. He pictured her there now, vacuuming the floors and the draperies, dusting the tables and cabinets, throwing open the refrigerator door, and tossing things into the garbage—changing her life in increments, the only way she knew how. He looked around the room but didn't know where or how to start. Finally, he found their old Hoover and started pushing it noisily around the house. When he was finished, he dusted, filling the house with the scent of lemon Pledge, a smell he'd always loved. Then, he cleaned out the refrigerator, tossing out a brick of hardened yellow cheese, a bottle of soda that had long ago gone flat, a package of hot dogs that he didn't remember buying, and a half can of soup. He then wiped the refrigerator down with a soapy sponge and carried the garbage outside. He took the garbage to the garage and set it in the can, overtop last week's bag, which stunk of rotten food. Disgusted, more with himself than the smell, Bernard dragged the can to the curb. He had missed the collection day again and now the can would sit on the curb all weekend, annoying the neighbors and attracting raccoons.

Bernard looked back at the house, not wanting to go back in. He wished there was another place for him. Somewhere else he could be. He thought of his kids in their separate corners of the country. John in Jacksonville, Pam in Chicago, and Daniel in Connecticut. Bernard had a hard time remembering why or how his kids ended up where they did. But he considered it an insult that they landed so far away from where they began. It was as if they were *trying* to get away. Bernard remembered the way Pam had laughed when he suggested she attend the University of Florida. "Why would I want to do *that*?" she had said.

One memory led to another and Bernard's heart broke in places he didn't know he had. There were doors deep inside him that were swinging open and slamming shut.

On a whim, he went back into the garage and dug through the detritus of the last five decades. He was looking for his bike, a silver Schwinn Continental that John had coveted but Bernard never let him ride. He decided that he would clean it up and send it to John, no sense in keeping it. It took him so long to find the bike that Bernard wondered if John might have taken it sometime or other, dissecting it while Bernard slept and stashing the frame in the back of his Subaru. Bernard pictured it so clearly he was sure it had happened and was angry with John for the theft. Then, he found the bike stashed behind a stack of boxes marked IRENE, and forgave his son in an instant.

The bike was in sorry shape. The tires were flat and the frame had rusted a bit where the paint had chipped; the chain sagged like the belly of a pregnant dog. Bernard thought about leaving it there, going inside and back to bed, but he thought about John, and how selfish he had been keeping it away from him all those years, so he pulled the bike out, cleared some space on his old worktable, and set to work on it. He oiled and adjusted the chain, reinflated the tires, and cleaned the frame with a wet rag. When he was finished, Bernard walked the bike out of the garage.

He was thinking he might test it out, but then thought about his knees and back, his blood pressure. Would a bike ride kill him? Did he care? He tilted the bike to one side and attempted to swing his leg over the bike, but he couldn't get his leg high enough and nearly fell backward in the attempt. Embarrassed, he looked around to see if any of his neighbors were watching. Then, he tried again, dropping the bike lower and bending over it; he swung his leg over the bike, this time connecting with the seat, and stood the bike up beneath him. Bernard was unsteady, but he lifted his feet to the pedals one at a time and rode uneasily down the driveway and out to the street.

Once he started, Bernard was not sure that he could stop, and he wasn't sure he wanted to. It felt good to move his old bones and muscles, felt good to feel his heart. He rode out to the golf course, which was situated in the center of the neighborhood and surrounded by a paved path, where people would jog and walk their dogs, and where he once taught his daughter to ride a bike without training wheels. Tonight, though, the path was empty. The sun had set and the sky was a cloudless purple dome, scarred by the occasional vapor trail. Soon, it would be dark.

There had been a cold winter a few years back that killed a lot of Florida's invasive species. Pythons in the Everglades were discovered dead on pine islands. Nonnative fish were found floating in tidal marshes. Iguanas fell frozen from the trees and died, not from the cold, but from the impact. To Bernard, it felt like there were dead iguanas everywhere that year. He'd round a corner and see another one—rotting, stinking, and half-eaten. They became so ubiquitous that they haunted him; he dreamed of finding them in his bed and in his bathtub and in the passenger seat of his car, curled and decaying. As

Bernard rode the path, the light fading quickly around him, it was the image of Adel that haunted him now. And not the woman he knew—the old battle-ax who had once found him with Vera behind the pool shed at Cal Hendricks's Fourth of July barbecue—but the woman he saw carried from her house. He half expected to see her, lying on a stretcher, sticking out from beneath a row of box hedges.

Bernard felt the strain of activity in his calves and quads and hamstrings. Felt the weight of his body on the saddle. But he was too afraid to stop, too afraid to give up momentum. Too afraid that whatever was out there would grab him too. It was fully dark now, and the path was illuminated here and there with the short electric lampposts they installed in the 1980s, after all those kids went missing. But the light only created shadows, and in them Bernard saw Adel, and Vera, and Irene.

He pedaled on, faster now, afraid of the shadows, of the darkness, of the night. When he finally did stop, Bernard found himself at home. He had done a loop and circled back to the most familiar place, and that most familiar feeling: Why hadn't he gotten cancer? Why hadn't the man come into his house? When would he drop, frozen, from a tree?

"Hi, Mr. White," he heard someone say.

Bernard looked up, startled, and saw his neighbor, the girl. "Oh, hi," he said, breathless. "Just getting home from work?"

"Yeah."

"Busy?"

"Yeah, Tuesdays usually are."

"My daughter worked there, you know. Back when she was about your age."

"Did she like it?"

"I don't know." He shrugged.

"Oh," she said. And then: "Hey, Mr. White, who do you think did it? Who do you think killed Mrs. Minor?"

"I don't know," he said, flummoxed. It had only been a week and he was already tired of the question.

MADDIE

THE CLOUDS WERE BUILDING AS MADDIE walked to The Smiling Pig that day from her school bus stop, large thunderheads rolling in from the west. Every May it surprised her—how hot and humid it could get; how bright everything was suddenly. She loved it when the rains came in the afternoon and the picture changed completely, everything going from light to dark, like flipping a switch. The challenge was getting to work before the rains started. Otherwise, she'd be walking around in swampy shoes all night.

That day, she arrived just before the clouds broke. Inside the restaurant, one of the police detectives she had waited on the other day was standing by the kitchen, talking to her boss.

"Hey, Maddie, come over here a sec," her boss said, beckoning her with a wave.

"What's going on?" she asked nervously.

"Hi, Maddie. Detective Stevenson," the man said, offering her his hand. "We just have a few questions for you."

Maddie looked up at her boss, who told her: "It's OK."

"Let's have a seat over here," the detective said, moving toward a booth near the back.

"How are you?" he asked when they sat down.

"Fine."

"How was your day at school?"

"It was fine," Maddie said, worried now—surely they didn't suspect *her* of anything.

"What do you do every day after school?"

"I come here Tuesday, Wednesday, and Friday. I usually go straight home Monday and Thursday."

"So you were here the night of May twentieth."

"Yes."

"Do you live at 4590 Southwest Seventh Avenue?"

"Yes."

"And you live there with your . . ."

"My dad and my brother."

"How old is your brother?"

"He's twelve."

"So you're the big sister."

Maddie was starting to get scared. She looked beyond the detective and scanned the restaurant. It was the time of day when all the tables were clean, the ketchup and hot sauce bottles arranged behind the salt and pepper shakers, like parents behind their children.

"Do you know this man?" the detective asked, sliding a photo across the table.

It was an old mug shot, but it was plainly Charlie. "Yes."

"How do you know him?"

"He comes in here almost every night. He's a customer."

"Around what time does he usually come in?"

"It depends. Sometimes he's here early. Sometimes he doesn't come 'til much later."

"OK," the detective started, "can you remember—?"

"But I see him all the time," Maddie said, interrupting him. "He stands at the intersection over there, collecting money."

"Collecting money?"

"Begging. From people in their cars. People coming home from work and stuff."

"OK. Now I need you to think really hard about this. It's important. Do you remember seeing him on the night of May twentieth?"

"The night of the murder."

"The night of the murder," the detective said, nodding.

Maddie looked down at the table, down at the mug shot of a young Charlie. She wanted to say that she had seen him, but she wasn't sure. She had a picture of him in her mind, standing at the intersection, holding an empty soda cup. In her mind, Charlie was always there. He was as much a fixture as the stoplight.

"I think so," she said finally.

"What time?" the detective asked.

Maddie liked to think that she had a good memory, but it had been a full week since the murder. She couldn't even remember what she ate last Tuesday, or what she wore. Finally, she told him what she thought to be true:

"I saw him when I got here, around four. He was standing at the intersection where he usually is. And then I saw him that night. Around seven, I guess. He goes over to the gas station and buys a beer, and then he comes here and orders the brisket."

"Do you ever talk to him?"

"Sometimes."

"Did he mention anything about the murder, like in passing?"

"No," she lied.

He pulled the photo of Charlie back toward him. "Thank you for your time. We really—"

"Is he a suspect?"

"I can't say," the detective said, getting up from the table. "But we should definitely keep this conversation between us."

After he left, she sat at the table for a while, looking through the window, which, by then, was completely gray with rain. All she could see was the washed-out daylight and the blur of cars as they passed.

Charlie wouldn't be out there now, not in this rain. Maddie wondered where he went when it rained. And where he slept, for that matter. She had a dream once that she was hiding him in her backyard, on the side of her house, where her father would never see him. She had lent him a tent, and snuck food out to him at night. She almost told Charlie about the dream, but she thought that it would be weird. What does it mean when you dream about someone? Maddie was afraid that it meant that you loved them.

She had to get her mind off of Charlie. And off of the fact that she had lied about him to the police. Of course he had mentioned the murder—everyone was talking about it—but that didn't mean that he had killed anyone. She could go in the bathroom and cut herself, but she worried that she was doing it too much—that it was becoming what her friend Stacia might call "a problem." So she stashed her backpack behind the counter and opened up her paperback, waiting for the rain to die out and the restaurant to fill.

But the more she read about Mrs. Pontellier, the more she thought about her mother. Had her mother been sad and Maddie not noticed? Had she felt trapped? Burdened? Unloved? If only they had read *The Awakening* at the beginning of the school year and not the end, Maddie might have looked at her mother differently. She might have asked her if she was OK, if she was happy, if she loved them. Since her mother left, Maddie had an almost-constant dialogue with her, imagining her mother's voice and then her own. But when she got to the question of why her mother left, the voice fell silent. Maddie simply couldn't supply an answer.

Her mother had worked in a dental office. From what Maddie knows, she left work that evening, got in her car, and headed up the turnpike, but missed her exit and kept going. They checked the records from her SunPass transponder, so they know that she blew through the tolls all the way to the Georgia line. Somewhere around Orlando, she tossed her cell phone out the window. Maddie knows because it was found on the side of the road, just north of Yee Haw Junction. Since then, Maddie had pictured her mother doing it a thousand times—tossing her phone out of the window and declaring herself *free*.

Maddie wished she could do the same thing. But you can't do anything when you're fifteen. And where would she even go?

◆　　◆　　◆

THE RAIN DIED out and the crowd picked up. They did a steady carryout business on Tuesday nights, so Maddie was busier, managing her tables and the single men (it was always men, for some reason) who stood at the counter, waiting for their takeout. Despite herself, she kept looking for Charlie to come through the door. Each time the door swung open and it wasn't him, her heart sank a little. She wondered if he had been arrested. And if he really had killed Adel Minor, and what would make a man like Charlie do such a thing. And then she remembered his favorite refrain: The desperate do desperate things. She thought about Mrs. Pontellier and Charlie and her mom, all doing desperate things.

A boy a couple of years older than she was came in to pick up his carryout, and when she handed over the bag and made change for him, he asked her name and what she was doing later.

"What am I *doing* later?"

"Yeah," he said, his smile exposing broad white teeth. He was taller than the boys Maddie was used to, more confident.

"Nothing," she said, looking at the carryout bag instead of at him.

"Why don't you come out with me? It'll be fun."

"Out, like . . . where?"

"I don't know." He shrugged.

"I think I'm busy later."

"OK," he said. "Maybe some other time."

"OK," Maddie said, and ducked into the kitchen.

This type of thing didn't use to happen, but now it happened all the time—men, curious about her, looking at her a certain way. Other girls she knew seemed better equipped to handle it—the attention. They knew what to say, what to do, how to laugh the way that girls of a certain age laughed. But Maddie wasn't like them, and didn't want to be. She bit the inside of her cheek, and peeked out into the dining room to make sure he was gone. He was. And Charlie was there, seated in his regular booth, waiting for her. Maddie was so relieved, she practically ran to him.

"Hi," she said when she was in front of him. "How—how are you?"

"How do I look?" he asked.

Maddie shrugged. "OK, I guess."

"How's the brisket?"

"It's *particularly* brown today."

"Good. Give me that, some greens, and some potato salad."

"OK," she said, and before she turned to go, she asked him: "Hey, Charlie, where do you go when it rains?"

He looked up at the ceiling, thinking about it. "Trees are good. The awning over the 7-Eleven is OK. Why? Where do *you* go when it rains?"

She pretended to think about it for a minute. And then she said, "Home. I go home."

"Ever been hit by lightning?" he asked.

"No." She smiled. "You?"

"Four times," he said. "Almost died the fourth."

WHEN MADDIE WALKED home that night, she thought about Charlie, and her mom and Adel and the cops, Mrs. Pontellier, and the boy from the carryout order, all connected but distant, like the shapes in a kaleidoscope. She saw her neighbor and she thought about him too. And then she thought about her father, who might be like Mr. White one day. Alone in the house by himself.

Inside, the house was dark. She heard her brother in his room, mimicking the lines of a favorite kung fu movie. She smiled and put her hand on his door, a gesture of affection. Then she pushed through her bedroom door, turned on the lights, and let out a howl.

Her room had been ransacked. Dresser drawers hung open, their contents spilling out onto the floor. Her closet door had been lifted off its tracks, her dresses and skirts and blouses thrown onto the bed and floor. Her shoe boxes and shoulder bags emptied, her jewelry box had been broken, its delicate glass doors cracked. It had been her mother's, as had much of the jewelry inside. But nothing, so far as she could tell, had been taken. She looked for, and found, her long leather boots. She reached down inside the left boot, found her stash of money, and sighed with relief. He didn't find it. She put the money back and went out to her brother's room and pounded on the door.

"Briiiaaaan!" she screamed. "Open up!"

"What, Brattie?" he asked, swinging the door open.

"What do you mean *what*? What did you do to my *room*?"

"What are you *talking* about?"

"You tore up my room, you little shit!"

He followed her into her room. "Whoa," he said.

"Whoa is right. Dad's gonna kill you."

"I didn't do it!"

"Really?" she said sarcastically, "Who did, then?"

"How should *I* know?"

"What time'd you get home from school?"

"Around three."

"Then what?"

"Then I made a Hot Pocket and went into my room."

"Then what?"

"Then I ate the Hot Pocket, but I was still hungry so I made some popcorn."

"You little pig, I don't care what you ate. Did you *hear* anything, *see* anything?"

"I got tired." He shrugged. "I took a nap."

"Then what?"

"I got up, made another Hot Pocket, and started watching *Rush Hour*, and then *Dragons Forever* came on. And then you started banging on my door."

She slid down the wall, defeated. "You really didn't do it?"

"Really, Maddie, I *swear."*

"I'm scared," she said, looking up at him.

"Don't be." He sat down next to her, took her hand.

"Don't be? Someone broke into our house and totally fucked up my room, and I shouldn't be scared?"

"Should we call the police?" he asked.

She thought about Charlie and the cops. She thought about her mom, out there somewhere. "Just help me clean it up, OK?"

AMY

FOR AMY, THE SCENES KEPT COMING. She drew constantly, filling sketch-books with moments from Adel's final day: folding laundry; eating cereal; cleaning a potato; setting an egg timer. She drew the murderer too, a shadowy figure entering the house; a figure that grew larger as he stepped from room to room. She dreamed in full color, but drew in black and white, often writing notes for herself in the corners of her drawings: Magenta, Ochre, Brown Madder, Ultramarine.

She hadn't returned to her studio since the morning she'd left the painting anchored to her easel and gone to work, exhausted but ex-hilarated. She was afraid to see the wreck she had made, afraid to see the painting too. She was haunted by her memory of the dream, and all the images that followed. Still, she wanted more than anything to do the work, to get the scenes down, to bring them to life.

And so on Saturday, she set out early to take her studio back from the years of depression and inertia, cleaning it so she could put it back to use.

She filled garbage bags with the rolls of moldy canvas, termite-eaten canvas boards, and tubes of dried paint, trying not to count as she did, trying not to say *$8.99, $10.99, $25.50,* trying not to think about all the wannabe artists who had come before her, handing over their hard-earned money to Utrecht to buy supplies that were like broken instruments in their hands. Trying to reassure herself that she was not them. That she was Amy Francis Unger, a painter who had, in graduate school, shown enormous promise.

Her second year at Antioch, Amy had won a juried prize for a body of work, a collection she called *Found Objects*. She had taken things she had found—a child's watch, a pair of glasses, a note hastily scribbled and then tossed—and painted the scenes in which she had found them: the pink child's watch in the gravel under a playground swing set, the broken bifocals on a window ledge in the public library, the crumpled note in the canopy of a mulberry tree.

The collection was written about in *Newsweek*, in an article about her teacher, the truly great Anders Kane. Amy had memorized and sometimes repeated the lines written about her in a kind of cadence: *Kane's students are going places too,* a photo caption read. *Here, second-year grad student Amy Francis Unger successfully explores the meaning of lost objects; her paintings, which are nothing more than moments in time, smack of timelessness.*

Now, of course, it felt like those words had been written about someone else. And other than the $3,000 she got from the juried prize, Amy had never made a dime off her work. Worse, in three years, she'd not painted a thing. This, even though Pete had turned his garage into a studio for her nearly the moment she moved in—installing windows and skylights to capture the northern light; finishing the walls, which had been bare cinder block on the inside and plywood on the outside, with Sheetrock and drywall mud on the inside and stucco on the outside, making the once haphazardly converted carport into a bona fide extension of the house. Inside, he'd added industrial fans, a utility sink, and cabinetry customized for Amy's supplies. He finished by painting the cement floor a brilliant, high-gloss white. Amy had loved that the floor, over time, would become a work of art in and of itself, an unintentional Pollock created with the mess from her work. Now, the paint splatters on the floor looked more like a Hirst than a Pollock, more like dots on a constellation than an explosion of stars.

As she cleaned, it felt like there was no end to it. With each item she moved, another revealed itself. There were stacks of latex paint cans left over from when they painted their bedroom a color called Elephant Tusk and their house a color called Storm Cloud. Next to them were stacks of terra-cotta planters, some still filled with dirt and dead plants. There were exotic gardening tools—a long pole with a serrated saw for trimming palm trees, a machete for beating back the banana and bamboo that might otherwise take over their yard. There were the things they had bought but never used, or used only once. The crutches from when Amy sprained her ankle years before, the longboard that Pete bought and rode for a month after watching *Lords of Dogtown* on Showtime. The wrought iron bench she'd bought at a yard sale and intended to refinish but never did. She carried the paint cans to the curb and sat them alongside the garbage bags she'd filled with the ruined art supplies. She emptied, cleaned, and stacked the terra-cotta planters, and put them in a corner with the lawn mower and other gardening tools. On a whim, and after twice tripping over it, she carried Pete's longboard out to the curb too. She hated to throw things out, especially perfectly good things, but she hoped some neighborhood kid would spot it and snap it up.

There were plenty of geckos and anoles hidden in the room, which, as she cleared it, were losing the dark cool space where they spent their summers, ducking in and out of the crevasses, chasing each other around, and shitting everywhere. As she exposed them, they nodded their heads up and down, robotically communicating the threat. They reminded her of the winter that Pete tried to save an iguana from dying after it fell from a tree, frozen solid. He wrapped it in a blanket and placed it in the garage, to help it warm up. The iguana died, but not before ripping through a prestretched canvas, climbing the walls, and chewing through some exposed wires on the ceiling. Luckily, there were no dead iguanas to dispose of today, just a few gecko carcasses, thin and brittle as burnt paper. Amy swept them up, along with the termite droppings she found in the corner between her supply cabinet and the door, black and gritty as ground coffee. *Call exterminator*, she thought, mentally adding it to her list.

When the room was finally cleared, it was time to contend with the dust. And there was so much of it! It was as if everything in the room died a little, letting go of parts of itself—plastics outgassing, woods decaying, metals rusting—everything becoming slightly diminished, weakening the way bones do. Or maybe, she thought, the dust was just from the road. They were hemmed in by highways, trapped in the cusp between one system and another. In the house, they vacuumed. But they never vacuumed out here. Amy had half a mind to turn the leaf blower on the room, picking up the dust and dead particulate in a great windstorm and blowing it out the door. But she took her time instead, using first a dustpan and broom, then switching to a Shop-Vac, and then a mop and a bucket. She then scrubbed the walls, taking a sponge mop to them, dirtying the bucket water quickly, and changing it, dirtying it, and changing it again.

When she was finished, when the walls and shelves and windows had all been scrubbed clean, Amy sat on one of the stools Pete had taken from the Green House, a bar they used to go to together before it was torn down, and looked around. The room itself was a blank canvas, not the varietal dump she'd imagined it to be when she told herself it was beyond salvage. She wanted to kick herself for being so foolish, so lazy. For allowing so much inertia to take over her life.

But that was then. That was before. And while she wanted to promise herself that it would never happen again, she knew herself too well to make that promise. Hadn't she similarly crumbled after her mother died? Hadn't she skipped a year of school, staying in her bedroom, listening to The Cure and smoking pot? This was her pattern; her dependencies her anchor, weighing her down like so many bad decisions, so many wrong moves.

Amy took a shower and ate some peanut butter on crackers, thinking that she really should go grocery shopping. Instead, she decided to drive out to Utrecht to replenish her painting supplies.

Because she was going to have to buy prestretched canvas, as opposed to building the canvas board and stretching the canvas herself, which Pete usually helped her with, she could afford, at most, fifteen colors. But her palette, she decided, really only needed five—red, yellow, brown, black, and blue—so she stuck to her budget and bought five hues of red, three of yellow, two of blue, three of brown, and two of black. She drove home with five eighteen-by-twenty-four-inch stretched canvas boards in her trunk and a plastic bag full of Cad Red, Crimson, Permanent Rose, Quin Violet, and Magenta; French Ultramarine and Radiant Blue; Brilliant Yellow Light, Brilliant Yellow Red, and Yellow Ochre; Burnt Umber, Brown Madder, and Brown Pink Lake; Paynes Grey and Ivory Black; Chinese takeout and a half bottle of sparkling wine.

As she ate, she stared at the back of Adel's house, wondering about the secrets it kept. When she finished dinner, she walked over to the fence and, without another thought, climbed it. Within seconds, she was in another world entirely.

IT HAD BEEN a little less than two weeks since Adel's murder, but her lawn had already been taken over by weeds, which sprouted triumphantly above the rest of the grass, their furry green and white faces shining toward the sun. The yard was full of the stink of rotting mangoes, which covered the ground under the tree, bug-eaten and fermented. It was just after dusk, and the mosquitoes were out in full force. One landed on Amy's leg and she smacked it, and wiped the resulting blood on the back of her shorts. She saw something move in the grass and realized it was the snake she had seen the other day, which must have taken up residence in the quiet and undisturbed yard.

Spooked, Amy walked toward the house, to where it had been burned and boarded up with plywood. She stood on her toes and tried to look in through the kitchen window, but she couldn't see much—just that the oven had been pushed out of the way, its back scorched and burned through. The house was dark, and she couldn't see beyond the kitchen—couldn't see the rooms where Adel had lived, or the spot where Adel died—and she wanted to. She didn't need the details, but she wanted them. She wanted her work to be true. And so she walked to the back door and tried the knob, but of course it was locked. It was an old knob, an old lock. She took her credit card from her back pocket, and pushed it between the door and the jamb, trying to trick the lock mechanism. When the knob didn't give, she tried it again, and then a third time. On the third try, the knob turned, and Amy took an excited breath. She looked behind her to make sure no one was watching, and pushed into the house.

There was an eerie silence, and an equally eerie darkness, and Amy walked around the house carefully, the way she would a museum, afraid to touch anything. She walked into each bedroom and bathroom, wanting to, but not, opening the medicine cabinet. In the master bedroom, she had an impulse to peruse Adel's closet, the way she used to peruse her mother's, paging through each dress and sweater and blouse, but she didn't. Instead, she sat on Adel's bed, and then lay on it, her feet dangling off of the side. The bed was firm, hard even, and Amy wondered if this was Adel's preference or her husband's. Amy didn't remember Adel's husband, and figured that he had probably been dead a long time. She thought about Adel living alone in that house year after year, sleeping in a bed that was too hard for her, all too aware that death would come. Amy wondered if Adel believed that death would reunite her with her husband. She wondered if it had.

In the living room, Amy stood in front of a shelf lined with framed family photos, and studied them, particularly Adel's face. Amy noticed that Adel did not smile for the camera so much as compose herself for it—stilling her body just long enough for the shutter to snap. Often, a child or grandchild clung to her, a fixture in their lives as permanent as a wall.

A few feet from where Amy stood, a taped outline marked the space where Adel had died. Her legs had been crossed, just above the ankles. One arm was raised in protest, the other, which was not traced, must have been beneath her body. Her head had faced the front door.

Amy approached the spot with deference. She kneeled, and then lay beside it, moving her arms and feet into place to re-create Adel's position. Adel was said to have been bludgeoned, that one half of her face was nearly unrecognizable. She would have fallen, then, on the side of her face that was fine; from there, she would have been able to see the hemline of her curtains. Amy closed one eye and tried to imagine what those final moments must have been like: the air-conditioning; the stillness of the room; the blood making its way down her ear canal, an irritation Adel could do nothing about.

Amy felt her breath catch in her throat. She jumped up and dusted herself off, as though she had gotten something of the moment on her. She quickly left the house through the back door, locking the doorknob and wiping it with the hemline of her T-shirt before climbing over the fence and back into her life.

THE NEXT MORNING, Amy sat outside, drinking coffee and meticulously sketching the scenes that would become her next project—*The Murder of Adel Minor.* The first was the original scene from her dream, the thin band of light squeezing between the curtains, between Adel and her murderer. In the second, Amy decided, the light would change; their faces graying as the murderer advanced toward Adel. The third frame would be the impact, the kettle against her face. The fourth would be Adel lying on the floor, bleeding to death. And the fifth, Amy decided, would be a self-portrait of sorts; she would paint herself as she was the night before, lying next to the outline of Adel's body, assuming Adel's shape.

Fortified with caffeine, she carried her canvases into her newly reclaimed studio and put her new paints away. She pinned her sketches to the wall and clamped a fresh prestretched canvas to her easel, removing the original painting and propping it up against a wall.

She transferred the first image onto the canvas, drawing Adel's kitchen, dining and living rooms as they could be seen from where she was murdered. She then roughed out the figures—Adel in the bottom-left portion of the canvas, her murderer in the center. Once the shapes were roughed in, she took out her reds, yellows, blues, and browns and started in on the painting, fleshing out the details of the room itself—the pictures on the shelves, the dark draperies, the tidy kitchen.

The painting would take weeks, maybe months. The series might take her a year. In that time, the murderer might be caught, tried, and convicted; Pete might move out for good, or sell the house out from under her. Her cancer might return—tumors forming islands in the dark, vast oceans of her body. But now, here, none of it mattered. All that mattered was the light squeezing through the thick, brown draperies, and the way it played off of Adel's face and the murderer's. The line it drew between them.

BERNARD

THE DAY WAS WARM, QUIET, AND still. The sky was a bright blue with perfect cumulous clouds passing, slow as spaceships, over the tiny houses. The thinnest of breezes rippled through palm fronds, which sputtered now and then, teased by the wind. The woman from the postal service arrived and began inching through the neighborhood in her tiny van. Rebecca Biggs arrived to take her mother to the doctor. She used her key to open the door, pushed into the small cool house, and screamed loud enough to scatter the birds that had been sitting idly on the telephone wires outside the house.

And then there were sirens, and then there were neighbors, and it was all happening again. That's what Bernard thought as he walked the side streets to meet Danny, who had called him after they knew what had happened. Together, with the small crowd of neighbors who were home during the day, they stood in the street and watched as Angela's daughter was questioned by police, as Angela's body was carried out, as another murder investigation began.

"I think I'm going to be sick," Bernard said, backing away from the scene.

"You're right," Danny said, "let's get out of here."

Bernard followed Danny down the street. At midday, they made almost no shadow. As they walked, Bernard felt heavy. The sun was so bright it seemed antiseptic. It warmed his skin and caused him to sweat at the neck and underarms and belly. *This is why they tell the elderly to stay inside*, he thought. Out here, he was liable to die of heatstroke.

Inside Danny's, Bernard remembered with a groan that Danny did not run the air-conditioning and so he settled onto the sunporch, accepting the whiskey that Danny offered him, and finishing it in a single swallow. His throat burned. But so did his eyes and ears and the palms of his hands. He didn't know what to say or how, even, to say it. Instead he sat back in the chair and closed his eyes, and when Danny asked him if he wanted more whiskey, Bernard said that he did.

Bernard held the second whiskey up to his forehead, and then pushed the glass against his cheek. He thought: *Adel, Angela, Angela, Adel*, turning their names over in his mind as though there was some puzzle to be solved. Bernard looked out to the golf course, which burned in the heat of the day, little lines of refracted light radiating off the lush green hills. There was a solo golfer out on the course and Bernard watched him swing.

Danny sat down across from Bernard and rocked noisily back and forth on his glider. Bernard looked at Danny and then beyond him, at the golfer as he stepped into his cart and drove away.

Bernard couldn't figure out what Adel and Angela had in common, only that they were old. And probably weak, and frail. Easy targets, he assumed.

"Were they friends, do you know?" he asked.

"Who?"

"Angela and Adel?"

Danny shrugged. "Friendly, probably. Both here from the beginning, just like us."

"Right," Bernard said, working it over.

Finally, he said: "What are we going to do?"

"Do?"

"About the *murders*. We have to do something."

Danny shrugged. "Like vigilantes?"

"Whoever is doing this is targeting girls our age. *Women* our age," he corrected himself. "They might be strangers to us now, but we used to know them. They used to be our friends. Our *wives'* friends. We can't just sit around while they're . . ." Bernard couldn't bring himself to say *beaten to death.*

Danny swished back and forth on the glider for a few silent minutes. Then, Bernard said: "Let's call everyone. All of the originals—everyone who's still here. Do you still have their phone numbers?"

"Some."

"I think I have some too," he said. "We'll meet this afternoon in the clubhouse. That way we can watch the news beforehand, see what happened."

BACK AT HIS house, Bernard dug through a half-century's worth of junk in the drawers of his old metal desk, looking for a list of phone numbers they'd had forever. There were old maps and magazines, extra buttons from shirts and pants he no longer owned, and takeout menus for restaurants that probably didn't exist anymore, but no list. He knew it was somewhere—he could picture the list in his mind's eye. Irene had balled it up and thrown it out during an argument the night after she found out about his affair with Vera, because she'd noticed that he had underlined her name and number. Later that night, after several gin and tonics, Bernard retrieved the list, smoothed it out, and stuck it in a folder marked TAXES.

Remembering this, Bernard found the list right away, opening a drawer in his old metal desk and paging through manila folders until he found the folder marked TAXES. He smoothed the thin, faded paper between his hands, and looked over the list of names. Every original resident of the neighborhood was here, written in an unfamiliar hand, photocopied and passed around for safety and party planning. They were all members of the same club; each had escaped their fates and moved to Florida, a radical idea they'd all had at the same time.

Bernard closed his eyes and exhaled deeply. He didn't want to call anyone, or see anyone. He wanted to lie back down in the well-worn groove of his routine—eating lunch, and watching television, and letting the world go on without him. But he wasn't hungry for lunch. And, really, what choice was there but to corral his old friends, and do what he could?

Before calling anyone, Bernard switched on the TV to watch the twelve o'clock news. It was grim enough to turn his stomach. Angela Greene had been beaten with a rolling pin. *Her* rolling pin, the woman reading the news made sure to mention.

He shook his head. Adel, he had learned, had had her face smashed in with a heavy kettle, and now Angela had been beaten with her rolling pin.

"Police are saying that these murders could be connected," the woman on TV said. "They're also saying that, given the choice of murder weapon, that this could be personal. And that these women—for some reason—are being targeted."

Before she could say more, Bernard turned off the TV and started dialing down the list, getting many disconnected messages along the way. Still, quite a few phones rang. When they did, Bernard's hands would start to shake, his voice to quiver.

"Hello, is this Louise? This is Bernard White from down the street. What's the *matter*? Have you seen the news? We want to get everyone together, all of the originals. What *for*? Do you want to get beaten to death with *your* rolling pin? In an hour. At the old clubhouse rec room."

After the first one he took a deep breath, told himself not to sound so threatening, and pressed on, this time dialing Marty Hines. "Hello? Marty?"

AN HOUR LATER the remaining originals assembled in the clubhouse rec room. While Bernard and Danny worked to arrange chairs in neat rows, the others tentatively and tearfully greeted one another. It was a reunion of sorts, and Bernard realized that so many of them had done the same thing that he had, isolating themselves inside their homes and lives. Together now, the women hugged and cried into each other's necks, or stood in groups of three or four, wringing their hands and quietly fretting. The men, generally, paced.

"Let's everyone sit down," Bernard said, moving uneasily toward the front of the room.

"Let's make this quick, White," Cal Hendricks said. "I've got tee time at two."

"Oh hush, you old bird!" a woman called out.

"OK!" Bernard clasped his hands together in a dull clap. "You all know by now what happened to Angela Greene." He paused a moment to look down at his shoes. "I think it's clear now that us old-timers are being targeted, and I don't want to scare anybody, but it looks like the girls in particular." There was a bit of buzz around the room as the crowd traded whispers. "Now, what we're going to have to do is come up with a solution so that what happened to Angela and Adel doesn't happen to any of us."

"Like what?" someone said.

"We already have a neighborhood watch," someone else said.

"The neighborhood watch is a joke!" another said.

"You're a joke!" someone fired back.

"I was thinking more along the lines of a buddy system. Both of the girls killed were widows. They lived alone. A good bit of us do."

"So what do you want us to do," someone asked. "Pair up?"

"Well . . . yeah."

"Excellent idea!" Danny said. "Pair the widows with the widowers." He looked around the room, lifted a shaky hand, and pointed at Roberta.

"Horny old dog!" someone said.

"It doesn't have to be quite so scandalous," Bernard said. "And it was just an idea. If anyone else has any ideas . . ."

"I'm going to shutter the house and move in with my daughter," Susan Boon said.

"Well how nice for you," Leslie Nelson said. "What about the rest of us?"

"Well, if the cops would just do a better job catching this guy . . ."

"The cops are all a bunch of stoners," Marty Hines said.

"Oh, Marty! That's not true," another responded.

"Sure it's true. I live next to one of 'em. I know reefer when I smell it," Marty said.

"I'm buying a gun," Cal said.

"No one's going to give a gun to a geezer like you," Roberta said.

"'Course they will! This is Florida!" Cal said.

Bernard continued: "So if anybody doesn't have any real ideas—*for the group*—I'd like to see a show of hands of the singletons in here. Who lives alone?"

About twenty or so hands went up.

"Now, who would like to participate in this buddy system?"

Danny's hand shot up in the air, a few others followed.

"Only six of you?"

Roberta and Leslie each raised their hands. Maryanne Wilkerson raised her hand reluctantly. "Only if it's with another woman," Maryanne said.

"Prude," someone muttered.

Bernard took a flyer from the corkboard and asked if anyone had a pen. Roberta emptied the contents of her purse onto her lap. Used wads of tissue, a half a banana, and several coins spilled out onto the floor. "Nope."

"I do," Leslie said, standing up to hand it to Bernard.

"If you're interested in doing this, write your name, address, and phone number on the paper."

The paper was passed around the room. By the time it found its way back to Bernard, nearly all of the singletons had signed it. "OK," Bernard said, studying it. "I guess I should have asked you your preference. Man or woman?"

"I want to live with Avery," Leslie said, naming her long-dead husband. The room fell quiet. "I mean—I'm sorry. I meant to say April." April, who was sitting behind her, squeezed Leslie's shoulder.

A few more people shouted their preferences. "How about it, Roberta?" Danny asked. Roberta gave him a sour look, her face pinched, but she couldn't hide the flush that came to her cheeks.

"All right," she said.

"It's settled," Bernard said.

Maryanne raised her hand. "I still don't have anyone."

"I don't either," Bernard said. "You can stay with me."

"But . . ." she said in a small voice, looking around at all the other women, who were already happily paired.

"OK," Bernard continued. "Everyone else—lock your doors, keep your porch lights on. Keep your curtains closed. And don't let anyone in!"

MARYANNE SAT ON Bernard's old dusty couch, reading the copy of *National Geographic* that she had brought with her, her legs crossed at the ankles, her eyes never moving from the page. She looked as though she were sitting in a waiting room, as though at any moment, someone would call her name and free her from this state of purgatory. After nearly two hours had passed (Bernard was keeping track of the time, wondering how he would ask whether or not she minded if he watched *Oprah*), Maryanne clenched a fist, stood up, and declared that her house had better light.

For Bernard, this was both a relief and a disappointment. He hadn't considered how unfit his house was for a woman. It had been five years since Irene passed, and in that time, he hadn't painted a wall, hadn't washed a drapery, hadn't beaten a rug. He had little food, and what he did have was frozen and probably had been for some time. Maryanne, on the other hand, had a cupboard full of food—foods he'd never tasted, or even known about. She had exotic rice, dried mushrooms, and pasta made from green vegetables. She even had her own vegetable garden. And, within an hour of him being there, she had whipped up the best meal Bernard had eaten in years.

"What do you call this?" he asked. He was sitting across from her in the brightly lit dining area, which, just as in his house, was a small space two feet from the kitchen.

Maryanne looked up from her plate in disbelief. "Eggplant Parmesan. You've never had it?"

"I eat a lot of frozen burritos. You can buy a pack of twenty-four for sixteen dollars at Publix. That's less than seventy cents a burrito."

"How do they taste?"

"OK, I guess."

"You say 'OK' a lot."

"I do?"

"You don't know?"

Bernard considered this. "I guess I do. Call it a verbal crutch. I probably go days without talking to anyone."

"You?"

He considered this for a moment and shrugged. "Probably."

"I find that surprising," she said. "You used to be so . . . social."

He thought about it for a minute, tried to remember a time when he was, in fact, social. Finally, he said, "That was a long time ago."

"Everything was a long time ago," she said, swirling a piece of bread around her plate to sop up the sauce.

"Do you want some wine?" she asked. "I forgot to offer you wine."

"No," he said. "I hardly drink anymore. It's a waste of money. I'm surprised you drink. You're so . . . um . . ."

"Uptight?"

He shrugged. "For lack of a better word."

"Thus, I drink."

"Well by all means," he said, doing a little flourish with his arms. "Don't abstain on my account."

"OK." She laughed. "Now I'm saying it!" She stood up, walked over to the kitchen, and uncorked a bottle of Chianti.

She returned with a very large glass.

"Maybe you should have gone with horny old Danny!" He wiped his mouth and threw his napkin onto his plate.

"Don't make jokes," she said.

"Sorry." Then, "Did you know Adel or Angela well?"

"I don't know anybody well. Not anymore."

They were quiet for a while, each with their own thoughts. "So!" Bernard said finally. "Where am I sleeping?"

"In my son's room."

"And where is that?"

"Down the hall." She pointed. "But give me a few minutes. I haven't changed the sheets in years."

"It's OK," he said, rising from the table. "Neither have I."

IN THE MORNING it was waffles with strawberry sauce, hot coffee, and Gershwin. Bernard heard it before his eyes were open, smelled it before he was awake. It caused him to dream that he was back in his mother's kitchen in Baltimore, the radio playing "Sweet and Low-down," the skillet sizzling around heavy Bisquick pancakes. He woke before he was ready, and spent the next few minutes with his eyes closed, trying to will himself back into that warm sunlit moment, seventy years behind him.

When he began to wake more fully, Bernard opened his eyes and looked around. The walls were blue, the sheets white. A fan whirred noiselessly above him. This had been a boy's room once. It must have belonged to Max, who had died young somehow, perhaps in Vietnam. The room had a large window that looked out into the backyard. The yard itself was a stark contrast to his own, which was dry and yellowed, the only green coming from invasive vines and weeds creeping in from other people's yards. Maryanne's yard was lush and green but not overly manicured. There was a Japanese orchid tree with a thick viney canopy and leaves the size of saucers, a large bougainvillea bursting with hot pink flowers, and a cluster of cabbage palms, each with a decade's worth of dead fronds hanging down the trunks like thick beards. There were butterfly bushes and birds of paradise and peace lilies. There were ferns in huge terracotta planters. There was a fountain off in the corner of the yard where birds bathed and squawked and drank. It was a sort of paradise, a realized Eden.

Gershwin played "Rhapsody in Blue." Bernard fell backward into bed, dizzy. His wife had gardened, and his own yard had once been almost as beautiful as Maryanne's. And so being there, seeing it all spread out before him, reminded him of his Irene, gone for so long now that it seemed she existed in a different world entirely. Being there, looking out into that yard, brought him back with such exacting detail that if you had told Bernard he'd traveled there in a time machine, he would have believed it.

He took his time getting out of bed, and by the time he made his way into the kitchen, Maryanne was already eating.

"Good morning!" she said. "I'm sorry I didn't wait. I thought you'd never get up. Here," she said, standing, "yours is in the oven." She went over to the oven and took out a pan and slid its contents onto a plate. "Strawberries?" she asked, turning her head around to face him. Bernard nodded, and she poured a generous amount of strawberry sauce over the waffles. "How do you take your coffee?"

"With cream, please," he said, and, looking down at her plate, at the half-eaten waffle, the half-drunk coffee, said, "You don't have to wait on me! Please," he said, taking the plate from her hand.

"It's all right." She blushed and looked down and then went back to the table. "I'm sorry," she said.

"No *I'm* sorry. I never—"

"I always waited on Gerald hand and foot." She shook her head and, as if reacting to something unspoken, said, "Of course I did! We *all* did."

"All did what?" Bernard was confused.

"Waited on our husbands!"

"Oh yeah," Bernard said, thinking of Irene. "I guess you did."

"I imagine that kind of thing looks silly now—a woman waiting on her husband. Of course, women today have more important things to do. And we had nothing to do but raise kids and tend house and wait on our husbands hand and foot."

"Are you OK?"

"Of course I am!!"

"Sorry," Bernard said, and cut at the edge of a waffle with the side of his fork.

"Do you want a knife?" she asked, and was up and in the kitchen before he could respond.

"This is delicious," Bernard said, his mouth full.

"Thank you."

There was silence for a while. Gershwin tapped away at "An American in Paris."

When Bernard was finished with the waffles and ready to drink the coffee, he looked around the room for the stereo, but couldn't find one. "Where's the music coming from?"

"My iPod," she said, pointing to a little green Nano sitting on a sound dock between books on a shelf.

"An iPod?"

"It stores music."

"Where?"

"On a little hard drive, I guess."

"How do you get it in there?"

"You have to buy it special."

"Special tiny music . . ." he mused.

"It's really something! You can find anything! Anything at all! Just think of something you'd like to hear."

Bernard sat back in his chair. He hadn't thought about music—*real* music—in decades. He had almost forgotten it existed. "Billie Holiday," he said finally, remembering his boyhood crush.

Maryanne got up from the table, walked over to the iPod, and put on "I'll Be Seeing You." "You and I have the same taste," she said. When she returned, Bernard was crying.

Embarrassed, he got up from the table and made some excuse about a contact lens—he had seen someone do this in a movie once—and dove down the hallway and into the bathroom. There, he took a long hot shower and pulled himself together for the second time that morning. He had thought it might be difficult to live with a woman again after all these years, but not for this reason. He thought he'd be impatient, moody; that he would miss his house, his solitude. Not that he'd be flooded with memories of happier times and happier places. Billie Holiday! Why had he said Billie Holiday? He had no idea that any of this was in him. But he cried and moaned and guffawed in the shower, playing "I'll Be Seeing You" over and over in his head, thinking of Vera and Irene and then of Billie herself, getting all the women he'd ever loved mixed up, until there was only one—a beautiful southern crooner who was also his wife.

By the time he was again ready for the world, the breakfast dishes were already done and put away, the crumbs already shaken from the tablecloth. He thought that Maryanne might have gone out, but her car—an old red Buick Riviera—was still in the driveway. He found her in the backyard, kneeling over a pot of yellow marigolds. To his relief, she didn't mention anything about what had happened. She looked up at him and smiled. "Would you do me a favor?"

"Sure."

"A toad laid some eggs in my potting soil," she said, gesturing to the bag on the other side of the patio with her shovel. "Can you take this shovel and scoop some dirt into this pot?"

She handed him the pot and the shovel and he walked over to the bag and reached his arm down into it. "Whoa!" he said, leaping backward, and tossing a shovelful of dirt onto the patio in the process. "There are frogs in there!"

She smiled at him. She looked like a knockout in her big hat and sunglasses. "Yeah," she said, "that's what I said."

"You said *eggs*, not full-size *frogs*."

"Well, they're toads, and I didn't think I had to draw you a picture. Do you think I'd be afraid of some silly little eggs?"

"What do you want me to do?"

"Just scoop some dirt into that pot."

"But there are frogs in there!"

She took off her sunglasses and looked at him. "Are you afraid of toads?"

"So what if I am, *you* are."

"Fine," she said. "Never mind."

"I'll do it, I'll do it." Bernard went back to the bag, scooped dirt into the pot, and flung the toads into the yard with the shovel. When he was finished, he handed the pot and shovel back to her and stood over her for a few moments, watching.

"Everything all right?" she asked, looking up at him.

"Yeah," he said. "OK. I, um, I think I'll . . ." He looked around, not sure what to do. "Say, do you have a pole saw?"

"I think so. Check the garage."

Bernard went into the garage and quickly found a pole saw hanging by a nail. With it, he returned to the backyard and started sawing off the old dead fronds that were hanging from the cabbage palms.

"What are you doing?" Maryanne called.

"I'm cutting away all this dead stuff."

"I like it the way it is."

"Oh." He looked up at the tree. "It's just that I saw on TV that some kids were driving around and setting them on fire," he called.

"How are they doing that?"

Bernard put down the pole saw and walked over to her. "Fireworks. They're pointing them right at the trees and setting them on fire."

"Well I'll be darned."

"So I'm just going to cut away at the dead."

"OK. Thanks."

He walked back over to the stand of trees, raised the pole saw to the dead fronds, and started sawing away, the large, dead, fanlike fronds falling to earth every now and again in a small papery crash.

MADDIE

IT WAS THE FIRST WEEK OF June and the graduating seniors were already gone—Maddie's best friend, Stacia, among them. So Maddie walked the hallways alone, and when she went to classes, her phone did not buzz with the occasional text message as she and Stacia traded stories about the things that happened to them while the other was not around. She dreaded the idea of being in school for two years without Stacia, who was in New York for the summer studying drama, and would be at Vassar after that, embarking on her real life while Maddie was still in this state of purgatory.

She was actually excited to get to The Smiling Pig that afternoon. Excited for the chance to talk to people—even if she was just taking their dinner orders. But as she turned the corner from Seminole Road to Highway 7, her excitement turned to dread. Three police cruisers had come out of nowhere and surrounded Charlie, boxing him in at the intersection. She watched as two of the officers got out of their cars and pointed guns at him. They shouted for Charlie to put his hands up, but Charlie just stood there, and the moment froze.

There was shouting, confusion, and Maddie didn't know whether to close her eyes or take it in. She was afraid that Charlie would be shot, and that her heart would explode with the trigger. Finally, he held a hand out to the officers and slowly crouched to put his cup down, the officers barking all the while. When Charlie stood up, Maddie could see by the dark stain on the front of his pants that he had wet himself, and she was embarrassed for him.

The officers shouted, "Hands! Behind! Your! Head!" And Charlie put them there, in a stance that reminded Maddie of the butterfly she had pinned to a corkboard in the eighth grade. The officers moved in, and Charlie was on the ground. There was shouting. A large crowd had gathered. There was a gun to the back of his head. Maddie couldn't see his face, but she pictured it—puffy, like bruised skin, in a kind of stunned wonderment.

Then, the officers picked him up, pressed the gun between his shoulder blades, and tucked Charlie into the back of the cruiser, efficient as a factory assembly line.

Maddie watched as the cruiser sped away, and then ran to the restaurant and marched into the kitchen.

"What the hell?" she screamed. "The police just arrested Charlie!"

"*Who?*" her boss asked.

"Charlie, the homeless man who comes here every night. The one they..." She stopped to catch her breath. "The one they asked me about."

"They arrested him? When?"

"Just now, right outside."

"I'm sure they wouldn't have arrested him without reason."

"Obviously!" Maddie barked. "They must think he's the killer." She looked down at her shoes, wiped a stray tear from her eye.

"It's just some homeless guy, Maddie. It's not the end of the world."

Maddie closed her eyes and shook her head. "I'm sure he didn't do it."

"I'm sure the police know more about it than you do. That mug shot they showed you didn't come out of nowhere. I heard he has a history of breaking and entering."

"He does?" she asked, thinking of her ransacked bedroom.

"You shouldn't feel sorry for people like that, Maddie. They're there because of their own actions. You don't see me out on a corner, do you?"

"No," Maddie conceded.

"And do you know why that is?" He put his hands on his hips.

"Because your parents gave you this restaurant when they died."

"You shouldn't be so goddamned smug," he said, letting his arms fall to his sides.

"Sorry," she said, looking again at her feet.

Maddie left the kitchen and went into the bathroom. She pulled the chain on the swinging lightbulb and looked at herself in the mirror. She wanted to cry. She could feel the urge stuck in her throat. It was the same as when the clouds built up in the afternoon and she waited for the rain. All of the ingredients were there, and still—sometimes, the rain didn't come.

She took her Swiss Army knife from her backpack and pulled her pants down to expose her thigh. She had cut herself just three days before in the bathroom at school, for no other reason than that she thought she needed it to get through the day. Her skin was pink and tender and swollen around the cut. Still, she cleaned the blade and didn't wait for the alcohol to dry before pressing it into her thigh. Maddie bit her lip and then exhaled. She thought: *pain pain pain pain pain pain pain.*

MINUTES. THAT WAS all the day was. She collected several of them in that bathroom. Five or seven or ten. Enough where, after she cleaned the knife, bandaged her cut, and went back into the dining room, there were five tables waiting for her. She sprung into a kind of autopilot and time seemed to burn around her, like so much fluorescent, so much neon. All the while, her leg burned right along with it, giving her something to think about, something to focus on other than the pain she felt but could not see. The minutes bled around her, and soon, the night was over. It was as if she put her head down for a few minutes and looked up when it was dark, the restaurant empty.

Maddie locked the front door and switched off the neon signs. She was just about to start cleaning when someone came behind her and put their hands over her eyes. She was sure it was one of the cooks, and that this was her worst nightmare come true, but she spun around to see the boy from the other night, the carryout customer who had asked her out.

"Where did you come from?" she asked, petulant.

"I hid behind the bar."

"You shouldn't be here. We're closed."

"I wanted to see you."

"Why?" she asked, and when he shrugged, she said: "I don't even know who you are."

"My name is Nate." He held out his hand to her, but Maddie didn't shake it.

"You should get out of here."

"You should come with me."

"I'm not in the habit of leaving my place of work with strangers."

"My name is Nate," he said again. "I live about ten minutes from here with my mom. I go to Broward Community and I work construction part-time."

"You're in *college*?"

"You're not?"

"I'm *fifteen*."

"All the more reason why you should come with me."

Maddie looked around the restaurant. There was a mess on every table and plates stacked high on the bar. There were fries and crayons and napkins on the floor.

"Help me clean up and I'll think about it."

And so he helped her, noiselessly clearing tables, stacking chairs, and sweeping. The restaurant was clean in half the time, and when she was ready to go, Maddie made Nate wait outside while she settled out with Bob and went into the bathroom to evaluate her appearance.

That night had been a particularly bad one for stains. She had a badge of barbecue on her chest and frank 'n' bean juice up her right sleeve. She had spilled Coke down her front, the result of carrying too many drinks on a tray. Aside from that, she looked OK. She washed her face and hands with the crappy pink hand soap and changed into the clothes she'd worn to school that day. She smeared lip gloss on her lips and rubbed some into her cheeks as well, doing what she could.

Before she left the bathroom, she took one last look at herself. She was leaving the restaurant with a stranger—a *male* stranger—who could in fact rape her and kill her and bury her in his backyard if he wanted to. Maddie decided that she was OK with that. That she would prefer almost anything to walking home alone, and being at home alone, and waking up and going to school the next day—alone. She took a deep breath and left the room.

NATE HAD A blue Ford pickup that was hard, at first, for Maddie to climb into. She had to put her foot on the floor of the cab and leverage herself against the door to climb in. Once she was up, Nate helped her by taking her arm and pulling her in. Then, he backed quickly out of the parking spot and peeled wheels as he pulled onto Highway 7.

"Where would you like to go?" he asked, his voice deep.

"I don't know," she said with a shrug. "Where do you go with a stranger at nine thirty on a Wednesday night?"

He drove her to the parking lot of an abandoned movie theater and parked under a sprawling laurel oak. "Do you want a beer?" he asked, pulling a can of Budweiser from behind the passenger seat.

Maddie had had beer exactly twice in her life. Once, the odd can that sat in the back of her refrigerator for months and months that Maddie drank one night out of boredom, and once at a party with Stacia. Both times, she hated the taste. Still, she said yes. The beers opened with a satisfying crack and Maddie sipped hers voraciously despite the taste, which was, as predicted, awful.

They opened the windows and talked for a while. She learned that he had graduated two years before and now attended Broward Community part-time. The rest of the time, he worked for his father's construction company. To prove this, he showed her his muscle and his farmer's tan line. When she asked him what he was going to college for, he shrugged and said, "So I don't have to work construction, I guess."

"I mean, what are you studying?"

"General stuff. I'm taking astronomy and statistics and the first part of U.S. history."

"Oh," Maddie said, disappointed. If she were in college now, she didn't know what she would be studying either. But she hoped to figure it out by the time she got there.

"So, am I the first fifteen-year-old waitress you've ever tried to pick up, or just the first one that said yes?"

"Both," he said, smiling.

She looked at him, but he didn't say anything. He seemed to be waiting for her to say something else, to give him some kind of signal, but Maddie didn't know any signals. So she watched him—watched his eyes as they went over her, watched his lips as he grinned at her. She thought about going for the door handle, jumping out and running away. She was afraid now, afraid that it really was his plan to rape and kill her. But she didn't, and he didn't. Instead, he slid across the seat until he was beside her and put his hand on her thigh. It was the same thigh she had cut that night, and the weight of his hand sent tiny waves of pain out from the cut, like radio or sonar. She gasped a bit and he must have taken this—this parting of her lips—as an invitation, because he leaned in and kissed her. The kiss was wet and soft and he moved his hand from her thigh to her breast and pressed her against the door, kissing her still, harder now. She could feel the door handle in her back. It hurt, but she didn't say anything.

Maddie liked the feeling of being kissed. She liked that it took away every other feeling she had, numbing them out to the point of fuzzy abstraction. Suddenly, the only things that mattered were physical—their lips, their tongues, their breath, the door handle in her back, the throbbing of her leg. He pressed her against the door harder, one hand on the inside of her thigh, the other on her breast, groping and squeezing as he kissed her hungrily and she tried to keep up.

He smelled of sweat and spit. He tasted like Budweiser, and Maddie wondered if he'd had more than the one beer that night, if he had been driving around, drinking, if he was more dangerous than he seemed. But right then, she didn't care. He slipped his hand under her shirt. It was rough and calloused. She felt as though she was caught in the undertow, as though she would drown or be taken out to sea. The cab was hot with their breath. It made her dizzy.

He dug his hand under her bra, cupped her breast, and pinched her nipple.

"Ow," she said.

"Sorry." He released his grip but left his hand and continued to kiss her.

Maddie wanted to pull away but there was nowhere for her to go. She was pressed against the window, against the door. Finally, she put a hand on his shoulder—it was thick and muscular, and she was surprised by it; he looked thin in his T-shirt and jeans, but underneath he was a man, muscular and powerful. She pushed against him, and he stopped.

"What's the matter?" he said.

"I have to get home."

"Oh," he said, regarding her. "OK." He slid back into his seat and combed his hair with his fingers before starting the engine.

"Where to?"

"Oh, um, straight down Seminole Road, left on Golf View Lane."

They drove in silence down Seminole. It was after eleven and she'd never gotten home so late. Her father was at work, but Brian would be waiting by the window, worried.

"This is where those old ladies were killed," Nate said, after they turned into the neighborhood.

"Yeah," she said. It was all she could think to say.

"Did you know them?"

"No."

"Are you scared?"

"No."

INSIDE, THE HOUSE was dark and messy. She tripped over a pair of shoes by the front door and picked them up and carried them into Brian's room. He was not asleep but pretending to be.

"Who was that?" he asked, opening his eyes and looking up at her.

"No one," she said.

AMY

SOMEONE HAD TAKEN A VIDEO OF the arrest and sent it into one of the local news stations, which played it—the police cars, the confusion, the arrest—in a loop. It happened so quickly that Amy had to pause her DVR to get a better look. She pulled her sketchpad onto her lap and started sketching the scenes, and then—only—his face.

He was a homeless man, a beggar. She had seen him a million times and would occasionally give him a dollar or two when she had cash, which she rarely carried. He didn't look like a murderer. He looked kind and sad and maybe somewhat disturbed. But not a murderer. As she sketched him—his round face, broad mouth, and thick eyelashes—she tried to place him in the scene she had imagined at Adel's. She tried to see his face going angry, tried to imagine him baring his teeth, the snarl of a dog. But that face—the face of the man who always said "thank you" or "God bless you" when she handed him a dollar—would not go that way. And so she wondered: *Why?*

On the news there was no discussion of motive. Only that police believed that this man—Charles Abbott—had beaten both Adel and Angela to death, Adel with a single blow from a heavy kettle, and Angela multiple times with a rolling pin.

Amy sat with the information for a while, running her fingers over the drawing of the beggar's face as the room grew dark. It didn't make sense to her, but Amy wondered if any of these things ever made sense.

You couldn't always draw a line between what had happened and the reason why.

Feeling restless, Amy put her sketchpad away and went outside. She supposed she should have felt better—safer—but she didn't. If anything, she felt more unsettled, more afraid. She felt, strongly now, that the thing that was going to happen hadn't yet. And that this, the hasty arrest of a homeless man, was not the end.

In the garage, she stood across from the painting she had finished early that morning, her first finished painting in three years, and studied it, particularly the murderer, who looked nothing like the man who had been arrested. Nothing like anyone she had ever seen. The man in her painting had a long, flat nose, and a long, broad, angry face, with features that bunched in the center, like a thumbprint cookie filled with jam. Amy wondered where in her imagination he had come from. Had she seen him somewhere before?

No. He was a figment, a character, a boogeyman.

She sighed deeply and picked up her brushes to feel if they were dry. When she found that they were, she removed the finished painting and anchored a clean prestretched canvas to her easel. She selected a #2 fine-tipped brush, and started on Charles Abbott's face. She painted his lips, eyes, and strong broad cheeks in black and filled them in with Quin Violet so that his face was ruddy and flushed. She painted his eyes brown with little flecks of purple. She took her knife and mixed some of the Quin Violet with crimson to stain his mouth a deep, dark, exaggerated red. She went over his face again and again, giving it shadow and definition. She selected a #6 brush and shaped his head and hair, giving him wispy bleached curls around his forehead and ears. She gave him fat, detached earlobes and a wide, broad neck.

When she was finished, she put her brush down and stepped back to look at him.

But the man she saw was not Charles Abbott. The man she saw— who stared back at her with stained lips and dark, angry eyes—was the same man from her first painting. He was a fiction. And yet, he was so real that if she listened, she could hear his voice. If she stood still, she could feel his breath on her hand.

Amy looked away but found him again in the first painting, which was now leaning against the washing machine. He seemed to want to leap out of the painting and come after her. Amy was afraid then to look away, to leave his angry gaze and turn to her left, for fear he might be standing beside her, or behind her, or completely encircling her, a ring of specters in a house of mirrors.

Spooked, Amy left the garage before turning off the lights and locked it at the knob and bolt. She then locked herself in her house and poured a brandy and drank it quickly. She found an old utility knife of Pete's, put it in her pocket, and carried the Maglite from room to room as she turned on lights.

BERNARD

BERNARD AND MARYANNE ATTENDED ANGELA GREENE'S funeral together, but skipped the postfuneral lunch in favor of leftover chicken potpie and the comfort of their mutual silence. Everyone, it seemed, agreed that it was best to wait a couple of weeks to ensure the police had the right person before returning to their lives and homes. They all remembered the serial rapist from the 1980s, who continued terrorizing the beachside motels long after the police had made an arrest. And so, to Bernard's relief, the buddy system would remain intact.

He had come, in the span of a week, to feel as though everything would be OK so long as Maryanne was five or ten feet away from him; so long as she would look up from her book every now and again, and remark about something she was reading. He was starting to think that a great correction was taking place in his life, some invisible hand reaching down and moving him several inches to the left or right, changing everything. Every day, they would do some wondrously simple thing around the house, and each night they would eat some wondrously delicious meal. It was amazing to him how you could establish a routine with a perfect stranger; how human beings, if they wanted to, could work together like machines.

After lunch that day, they put on work clothes and went into the front yard to weed Maryanne's huge front garden—Bernard hacking away at the dead undergrowth in a small grove of banana trees, and

Maryanne pruning butterfly bushes and pulling weeds from between the ground orchids and betonies. It was brutally hot outside, but it felt good to be working. If you stayed in the garden long enough, Bernard realized, the work would take over and your mind would go blank. This was probably why Irene spent so much time outside, why her garden always looked so lovely. She had needed an escape just as much as he had—maybe more.

He was pulling the last of the dead leaves from the banana trees when a bolt of lightning split the sky.

"Hey, Maryanne!" he called across the yard. "Better head in."

She shrugged. "It's miles away."

Bernard, who had seen someone struck by lightning at a carnival when he was young, shook his head, and repeated the words Maryanne had used a few days before when discussing the specifics of her compost pile, "Respect nature and it'll respect you."

"All right, all right," she said, standing up. "Help me take all this stuff around back."

He pushed her wheelbarrow into the backyard, and emptied its contents into the compost pile, turning it over a couple of times with a hoe to mix the dead plants in with the dirt and food scraps Bernard recognized from the meals he'd enjoyed over the last couple of days.

They made it in just before the rain started to fall and settled on the screened-in porch.

"Shoot," Bernard said, looking at his watch. "Missed *Oprah*."

"Safe to say Oprah didn't miss you," Maryanne said, picking up a book and finding the page she'd marked.

Outside, the wind picked up and blew the long flat leaves of the banana trees open like sails. Within seconds, the sky broke open and it began to rain.

"Think everything will be OK in the pile in the backyard?"

"What's that?" Maryanne asked, looking up from her book, her red drugstore reading glasses at the end of her nose.

"The pile, the heap, the what-do-you-call-it, where you throw the scraps."

"The compost? It'll be fine."

She looked back down at her book, but Bernard didn't look away. Every time he looked at her she looked less and less like herself and more and more like Vera. They were both redheads, after all, both tall and fair skinned too. For all anyone knew, this is what Vera would look like at seventy-some. As it was, Vera was still thirty-five, frozen in time for anyone who still remembered her.

"What?" Maryanne asked, noticing that he was staring.

"Sorry . . . it's just . . . you remind me of someone."

"Don't say your wife," she said with an air of annoyance.

"No, not my wife. My, um . . ."

"Sister?" she asked, an eyebrow raised.

"Of Vera. Vera Johnson. You may not remember her. She lived . . ."

"Oh, I remember her."

"Oh?"

"Oh yes—and I should hope I don't remind you of her."

"Why not? She was a beautiful woman."

"She was that and more."

"What do you mean?"

Maryanne shook her head. "You can't think that you were the only one."

"What do you mean, 'the only one'?"

She took off her glasses and looked at him. "You really don't know."

"I really don't know what?"

She exhaled audibly and looked down at her lap.

"Vera was sleeping with *half* the neighborhood. Before she killed herself, it was . . . a running joke."

The wind picked up and the rain changed direction, spraying them with a fine mist. Bernard felt heavy, sick.

"Well I'm sorry if that's some big revelation for you," Maryanne said. When he did not reply, she reached over and put her hand on his.

But Bernard was already gone, back to the day it happened, and all the days that led up to it.

◆　　◆　　◆

THAT FIRST NIGHT, walking back to her house, the skirt of Vera's dress swinging as she walked. The sound of the ice cubes clinking against glass as she made their drinks. The way her hair released wafts of Prell as it came tumbling down to her shoulders in broad red tendrils.

"I . . . I've never . . . ," he said, wanting to say something about his marriage, and the fact that he'd never cheated on his wife.

"It's easy," she said. "Just close your eyes and go."

And so he kissed her, and her body eased beneath him.

Afterward, she pinned up her hair, asked him if he wanted another drink.

"I should probably be getting back," he said.

"You should leave through the backyard, through the gate."

"OK," he said, standing to tuck in his shirt and zip up his pants. "Can I see you again?"

She seemed to examine him—to look at his waist, his chest, his face.

"I'll leave the porch light on," she said. "If it's on, come around through the back. If it's not, don't."

The next day at work, he thought of almost nothing else. An accountant for Florida Power & Light, he spent the day preparing an internal audit, and thinking of her—the memory and anticipation nearly as thrilling as the act itself.

That evening, at home with Irene, he didn't taste the meal she had made, or hear his kids as they told him about their art projects and spelling tests. He thought of red hair spilling over white shoulders, and how he might get out to see her later.

"I'll do the dishes," he said, standing after the meal.

"Really?" Irene said to him, her head cocked in surprise.

"Sure," he said. "Why don't you all go for a walk or something? It's a nice night."

"Why don't you come with us?" she said, her arm around his waist now.

"Go on ahead," he said. "I insist."

They left the house, and he did the dishes, imagining Vera doing the same, a strand of hair coming loose from her twist. At the sink, he waited for the daylight to go, for the night to fully come. But what would he say when Irene came home with the kids? *I think I'd like a walk.* Or, *I think we're out of milk.* He checked the fridge. They had a full half gallon.

When he heard Irene and the kids at the door, he still didn't have an excuse. How would he see if her light was on? How would he get out?

Quickly, Bernard went for the milk, poured it down the drain, and crushed the container.

"Wow," Irene said, coming into the kitchen and putting her arms around his waist. "I can't believe how fast you cleaned up."

"No big deal," he said. "I'll do it again tomorrow if you want."

"I do want," she said, putting her arms around his neck and kissing him.

"I think we're out of milk," he said. "I can go get some."

"I just bought milk," she said, opening the refrigerator door. "Huh," she said, a hand on her hip. "I could have sworn . . ."

"It's no trouble," he said. "I'll just pick some up."

"Could you get me some cigarettes, then? And a magazine or something?"

Once he backed out of the driveway, Bernard realized the mistake he'd made. He couldn't go to Vera's like that—with his car and an errand to run.

But it was for naught. When he passed her house, he saw that it was dark—there was no light; no invitation in.

At Publix he bought a gallon of milk, which cost $1.12, and a pack of Salems, which cost $.50. He was down $1.62 for the night, not including tax, and wouldn't even get to see Vera.

In the magazine aisle, he picked up copies of *Women's Day*, *Look*, and *Life*, but put *Life* down when he discovered the cover story was about an extramarital affair. In the checkout aisle, he also put down the copy of *Women's Day*.

"For your wife?" the woman in front of him had asked.

"Yes."

"A man should never bring home a magazine that offers diet tips," she'd said.

And so Bernard stuffed *Women's Day* behind a tabloid and grudgingly handed over $2.75 to the cashier.

He left the store, angry at himself, at Vera, and strangely, Irene, if only for being the thing that stood in his way. But when he turned the corner from Golf View Lane to SW Seventh, his anger faded. Vera's light was on.

He pulled into his driveway, everything in him suddenly tingling.

"I got you a copy of *Look*," he said to Irene, handing her the magazine as she sat in front of the television.

"Thanks," she said. "And the cigarettes?"

"Yup." He handed over the pack of Salems and a book of matches.

Bernard put the milk in the fridge and came back to the living room. He stood with a hand on the back of Irene's chair, and looked at the television, which was playing a rerun of *Gunsmoke*.

"Do you want to sit here?" she asked, looking up.

"No," he said, "you stay put. I think I'll go for a walk. I'm feeling a little . . . restless."

"Is everything OK?"

"Of course! It's just . . . such a nice night."

Finally out of the house, Bernard practically sailed to Vera's. Once in front of her house, he looked up and down the street at the dark porches and through the lighted windows to make sure no one saw him when he opened the gate and disappeared into her backyard.

He found her on the porch, reading a magazine, the radio on.

"I was beginning to think you weren't going to show," she said.

"I had to run to the store. Is your husband, uh . . ."

"Working, yes. Can I get you something? Gin?"

"That would be great," he said.

"Have a seat, then," she said. "You're making me nervous."

Vera returned with his gin and sat next to him on the wicker sofa.

"I'm not going to ask you how your day was. But you can ask me about mine, if you want."

"How, um, how was your day?"

"Ordinary," she said. "The kids like it here. They're not in school yet, because of the move, so . . . they're here all the time. I'm thinking of getting a nanny. Get some time to myself. But that's probably boring to you, the talk of a housewife."

"Not at all," he lied.

"It is. It's fine," she said, putting down her drink. "It bores me too."

"I thought about you all day," he said. "Wondered what you were doing, what you were thinking. What your life is like."

"My life is the same as your wife's, I'm sure."

Bernard downed his gin and put his glass down. "Let's start over," he said, turning to her. "I thought about you all day—what you must look like under your clothes. And the way your hair smells. And the way it feels to be near you."

"I'm surprised," she said, moving closer to him. "You don't seem like a brave person, but that was a brave thing to say."

"I'm not brave," he said, their faces so close together he could smell the gin on her breath.

"Then why are you here?"

He could sense her vulnerability, her sadness.

"Because," he said, "you invited me."

They kissed, and she climbed on top of him, straddling his lap.

"Can I take your hair down?" he asked.

"No," she said. But unpinned it herself, and the red tendrils came tumbling down.

In bed that night with Irene, he didn't feel the weight of the things that he'd done. Didn't feel wrong. He felt like a man about to embark on a great journey. Like Christopher Columbus, or the men at NASA. He was going somewhere foreign, somewhere he had never been.

He saw her three times a week for nearly a year. Each time, it was gin and tonics and easy, if not superficial, conversation. He could always tell that she'd made herself up for him, that she'd put on a clean dress and dabbed some Réplique behind her ears. They'd finish their drinks and tug at each other's clothing, and suddenly everything in his life would fade into the background. He wasn't a husband, a father, or even an accountant. He was only a man, only a body. And she was . . . this *perfect, perfect* woman. He didn't know he needed her until he had her. Didn't know his life was black and white until he stepped into color.

THE RAIN CAME down in curtains and Bernard watched it through the screen.

"How many other men was it?" he wanted to know.

"What?" Maryanne asked, looking up from her book.

"With Vera?"

"How should I know?" She shrugged.

"Never mind," he said, shaking his head. He felt somehow paralyzed, like he couldn't move even if he wanted to. "It's just that . . . we were together all the time. We were in love. I don't know how she could have . . . where she would have found the time."

Maryanne shook her head. "Things aren't always what they seem."

"Things," he said, agitated.

"People, OK?" She closed her book, muttered: "I'm sorry I said anything."

"Was it Cal? Cal Hendricks? Was he one?"

"I don't know," she said. "I doubt it."

"Doubt it why?"

"Too confident," Maryanne said, standing up. "Not her type."

She walked away, leaving him on the porch by himself.

Outside, the sky brightened as the storm rumbled northward, and life returned to the yard. Songbirds bathed themselves in puddles, and geckos hopped happily from leaf to leaf of the potted colocasia, drinking from droplets that formed on the surface of its large flat leaves. Bernard watched as a white ibis swooped down and peeled a black snake off the ground. The snake hung like a cord from its beak, and a gaggle of birds collected around the ibis, tearing at the snake. The ibis, flustered, dropped the snake, only to swoop down upon it again and carry it away.

MADDIE

THAT NIGHT, MADDIE DREAMED THAT CHARLIE was at her window. He tapped on it to wake her, and spoke, but she couldn't hear him through the glass. *You're in jail*, she thought. *I'm dreaming.* She put her hand on the glass and he did the same, his mouth moving all the while, speaking words that Maddie couldn't hear. When Maddie woke shortly after, she was both relieved and disappointed. She thought of him, sleeping on a bunk in jail, and wondered what he dreamed about. Did he dream about freedom—standing on the corner again? Eating brisket? Seeing her? She imagined him there, in bed with her, his head on her shoulder, and wished that he could be. She wished that she could be something to him, some love or comfort. Maybe she would visit him in jail. Maybe they would become friends, or something more. She imagined him on top of her, doing things that Nate might do, if she let him.

She hadn't spoken to Nate since that night in his truck. He'd texted her, but Maddie hadn't responded. She felt embarrassed for what she had done, what she'd let him do. She felt foolish and fifteen, out of her element. She missed Stacia. They'd sit up nights together, talking, sometimes Maddie sleeping at Stacia's and sometimes Stacia sleeping at Maddie's. There was comfort from having a friend you loved and who loved you. Without her, and without her mother, Maddie felt completely alone. And the daily Facebook posts that Stacia was tagged in—pictures of her onstage and in the park with her theater friends—made Maddie feel even more alone. Maddie had recently stopped commenting on and liking the posts, because doing so made her feel desperate. She had stopped texting when Stacia stopped responding. Maddie was angry with her for dropping off the way she had. It was too similar to what her mother had done, and Stacia, if she had been thinking at all, would have known that.

Still, as she lay there in the middle of the night, she wanted nothing more than to talk to Stacia or her mother—someone. If she could talk to Stacia, she would tell her about the things that had happened in the truck with Nate. If she could talk to her mother, she would tell her that she was in love with Charlie.

She said it out loud: "I'm in love with Charlie."

Charlie brought her a bracelet once. He had probably found it on the ground somewhere, but still, he brought it to her. He'd held it up and said, "Look. Pretty." It had a broken clasp and rusted charms. She'd never worn it but had kept it hidden in a drawer of her mother's jewelry box. Maybe she should wear it now, out of solidarity. Maybe she could have T-shirts made that said: CHARLIE IS INNOCENT.

But she didn't know that to be true. She didn't know anything. She tried to imagine him doing the things they said he had done, but couldn't—she couldn't picture Charlie as a murderer or a thief.

"You don't know anyone," she said to herself. "But everyone knows you."

LATER, WHEN THE sirens started, she was standing behind the bar at work, breathlessly reading the final pages of *The Awakening*, and crying, thinking of her mother. She looked up to see the parade of police cruisers speed past, and ran out to watch them turn, one at a time, down Seminole Road.

"What's happening?" she asked a man who was standing at the corner. But he only shrugged, stepped on his cigarette, and walked away.

Maddie ran back to The Smiling Pig. She looked briefly into the empty restaurant, and ran home.

At home, the door was unlocked, but the house was empty.

Brian had left the television on in his room, a plate of half-eaten grilled cheese on the floor. Maddie called for him and searched the house. When she couldn't find him, she ran up the street, following the sound of the sirens, and found her brother in the crowd that had gathered outside the house the police had surrounded. She wanted to yell at him, to pull him out of the crowd and bring him home, but she didn't. She took her place beside him instead, and stood with the others, watching the house.

"What happened?" she asked him.

Brian shrugged, not looking at her.

It felt wrong to be there, but she couldn't move. She was terrified by the possibilities.

"Do you know who lives there?" she asked someone else in the crowd.

"An old lady," he said. "I don't know her name."

Maddie started to cry. She wiped her tears with the back of her hand and pulled her brother out of the crowd.

"Stop, Maddie!" he whined.

"This isn't right," she scolded him. "Go home and get your schoolbooks. You're coming with me to work."

Brian rolled his eyes and shook his arm free but didn't protest. They walked together in silence for a while and then he said: "What do you think happened?"

"What do *you* think happened?" she asked.

"I think . . . another woman was killed."

"I do too," Maddie said.

He took her hand. "I wish Mom was here."

"I do too."

When she got back to The Smiling Pig, her boss was waiting on two tables.

"What the hell, Maddie?" he asked.

"Go sit at the bar and do your homework," she told her brother. "I'll get you a Coke."

"I'm sorry," she told her boss. "I had to go and get my brother."

"So what now? You're babysitting?"

"I don't want him to be at home alone."

"Just make sure he pays for that Coke," he said, and went back into the kitchen.

"Your boss is a jerk," Brian said.

"Just do your homework."

It was slow for the next hour, and Maddie busied herself with side-work. She thought of Edna Pontellier, and of her mother, out there somewhere. She watched her brother sitting at the bar, chewing on the end of his pencil. School would be out in a week. She wondered what they would do all summer—the first since their mother left.

"Hey, Maddie?" her brother called. "Can I order some food?"

"Yeah," Maddie said, and went to take his order.

The restaurant started to fill. Everyone seemed to know the details of what had happened in the neighborhood. Another old lady was murdered. Beaten, they said, with a golf club. The idea of it was so horrible that Maddie thought she might throw up. She felt fuzzy all over, like she was full of static. She wanted a way out of that feeling—out of all of those feelings. She decided that she would go home and cut herself over and over until the feelings went away.

"Can I leave now?" Brian was asking her.

"*No,*" Maddie said. "You can't leave."

"Why not?"

"Because," she said impatiently. "There's somebody *out there.*"

"But he's killing old ladies," he said dismissively.

"You can't leave."

The restaurant was bright and loud. Maddie was grateful for it, and for the busy night that kept her moving between the kitchen and dining room, carrying plates. But every time she passed her brother, he seemed to have another request. "Can I have more Coke?" "Do you have dessert here?" "Are you sure I can't leave?"

Finally, she dropped a stack of plates next to him and looked at him, exasperated. "Is this what you did to Mom?"

When Brian started to cry, Maddie rolled her eyes and carried the plates back to the kitchen. When she returned, her brother was gone and Nate was there, standing where her brother had been just a moment before.

"Hi," he said, smiling.

"There was a boy here," she said. "Did you see him?"

He shrugged, stupidly. "I just got here."

"Damn it!" she yelled, and ran out of the restaurant.

"Brian!" she called, looking up and down the street. "Brian!" She ran to the corner and looked down Seminole, but he wasn't there, so Maddie ran home, leaving the restaurant as it was, full of dirty tables, plates of barbecue, and people.

She found Brian on their front stoop, sobbing into his hands.

When Maddie sat next to him, Brian slumped against her and cried into her lap.

"Why would you say that?" he cried. "Why would you *say that*?"

"I'm sorry," she whispered, petting him.

"It's not fair!"

"I know."

"I miss her," he whimpered.

"I miss her too," she said, petting him. His hair was long around his ears and neck. She wondered when was the last time he had a haircut, and decided that she would take him for one that weekend. That she would take care of him.

He sat up after a while and wiped his face on her shoulder. "When you get your license, can we go somewhere?"

"Like where?" she asked, looking out onto the dark street.

"Like . . . where do you think she is?"

"I don't know, Brian. Where do *you* think she is?"

"Georgia," he said.

"I don't think she's in Georgia," Maddie said. "I think she's . . ." She tried to imagine it. Where *was* her mother? "I think she's just . . . gone."

"No she's not!" Brian said. "She's not *gone*."

"Think about it. If she was around and she heard what was happening here, wouldn't she come home?"

Brian shrugged, looked down at his shoes.

"She can't be," he said.

"Why?"

He shrugged again. "Just because."

"I have to go back to work."

"Don't make me go with you."

"Will you, please?"

"I'll be fine. I'm *always* by myself."

"I know you are."

"Please?" he asked. "I just wanna eat ice cream and watch TV."

Maddie smiled at him. "That sounds really good."

"You wanna stay here with me?"

"I'll get fired if I don't go back. Just make sure you turn on all the lights in the house, OK? And lock the doors."

Maddie walked back, worried about her brother, the state of the restaurant, and the dark streets. If someone else had been killed, then it wasn't Charlie. She wondered if he would be released, and what she would say to him if she saw him.

Two blocks from the restaurant, Nate pulled up beside her in his truck. "Where'd you go?" he asked. "Your boss is pissed."

"Great," Maddie said.

"You want a ride?"

"No," she said. "I'm almost there."

THE RESTAURANT WAS mostly empty, and a mess. Maddie scanned the room, looking for Charlie. When she didn't find him, she went back into the kitchen to find her boss.

"Well if it isn't the disappearing, reappearing waitress," he said.

"I'm sorry."

"What is it with your generation anyway?"

"I don't know," she said, looking down.

"Get out there and clean up."

When Maddie left the restaurant an hour later, Nate was waiting for her in the parking lot.

"What are you doing here?" she asked.

"You keep blowing me off. I want to talk to you."

"What about?"

"I don't know." He shrugged. "Do you want to hang out?"

Maddie looked down the street. The light in front of the firehouse was flashing yellow. A few cars passed.

"Why don't you get in the truck? I'll take you home."

She looked at him, frowned. "I don't want to go home."

"Where do you want to go?"

Maddie shrugged. "I don't know."

They drove out to the beach, sat in the sand, and talked. He told her that his parents had gotten back together that week after a long separation, and she told him about her mother.

"My dad works at the airport, second shift," she told him. "He's gone a lot now—working extra hours and stuff. He says it's because we need the money, but I think it's because he can't face being at home without her. The weird thing is, we're *all* alone with it. Alone with the same thing. You know?"

She looked at him. He was staring out at the lights on the ocean—cruise ships coming in or going out.

"Yeah," he said. "I think I know what you mean."

"What's it like for your dad to be back?"

"It's, um . . . it sucks, actually. My mom is so happy about it, but I'm still mad at him. He lived with another woman for, like, four years. They had a kid together. How can you just . . . You know?"

"Yeah," Maddie said.

"Whatever," he said, standing up and dusting sand from his backside. "I'm tired of thinking about it."

Maddie stood up too. "Where would you go if you could go anywhere?"

"I don't know," he said. "I mean, I have a car. I guess I could go any-where."

"Why don't you?"

He shrugged. "Habit, I guess."

He took her hand and they walked down the beach together.

"It's nice to talk to somebody," he said. "My friends are . . . kind of Neanderthals."

"Yeah?"

"My friend Teddy put his fist through a wall the other day, mad about something."

"What about?"

"Who knows?" He shrugged.

"I feel like . . . there's violence everywhere now. I'm afraid all the time."

"Don't be," he said, putting an arm around her.

It was dark on the beach, the new moon a sliver in the hazy, humid sky.

"Are you hungry?" he asked. "I was gonna get some food at The Smiling Pig but then I never did."

"Not really," she said. "I'm always kind of sick of food after work."

She stood at the surf and looked out at the ocean. All she could see was blackness.

"Someone broke into my house," she said. "Like . . . two weeks ago. I didn't say anything. I didn't tell my dad or call the police."

"Why not?"

She shrugged. "I was afraid."

"Afraid of what?"

Maddie frowned, shook her head. She didn't want to tell him about Charlie. It felt like a violation, like she and Charlie had a secret to-gether but only Charlie knew what it was.

"It's just that . . . what if the person who broke into my room is the same one that's doing this? Like it's related somehow."

He shook his head. "It's probably not. It's not the same thing."

"But what if it is? And what if there are clues in my room?"

He shrugged. "When was it?"

"Two weeks ago."

"But you've cleaned your room since then, right?"

"Yeah, but not, like . . . doorknobs and stuff."

"Do you want to call the police?"

"I'm afraid to. Afraid I'll get in trouble for not calling when it happened. Besides, it could have been my brother. He could have been lying to me. I don't want him to get in trouble."

"Don't worry," he said. "Even if it wasn't your brother, it probably wasn't the same person. But call me if it happens again, OK?"

"Sure," she said, and fell into step beside him as he continued on down the beach.

AMY

AMY HEARD ABOUT THE THIRD MURDER during her commute from Miami. For a second, she thought about not going home. She imagined instead that she would drive to the airport and catch a flight to San Juan, or New York, or Cincinnati—anywhere. She imagined bailing off the highway and getting a room at a hotel on the beach; one with a nice, quiet hotel bar where she would meet a man and take him back to her room. She imagined, with horror, that she would jerk the wheel on the highway overpass and smash onto the surface street below. She was tired of being afraid, tired of being alone, tired of being at all.

When she got home, there was a note on her front door, and Amy brightened.

> IT'S TIME WE GET TO KNOW OUR NEIGHBORS.
> PLEASE JOIN US FOR BRUNCH, THIS SUNDAY, 11 A.M.
> BRING YOUR APPETITE.
>   —CARLOS AND GLEN, 4593 SW 8

Amy had spoken to Glen once, when he and Carlos moved in, and again one morning after she woke up in their backyard covered in bug bites, the result of a sad, drunken night she'd just as soon forget. Given that, she'd rather *not* go to the party. But she was lonely, so she dismissed the previous embarrassment and waited for Sunday as though she was holding her breath. When the hour arrived, she walked down her driveway, across the sidewalk, and up Glen's driveway, carrying a bottle of dessert wine she and Pete had received once as a gift. Maybe, she thought, the entire life of a bottle of dessert wine was spent this way—moving from one party to the next, changing hands, the host frowning at it, shelving it, and regifting it some months or years later. These thoughts were quashed when Glen looked down at the bottle and exclaimed, "Château Rieussec! You shouldn't have!"

Inside were clusters of neighbors, families talking only among themselves. Seeing them, Amy wanted to back out of the door and walk home. But Glen had his arm around her waist and was guiding her through the crowd. Soon, she had a mimosa in her hand and was standing with Glen's friends.

"This is Kenny and Steven. They're here to make sure we don't get into too much trouble," Glen teased, explaining that they were the only people there who did not live in the neighborhood.

"We're really just curious," Steven said.

"We're treating it like a game of Clue," Kenny added, oddly giddy.

"I'm sorry," Amy said, shaking her head. "You think the murderer might be *here*?"

"Why not?" Steven shrugged.

"It just hadn't occurred to me," Amy said, canvassing the room with fresh eyes.

"Plus," Kenny said, "there's just something . . . *fun* about a mystery."

"There's nothing fun about sleeping with your eyes open," she said.

Glen took her by the elbow and leaned in. "Can I tell them about your catnap?" he asked conspiratorially.

Amy stammered by way of response and blushed as Glen let loose with the story.

"I found her asleep on our patio one morning, *covered* in bug bites."

"Ambien," Amy said, relying on the old lie.

"Oh, I've heard about that stuff!" Steven said. "They should change their ad campaign. Tagline: 'What will you get into next?'"

"And show a woman asleep on her neighbor's patio!" Glen said.

"A man waking up in the wrong bed," Steven said.

"A dog shitting in the cat box!" Kenny said.

The three of them roared with laughter.

Glen soon left them to respond to some pseudo kitchen emergency, instructing them to "Eat!"

"So, Amy," Steven said after Glen left, "tell us who we're looking at."

Amy looked around at the strangers she recognized only by sight. The neighborhood was a tapestry of races, classes, and generations. There were younger couples, who had found in the neighborhood an affordable alternative to the high-dollar homes in Fort Lauderdale, and who had moved here with an eye toward remodeling the classic 1950s-style atomic ranchers, as Pete had done years before. There were the families who, it seemed to Amy, were barely getting by, who lived too many to a house, and spent evenings and weekends drinking beer and yelling at their children. There were the old-timers, like Adel, who, Amy imagined, had moved to Florida from somewhere else during the 1950s and 1960s, for a warmer, if not better, life. They were all in the same room now. All eating eggs and fruit and French toast. All trying to make sense of what was happening. Amy tried to listen to snippets of conversation, but there was nothing discernible, the room was a constant, low buzz.

"I'm not sure I know anyone by name," she said. "They live next to me." She pointed to a large Latino family, who were talking with a family Amy recognized from down the street. "He lives a few doors down," she said, pointing to Angry Dad. "He's the one who first told me about Adel."

"Did you know her?" Kenny asked.

"No. She lived behind me, but . . . no, not really."

"I don't think we know any of our neighbors either," Kenny said.

"Where do you live?"

"Wilton Manors."

"Oh," Amy said, and stopped herself before saying "of course," of the mostly gay, recently gentrified area.

"What is it that you do?" Steven asked.

"I'm . . . an artist," she said hesitantly. "I do graphic design for an ad agency in Miami. I also paint."

"What do you paint?" Kenny asked.

"Found objects," she said, falling back on her old explanation for her work.

"Do you ever show any of your work?" Kenny asked.

"Not since I've moved down here," she said. "I've been kind of . . . *stalled*."

"Florida will do that to you," Steven said. "Too much sun. It makes you stupid."

"Is *that* what it is?" she asked teasingly.

"And what is it that you do?" she asked, after the conversation lagged.

"I'm a reporter, actually," Steven said.

"For?"

"The *Daily Brain*," he said.

"Is that a zombie paper?"

"No," he said without a spot of humor. "It's a blog. We do local, muckraker stuff."

"So you're not just here for amusement . . ."

"*I* am," Kenny said, chiming in.

"More curiosity," Steven said.

"What did you think about . . . the arrest?" she asked, not sure how to characterize what had happened to Charles Abbott.

"What did I *think* of it?" Steven asked. He thought for a moment, then said: "To be honest, I thought, 'Where's the evidence?'"

She looked down into her drink. Charles Abbott had been released that morning. She'd seen the press conference on television. The police spokesman offered a hasty apology, while the beggar's court-appointed attorney talked about justice for the maligned. "And now we know there wasn't any," she said.

"The truth is," Steven said, "the police are clueless. They can't get a bead on the guy—the murderer."

Amy frowned at Steven, who shrugged and said, "Not to make you hit the Ambien harder than you already are," before following Kenny back into the kitchen.

The next thing she knew, Glen was at her elbow. "While you're here, Amy, can I talk to you about your tree?" With that, they were outside, staring up into the limbs of her live oak.

AFTER THE PARTY, Amy wanted nothing more than to take a nap, but she also wanted, more than ever, to get back into her studio and continue working. She had finished the second in the series depicting the murder of Adel Minor that morning, having worked on it every evening after work, and she was eager to start on the third. It felt good to be painting again—it was like an old, dear friend she had been ignoring, a really good drug she had forgotten to take. And so, when she returned from the party, she changed into a pair of shorts and an old Led Zeppelin T-shirt and made her way into her studio. There, she anchored a blank canvas to her easel, and started roughing in the shapes of the next painting, transferring the drawing onto the canvas.

In the first painting, Adel and her murderer were each shocked-still, a thin bar of light dividing them. The second was full of fear— gray faces and red cheeks, the murderer advancing toward Adel, and Adel taking a step back, the cast iron kettle on the corner table bluer than it had been in the previous frame, glowing almost, ready to be taken up by the murderer. The third would be the impact, the cast iron kettle slamming against Adel's face. This painting would be the most visceral in the series, and as she worked, Amy had a hard time keeping her hand steady. She imagined the person who had killed Adel standing around the party, chatting up neighbors while he pushed bits of French toast around with a plastic fork. She imagined him sipping champagne, relishing the spectacle caused by three unsolved murders.

When Amy was finished transferring the drawing to the canvas, she opened the barn-style garage doors for ventilation and began mixing paint. She was tired but wanted to get the background shaded in, the deep grays and blacks that close in on the figures, so that she could, in the hours of daylight she had after work each evening, do a bit of concentrated work on the details of the painting—Adel's face, the murderer's face, the murderer's hand, the teakettle, the impact.

She was just beginning to put brush to canvas when someone called her name.

"Hello? Amy?"

Amy spun around. It was Kenny and Steven, Glen's friends.

"I thought you said you didn't have anything to show," Kenny said, looking around.

"I don't," Amy said, trying to block their view of her canvas. But the others, which were leaning against the wall, could be plainly seen. "These are new," she said finally.

Steven looked around, likely noting the sketches that were pinned to the wall, versions of Adel as she lived and died. "You're painting the *murders*?"

"I can't stop thinking about them," she said by way of explanation. "They're . . . haunting me."

"Well," Steven said, raising his eyebrows, "at least you're not *stalled* anymore."

Amy put her brush down. "Can I help you with something?"

"We just thought we'd say good-bye," Kenny said. "We didn't have a chance at the party."

"Well"—Amy shrugged, annoyed by the distraction—"good-bye."

Steven, who couldn't take his eyes off the paintings, said, "Can I interview you? About your work?"

Amy shook her head. "It's all very fresh. I don't know what I would say about it."

Steven sighed, rolled his eyes, looked at Kenny. "Artists."

"He's doing stories about other people in the neighborhood," Kenny offered. "Tell her about the old people."

"There's a whole group of people who are living together now, because of this."

"Not living together," Kenny corrected. "They *paired up*. Like on the *ark*." He smiled, clearly delighted.

"It's very interesting," Steven said. "People's reactions . . . *Your* reaction in particular."

Amy shrugged, self-conscious. "I'll think about it."

He handed her his card. "Call me."

THE NEXT EVENING Steven returned with a camera and a tape recorder.

"I was just in the neighborhood," he said. "I thought I'd see if you were up for an interview."

Amy, who had worked that day and hadn't yet gotten out of her skirt and blouse and into her painting clothes, shook her head. "I just got home . . . I haven't even had a chance to change."

"This is good," he said. "You look nice. Perfect for this kind of thing."

Amy looked down at herself. She had worn a white silk blouse that day with a black skirt and kitten heels. She liked what she was wearing, liked that it was "perfect for this kind of thing." So she unlocked her studio and let him in.

"It started about two weeks ago," she said, leading him in. "I had a dream and came out here in the middle of the night, to paint the scene." She showed him that first crude painting, and then the refined version of it, completed after she'd gotten her studio together.

"Before then, I had been drawing her, the house—anything and everything. I was just, you know, processing it."

As Amy talked, Steven fumbled with his tape recorder, his notes.

"How long have you been painting?"

Amy shrugged. "Fifteen years."

"Did you dream all of the scenes, or just the first one?"

"Just the first. The rest just kind of . . . *came*."

"In your waking hours."

"Yes."

"Why do you think it's happening?"

"Why do I think the murders are happening?"

"Yes."

Amy looked down at her paintings.

"At first I thought it was just a mistake, you know? Just a line that was crossed. I didn't think that whoever killed Adel intended to do it. See?" She said, pointing to the first painting. "There's a lot of surprise, a lot of fear."

"But now?"

"Now I'm not sure." She looked at him, noticed the gray in his eyes. "Sometimes I wonder if it's really happening. If it's not some dream we're all having at the same time."

"But the women who are dying—they're really dying."

"Yes, but . . ." She shook her head. "They're *old*."

Steven looked at her as though she'd said something heinous.

"Tell me about your murderer, the man in your paintings."

"I tried, when Charles Abbott was arrested, to paint his face. But"—she hesitated—"it just wouldn't *go* like that." Amy showed him the painting she'd done of the murderer's face on the evening Charles Abbott was arrested. "I don't know who the murderer is, but for me it can't be anyone else. It's this . . . *fiction*. At least this part of it."

"And the scenes themselves? Where are they coming from?"

She shrugged. "I don't know. Like I said. They're just . . . coming to me."

"What do you think the police would say . . . if they saw your work?"

"I don't know," Amy said. "I never thought about it."

"You don't think your work makes you look kind of . . . guilty."

"Guilty of what?" she asked, nonplussed.

"Murder!"

Amy looked down at herself, her small body, her thin arms. "Not likely anyone would believe that."

She walked him to the door, expecting him to follow. When he didn't, she said, "I'm losing daylight."

"I just want to get some photos. It's a little dark in here. Can you turn on a light?"

AFTER HE LEFT, Amy felt foolish. She felt she had said too much, and she regretted allowing her paintings to be photographed. They belonged to her, and she wasn't ready to give them up yet—to let others see what she had done, who she was.

She decided to give herself a night off. She took a shower, put on some music, ordered a pizza, and opened a bottle of wine. She was deep into an interior design magazine and halfway into the bottle when the pizza deliveryman knocked on her door. When she opened the door, Amy froze. There, staring at her over a medium fig and prosciutto pizza, was the man from the paintings. He wore a red and white ball cap and a smile, but it was plainly him—broad face, flat nose, mean eyes.

Shaking, Amy dropped her wineglass. It smashed at her feet.

"Did I scare you?" he asked. "I'm sorry. Let me help."

With that, he was in her house. He put the pizza on the kitchen counter and handed Amy a tea towel.

"No," she said, "it's fine. Please . . ." She picked up the stem, which was jagged where the glass had broken, and tightened her hand around it. "What do I owe you?"

"Fifteen forty," he said. "Not including tip."

"Here," she said, offering him twenty. "It's fine. Just go."

"OK," he said, stepping over the glass and the puddle of wine at her feet. "Be careful."

"Careful?" she asked, still shaking.

"Wouldn't want to cut your feet."

After he left, Amy locked herself in the house and paced. She thought about calling Steven back, telling him what had happened, but she felt foolish, wrong. She had probably seen him before, dozens of times. He was the deliveryman at one of her favorite restaurants. Not a fiction, but not a murderer either.

BERNARD

OF ALL THE FUNERALS BERNARD HAD attended that month, Helen Johnson's was the most gut-wrenching. Her son, nieces, and grandchildren each took their turns, sobbing at the lectern. A friend spoke of a devoted scientist and researcher, who studied the effects of psychopharmaceuticals like Miltown and Valium in the 1960s and 1970s, and in the 1980s led the charge against their widespread use. Then, one by one, women from Helen's golf foursome and water aerobics class spoke of their energetic friend.

It was all too much, and by the end of it, Bernard *wanted* a Valium, wanted a drink, a nap—something.

"How about it, Danny?" he asked afterward. "Want to go somewhere, get a drink?"

"Let me ask Roberta," he said.

"What do you mean, 'ask her'?"

"Well I can't very well leave her alone, can I?"

"I suppose not," Bernard said, looking out into the parking lot—the sunlight on windshields.

And so they did a group thing, a lunch thing, and everyone had whiskeys, even the women. They wondered why Helen hadn't been among them, hadn't been called for that first meeting in the clubhouse, hadn't paired up.

"She wasn't like us," Elaine Trawlers said. "You heard them at the funeral. She was like women today—busy and . . . confident."

"Plus," Leslie Nelson said, "she wasn't one of the originals. I may have seen her around the golf course once or twice, but I didn't know who she was."

"Who else haven't we thought of?" Elaine Trawlers wondered.

April Oppenheimer shook her head. "We'd have to go back in time, count house by house—who is here, who is gone."

"And who's moved in, for that matter," Maryanne said. "It's retirees, like Helen, new arrivals."

Cal shook his head. "We can't be responsible for everyone. I sure as hell don't want that burden."

"What are we going to do, then?" Bernard asked, fuming. "Let them die?"

"Why the hell can't the cops *find* this guy," Harry Trawlers asked, to which the others responded with a collective shrug.

Feeling loose and low, they ordered another round of whiskeys and drank them with resignation.

"We should all get guns," Cal Hendricks said. "Go hunting . . ."

"Come on, Cal," his wife said. "You're drunk."

He looked at her, angrily at first, then softened. "My wife is right, as usual." He looked around the table. "To happier times," he said, raising his glass and swallowing his last bit of whiskey.

"Say," he said, perhaps having remembered a happier time, "the Fourth of July's around the corner. We should have a party, like we used to."

To that, his wife brightened. "Yes!" she said, thumping her fist on the table. "A party!"

Bernard's stomach turned at the mention of it. He thought of Vera—he *always* thought of Vera when he thought of Cal—and then of Maryanne's insinuation that she had been sleeping with "half the neighborhood." He had half a mind to bring it up now. He wanted to know *who* was "half the neighborhood"? Was it Cal? Was it *Harry*? Bernard shook his head. He was going to be sick.

"You all right there, buddy?" Danny asked, his hand on Bernard's back.

"Yeah," Bernard started, but before he'd known it, he had thrown up onto his plate, which had not yet been cleared from the table.

The ladies gasped and pushed their chairs back from the table. Danny and Harry jumped out of theirs to help him up. They walked him, each on either side, to the bathroom, where Bernard kneeled in front of a toilet for a few embarrassing minutes, his friends behind him.

"I'm fine," he said, standing only after he was sure he wouldn't vomit again.

"It's been a terrible couple of weeks," Harry said, staring into the mirror at him while Bernard washed his mouth and face.

"It's not that," Bernard said, turning to face them. "It's just . . . I've been thinking a lot about those days. And . . ." He hesitated. "Something Maryanne said . . ." Bernard felt himself swoon, and turned back toward the sink.

In the mirror, Danny and Harry looked like themselves, but Bernard did not look like himself. He looked old and alien.

"What is it, buddy?" Danny asked.

Bernard shook his head. "It's nothing."

"You're just not yourself," Harry said. "None of us are."

BACK AT MARYANNE'S house, Bernard took a shower and a nap. When he woke he felt almost new, almost human.

"I had a feeling a second round of whiskey was the last thing we all needed," Maryanne said when he joined her out on the porch.

"I'll say," he said.

"Can I get you anything? Ginger tea, maybe?"

He shook his head. "Just tell me. *Who* is 'half the neighborhood'?"

"Oh," she said, "*that.*"

"It kills me," he said, "to think of her with someone else."

"She was someone else's wife!" Maryanne said, angry now.

"Other than that!" Bernard said, waving an arm dismissively.

"For one," Maryanne said, standing up, "she was with my husband.

Other than that," she said, folding her arms, "I don't know. I was being hyperbolic."

With that, Maryanne walked away, allowing the screen door to slam behind her.

Stunned, Bernard looked out at the garden as it burned in the heat of the day.

THEY ONCE SPENT an entire day together, he and Vera. It was a rare Sunday afternoon when Irene had taken the kids to the beach, and Vera's husband had taken theirs up to Cypress Gardens alone, after Vera feigned a headache. They spent the afternoon in bed together, and ate scrambled eggs from the pan while standing in her kitchen. She told him about her childhood in Macon—her workaholic father and bored mother. How the only thing she ever wanted was to get out of there, to go and be a singer, or an actress or maybe even a writer. She didn't know what she wanted to be, just that she wanted to be *something.*

"But you *are* something," he told her, wrapping his arm around her waist and pulling her close.

"What?" she asked, pulling away, her gray eyes suddenly steely. "*What* am I? I'm nothing."

"What are you *talking* about? You're the only thing *here.*" He made a flourish with his arm. "Look around. Everything is . . . dull and useless, and then there's *you.* You're like . . . this *dream* I keep having. And every time I wake up I . . ."

She shook her head. "Being a *diversion* for a married man is not what I mean."

"You're right," he said. "I'm sorry."

"What did *you* want to do, before you became . . ."

"An accountant?" He frowned.

"Husband, father, accountant . . ." She shrugged.

He thought about it for a second, looking up at the ceiling and then down at the floor. "I only knew what I didn't want."

"Which was?"

"I didn't want to be a chicken farmer, for one. I didn't want to be stuck out in the middle of nowhere, slinging shit." He looked up at her, and then down again. "And then I didn't want to be stuck in Baltimore. And now . . . I don't want to be stuck here."

"Well congratulations," she said, holding up a glass of water, as though to toast him. "You're not a chicken farmer."

He took her hand. "Let's go away together."

"Away where?"

"I don't know, who cares? Chicago, New York, LA. Let's just *go.*"

"And then what?"

"And then nothing. And then we're already there and . . . it doesn't even matter what happens."

"That's where you're wrong," she said, pulling away from him.

"Why?"

"Because the same thing will just keep happening over and over again. You're an accountant here, you'll be an accountant there. I'm a wife here, I'll be a wife there. It's like . . . our fates are already decided."

"Don't you like your life?"

"No," she said firmly.

He squeezed her hand, and she pulled away.

"We can do this, Vera. You might not think so, but we can. You'll see."

"What? You're going to club me over the head and drag me to Chicago, New York, LA?"

He shrugged. "I might."

"Your problem is that you think things are going to be different. And my problem is that I know they won't be."

After that, her porch light was on a lot less. Bernard would drive up and down the street, watching for the light to flick on. Then he'd drive to the supermarket, buy whatever he'd claimed to be out of, and then come home to Irene, who was usually already asleep. Bernard would make himself a drink—he'd developed a taste for gin—and would sit on the screened-in porch, ablaze with grief.

"What happened the other day?" he'd ask the next time he saw her. "I thought we had a date."

"We always have a date," she'd say wearily.

"Then what *happened*?" he'd ask again, taking her by the elbows.

But she would shrug him off and tell him that she wasn't looking for a drag. That if he wanted to be a drag he should go home to his wife.

"But I want to be with *you*," he told her once. "I want *you* to be my wife."

"I'm already somebody's wife," she said, turning away from him.

AN HOUR LATER Bernard found Maryanne in the kitchen, pouring batter into a cake pan.

"What's that for?" he asked.

She shrugged. "I was hungry for something sweet."

"What is it?"

"Pineapple upside down."

"Sounds amazing."

"I'm not sure yet if I'm going to let you have any."

"I deserve that," he said, looking down at the counter. "And I'm sorry. And if Gerry were here—"

"You don't get to speak for my husband," she said, pointing a spatula at him.

"Irene and I never talked about it. Not in any kind of real way."

"I'm not your do-over," she said. She put the cake in the oven, filled the sink with water.

"I know that. It's just that, I thought you might want to talk about it."

"I don't want to. Not with you or anyone."

"She was everything to me," Bernard said softly.

"That's sad, because she was a tramp."

"You didn't know her."

"Don't defend her!" She threw her arms up and settled them onto her hips. He had never seen her angry, and now she looked like she was ready to charge.

"How about this," she said, more calmly than he might have imagined. "Let's agree that she might not have been the angel you thought she was or the evil temptress I thought she was. Most important, let's agree that it was a long time ago and is now enormously unimportant."

Bernard pouted. "I just wish I knew more. Understood more about her . . . About why . . ."

She shrugged. "You're probably never going to. You'll never know what was in your wife's head either. Or in mine. Or in the killer's, for that matter! The point is, it's immaterial."

He stared at her, afraid to even blink.

"I'm going to make some decaf to go with this cake. Do you want some?"

He reached across the counter and took her hand.

"I'm sorry," he said.

"Stop being sorry," she said, and shook her hand free.

MADDIE

IT WAS AN ORDINARY DAY, THE day her mother left. They had shared a rushed morning routine and offered quick good-byes. Then, everyone was off inside their separate lives—Maddie and Brian at school, George at the airport, and Caroline at the dental office, peering into other people's mouths. Every day since, Maddie has wondered what happened to cause her mother to miss the exit for Seven Springs and sail up the highway, pushing north to some unknown destination. Was it a bad day at work? Something Maddie had done? Or was it nothing at all? Just a whim Caroline had; just a way to break up the monotony.

Maddie would think about it until her mind seemed to explode with little fireworks of love or hate for her mother. Each day it was with her more intensely than the last, the longing, the anger. Always, she pushed the thoughts away, focusing instead on some other, more immediate thing. Some algebraic equation that had to be solved, some piece of flesh that had to be cut or healed, some question she was worrying over, about Charlie or the murders. She thought about them now in sound and pictures—a woman shrinking beneath the weight of an object; a man breathing heavily, red-faced, desperate.

Now that school was out, she had more time to think about it, more time to worry. She'd gotten into the habit of pacing between the front and back doors at night before she went to bed. She'd think: *Back door, locked; front door, locked; back door, locked.* Often, she'd check the doors several more times in the night, always returning to her bed, lying back down, and listening for noise. Sometimes, just as she was about to drift off, she'd hear a familiar voice calling her name and she'd spring out of bed, fully awake. Other times, she'd sit in the dark and think of Charlie, out there somewhere. She sometimes imagined him standing on the other side of her bedroom window, waiting to break in and ransack her room as she slept.

She had seen him twice now since he was released.

The first was like any other day. She watched him all afternoon from her perch behind the bar, looking up over her paperback and out the window. He seemed to be having a hard time, and Maddie wondered if he'd be able to collect enough that night to come in and eat. When he did come in, she was so relieved that she practically ran to him, but her boss beat her to it and greeted Charlie himself.

"I don't know what you did or didn't do," she heard him say, "but I don't want you in here."

Charlie looked up at him, and there was a moment where Maddie wasn't sure what would happen. But Charlie simply nodded, stood, and left.

Maddie wanted to rush after him, or at least run to the window, to see where he went. But Bob turned around, looked down at her, and frowned.

"You ever see him in here again, call the police."

"But he didn't do anything," she said.

"You don't know that," he said, slowly shaking his head.

Before the end of her shift, Maddie ordered the brisket to go, and walked up and down the street with it, looking for him. She called his name a few times, shouting into the night, but he didn't materialize. Maddie thought of him, lonely, tired, hungry, *some*where. She wished that she could put her arms around him the way a mother or girlfriend would, and soothe him. Instead, she walked to the intersection and left the brisket.

The next day, she saw him again. He was at the intersection, like always, waiting for the light to turn and the cars to stop. Maddie stood at the corner and stared at him for a few minutes, waiting for him to look at her. In her mind she called out, "Charlie!" but in reality she said nothing. When he would not meet her eyes, she went into the restaurant and started her shift.

FOR THE REST of the night, Maddie felt like she was walking a tightrope. She was afraid that he would come into the restaurant and afraid that he wouldn't. She didn't know what she would say to him, or what the situation would call for, and so she practiced various lines in her head:

Go outside and I'll bring you something.

I'm sorry, but I can't serve you.

My boss told me to call the police if you ever came in again, but I told him to fuck off.

But she never got to use them. Charlie never returned.

That night, Maddie sat in the back of Nate's pickup behind the abandoned movie theater and stared up into the laurel oak, her head resting against the edge of the bed while Nate groped her. "What would you do if you were homeless?" she asked. "Like . . . how would you live?"

"I don't know," Nate said. He slipped his hand up underneath her shirt, and tried to move her bra out of the way.

"Stop," Maddie said, elbowing him.

"What's the matter with you?" he asked. She was surprised by how angry he seemed.

"Nothing," she said. "I just don't want to be . . . *touched* all the time."

"Then what are we doing here?"

Maddie shrugged and pushed away from him. "Can't we just talk?"

"What do you want to talk about? Homeless people? I don't know what I would do if I was homeless . . . Eat garbage, I guess."

"Be serious," she said.

"I am," he said. "I seriously don't know."

"Never mind," she said, shaking her head slightly but not getting up. She liked the way the moon lit the tree's branches so that their silhouettes were accented against the night sky. She wished that she could draw so that she could re-create it, and thought about it for a few minutes, the lines she'd have to create, the mood. Then she thought about drawing Charlie, hunched over at his intersection, the streets stretching out around him to infinity.

Nate climbed on top of her and straddled her body. He was heavy, and his weight pushed her lower back into the hard plastic bed liner beneath her.

"That hurts," she said.

"Sorry," he said, but didn't move.

"Can you get up?"

"Kiss me and I'll think about it."

He leaned into her and she kissed him halfheartedly.

"High school girls," he muttered, climbing off of her.

"That's right," she said, sitting up. "I am in high school."

"But why do you have to *act* like it?"

"What am I supposed to act like?"

He climbed out of the bed and got into the cab, turned on the ignition.

Maddie climbed out of the truck, crossed the parking lot, and headed for the street.

"Get in the truck!" he called.

"I'd rather walk," she called back.

He pulled up next to her. "Your house is, like, *miles* from here."

"I'll be OK."

"Let me drive you," he said, serious now.

Maddie looked down the dark path. Beyond it were the streets through the commercial district, and then the neighborhoods, one after the other, for miles until she got to her own, which was the scariest of all.

"I'm not afraid," she said, but her voice cracked when she said it, giving her away.

"Just let me take you."

"Fine," she said, and climbed up into the cab.

As Nate pulled slowly out of the parking lot, Maddie couldn't help but feel like she was a little kid being punished for something she'd done.

In front of her house, he said, "I'm sorry about earlier."

"It's fine," she said, pulling the door handle.

"My parents are going away for the Fourth," he said. "You could come over."

"We'll see," she said, and left it at that.

In the house, she locked the door and went into her bedroom. She hadn't cut herself in two weeks, and had, in fact, promised herself that if she didn't she could dip into her car savings and buy herself some summer clothes. Tonight, though, she didn't care about summer clothes or promises made or kept. She wanted to be able to go into her parents' room and lie in bed with her mother and tell her about what had happened.

Instead, she locked her bathroom door, took off her pants, and looked at her cuts. She remembered almost every one, the when and where and why of them, and the way she felt after, fuzzy, like static on the TV at her grandmother's house.

Maddie squeezed her eyes shut and then opened them again. If she cut herself now, she would always do it. She would be in college cutting herself. She would get married and cut herself. She would be a mom to little kids and have to steal away to the bathroom every now and then to cut up her thighs. Instead, she put on the shower, sat in the stall, and cried, letting the water run over her until it was cold.

THAT NIGHT SHE dreamed that she bought a car, a used blue hatchback with a broken window. In it, she drove around town looking for Charlie. When she found him, he got in the car with her and she drove away. "Where are we going?" he asked.

"To look for my mom," she said.

"Can we look for mine too?" he asked.

In the morning she felt sore, as though she had been beaten in the night. Her eyes were puffy and creased. At breakfast, her father said, "What happened to you?"

"What do you mean?" Maddie asked, looking down into her cereal bowl.

"You look different," he said, his voice heavy with concern.

"I'm not," she said, her voice barely above a whisper.

"How about getting out of here for a little while?" he asked.

"What do you mean?" she asked, looking up at him.

"I was thinking that you and Brian could go to Ocala, spend the summer with your grandma."

"I'm not spending the entire summer in Ocala, Dad."

"What's wrong with Ocala?"

"It's . . . boring. And I don't have a job there. And . . ." She wanted to say "all my friends are here," but she realized that wasn't true. She didn't have any friends, not with Stacia gone.

"You could work at the scoop shop. I'll come up on the weekends. We'll go hiking like we used to."

"No," she said, standing up from the table.

"Madeline," he said, his voice firm.

"Dad," she said, stiffening.

"It's been a shitty year. You and Brian need more attention than I can give you. And this, this *thing* is happening. I'd be a bad parent if I didn't send you away. I should have sent you a month ago." George shook his head, frowned. He looked old now, the lines on his face all pulling downward. "It was just an idea," he said. "Maybe we can figure something else out."

Maddie crossed her arms. "What needs to be figured out?"

"I can't have you guys alone here while . . . somebody runs around killing people. If you don't want to go to Ocala, maybe we can bring Nana down here."

"*No,*" Maddie said. "She's *old*—the people being killed are *old.*"

"Fine," he said, sighing again. "I'm out of ideas."

"Send Brian, OK? Let me stay."

"He'll never go without you."

"He will if you tell him to."

"We'll talk about this later, OK? I'm tired." George stood up, put his cup in the sink, and left the room.

Maddie couldn't help but feel his anger, his disappointment, and she wished she could take it back, the way she had been. But she couldn't go to Ocala. Not without him, and not without her mother.

FOR A COUPLE of years, they went every summer and rented a cabin that had a kitchen and beds but no TV. George taught her how to thread a hook to catch fish, and then what to do with the fish once you had it, which was to slice it down the center and clean everything out, so all that was left was the kind of thing you might buy in a package at the supermarket. They'd hike in the national forest, and Caroline would point out the species that were native and the ones that weren't. The bright green anoles the size of Maddie's forearm were native, the smaller brown anoles were not. The razored sawgrass was native; the softer cogon grass was not. The slash pine was native; the kudzu that covered them was not. For a while, Maddie looked at the world like this—native, not native. She was a Seven Springs native; her parents, both from Ocala, were not.

Once, Maddie was hiking alone with Caroline when Caroline disappeared. Maddie had been looking down at the path, watching for snakes and roots as she walked. When she looked up, her mother was gone.

Maddie spun around, looking up and down the path and into the trees, calling, "Mom! Car-o-line!"

There was nothing, just some hoots of nearby birds. How long, she wondered, had she been walking alone?

"Mom!" Maddie called again, panicked.

She backtracked, walking in the direction she'd come from for a minute or so, spun around, and called for her mother a third time.

Then, Caroline came walking from a path Maddie hadn't seen before.

"What *is it*?" Caroline asked in a sharp whisper.

"Where'd you go?" Maddie asked.

"Just down here a ways. I wanted to see if we could get to the river."

"Oh," Maddie said, bruised. "Can we?"

"Yeah," Caroline said. She took her hand, and Maddie followed, feeling small.

At the river, Caroline taught her how to skip stones.

"You have to choose the flat ones, see?" she said, picking up a stone and showing it to Maddie.

"Hold it like this," she said, the stone between the pad of her thumb and her middle finger.

Maddie tried it a few times, but she couldn't get it right. All her stones hit the water with a *thwack* and did not reemerge. Her mother's stones would skip five and six times, going all the way across the river in some cases.

Caroline was beautiful that summer. Her hair was long and her face tan. Maddie remembered shielding her eyes from the sun and looking over at her mother.

"I want to be like you when I grow up," she said. And when it seemed like Caroline didn't hear her, she said it again. "I want to be like you."

"No you don't," Caroline said, frowning. "You don't even know who I am."

AMY

STEVEN'S ARTICLE ABOUT AMY APPEARED IN Thursday's edition of the *Daily Brain* under the headline: LOCAL ARTIST ENVISIONS GRIZZLY MURDERS. Beneath the headline was a photo of Amy in her studio, her paintings leaning against the wall behind her. At first, she couldn't bring herself to read it. Then, she read it six times, three times to herself and three times aloud. It was a nice article; he left out most of the things she wanted him to, and said some complimentary things about her work. The attention excited Amy and she half expected something to come from it. She imagined a gallerist or someone from the local arts council might see it and call her. But nobody had. Nobody at work had noticed either, and Amy started to wonder whether anyone was even reading Steven's blog.

Two days after it appeared online, Steven called her to ask her what she thought.

"I thought it was fine," she said, holding the phone to her ear with her shoulder as she stirred a pot of onions.

"Just fine? I said good things about you."

"You did," she agreed.

"Any, um, blowback?"

"Not on this end. I'm not sure anyone I know has read it."

He was silent for a minute. "So," he said, "any other visions?"

"No," she said, annoyed by his characterization of her work. "And I wouldn't call them visions. Only that . . ."

"Only?"

"I think I may have seen him. The murderer from the paintings."

"Where?" he asked urgently.

"He was here," she said. "He delivers pizza for Gianni's on Second."

"Are you sure it was him?"

"I'm sure that the man at my door strongly resembled the man in the painting, yes."

"Why haven't you said anything?"

"To whom?"

"The police!"

"Why would I?" she asked, incredulous.

"Seriously, Amy."

"Because I'd sound like a lunatic, that's why."

"But I think I believe you," he said.

"*I* don't believe me," she said. "Besides, who cares what *you* think?"

"What are you doing now?"

"Cooking dinner."

"I'm sending Glen over."

"Why?"

"I'm *afraid* for you."

"No you're not," she said. "You just want to find a way to get closer to the quote-unquote story. Only there is no story."

"There's somebody *out* there, Amy."

"There's *always* somebody out there," she said, with a certainty she hadn't realized she possessed.

He sighed. "What's for dinner?"

"Curry."

"Kenny loves curry . . ."

"Come over, then, if you want," she said on a whim. When he agreed, she wasn't sorry. She was lonely. And the deeper she dove into her work, the more isolated she became. It would be nice to sit with people who knew what she was doing and had some understanding as to why she was doing it.

Amy put on a pot of rice and spot-cleaned the house. She threw a tablecloth over the old sun-stained teak patio table, and took out all her wedding-gift tableware—the thin Riedel glasses she never used for fear they might break; the large glass votive hurricanes; the silver-plated ice bucket. When Steven arrived, it was as though she had planned the dinner for weeks.

"Where's Kenny?"

"He wasn't feeling up to it. Too much sun today."

"That's too bad," she said, and deftly removed the third plate from the table, her time as a waitress having served her well.

When dinner was ready, Amy took her usual seat at the table, facing Adel's house, and Steven sat to her left.

"Interesting view you have."

"I suppose it is," she said, frowning up at the house.

"I think you should call the police," he said, taking a sip of red. "Tell them what you know."

"But I don't know anything."

"You said yourself you're having dreams."

"It was only one."

"So the man that you mysteriously painted into the scene . . ."

"I must have remembered him. I order from there a lot."

"What does that have to do with your painting?"

"It's like in dreams where people show up where they're not supposed to—all the details of your life jigsawed together. Art is like that."

"So you don't believe that the man in the painting could be the murderer?"

She shrugged. "I don't know what to believe."

"That's why you should go to the police."

"And tell them what? I painted this picture of a pizza deliveryman as murderer?"

He shrugged. "Why not?"

She sat a moment and thought about it, thinking back to the night she tried to paint a portrait of Charles Abbott, how one face pushed through the other.

"Let's change the subject," she said, raising her glass.

"What are we drinking to?"

"To company. It's been a long time since I've shared a meal with someone."

He raised his glass to hers and took a sip. "Can I ask where your husband is?"

"No," she said, taking a sip. "It's a closely guarded secret."

"Really?"

She shook her head. "He's in San Juan. Working."

"What kind of work?"

"He's an architect."

"That's the kind of answer that sounds like a lie."

"It's not."

They ate, for a few minutes, in silence, Adel's burned house in the background, the flickering candles in the foreground. Steven told her about the quirky billionaire that Kenny worked for, who was currently spending six months in the Arctic.

"He wants to, in his words, *see for himself,* whether or not the ice is really melting."

"But it's summertime. The ice always melts in summer."

Steven shrugged. "You can't apply logic to ignorance. Anyway, he left Kenny in charge of his yacht."

"Like he has to scrape the barnacles from it?"

"Like he gets to take it out. That's where we were today. You should come with us sometime."

In all the time Amy had been in Florida, she'd never been on a proper boat in the Atlantic. "Where do you go?"

Just then, a crash came from inside the house.

"What the hell was that?" Steven asked.

"Probably just my cat," Amy said, getting up from the table.

Steven followed her in and together they checked each room. But everything was just as it had been. Nothing fallen, nothing broken. The cat was hiding under the bedcovers, having been spooked by the noise.

In the den, Steven checked behind the sofa, and Amy checked the closet. "Nothing," she called to him.

Then, a crash came from the garage.

"My studio," she said.

"Stay here. I'll check it out."

But she followed him. Through the window, they saw that the lights in her studio were on, the door ajar.

He said, "Stay here, lock the doors, call the police."

"Where are you going?" she asked.

He held his finger up to his mouth and advanced toward the studio. Amy locked the door behind him and dialed 9-1-1.

"Hi," she said to the 9-1-1 operator. "There's a . . . man."

"A man?"

"A noise, I mean. There's a noise, and . . ."

"Ma'am, I can't send patrol out for a noise."

"But there's somebody in my garage!" she said.

Then, Steven was on the other side of the door, knocking.

"He's gone," he called.

"He's gone," she said to the operator. "Are you happy? He's gone."

"We'll send a car," the woman on the line said, and Amy gave her the address.

Amy opened the door for Steven. "He took some things," Steven said.

"What things?"

"Come see."

He had taken her brushes, paints, and palette, and put a knife's gash through her last prestretched canvas. But her paintings were left untouched.

In a few minutes, the police were there, stepping through her studio, taking pictures.

One, an officer named Gonzalez, stood over her paintings, curious. "Where'd these come from?" he asked.

"I painted them."

"How?"

She shook her head, not sure what he meant. "With paintbrushes."

"I mean with what knowledge?"

"With . . ." She shook her head. "I just imagined them."

Gonzalez called over his shoulder. "Bag up the paintings."

"No," she said, advancing toward them, "please don't."

"I think you better come with me," he said.

"Why?"

"Reasonable suspicion." Gonzalez then called over another officer, who came behind her, spread her legs, and patted her down.

"But . . . I didn't do anything."

She looked helplessly at Steven, who seemed to be taking mental notes of the scene—the mess, the arrest.

"It'll be OK," he said. "I'll follow you in my car."

"CAN YOU REALLY just . . . *hold* somebody like this?" Amy asked. She sat in a gray room, across from a gray-faced detective.

"I just need you to tell me what you know," he said.

"But I don't *know* anything."

"Just walk me through it," he said. "Who was Adel Minor?"

"She was my neighbor," Amy said, and recounted the night of the fire and the time Adel had given her mangoes.

"And Helen Johnson?"

"I didn't know her."

"What else? Think. Tell me about the paintings."

"They just . . . came to me. The ideas. I just painted the scenes as I imagined them."

"What about the portrait? The one of the man."

Amy looked down at her hands. She was embarrassed. "It was supposed to be Charles Abbott. But when I painted it, the other face came through."

"Another face?" he asked skeptically.

"Yes."

"Are you on any medication, Ms. Unger?"

"No," she said defensively. "It was just a mistake. He delivers pizza to my house."

"Who does?"

"The man in the painting. The face that came through."

"Pizza," he repeated. His voice was flat, his face expressionless. "Where did you say he worked?"

"Gianni's on Second."

Gonzalez walked in, whispered in the detective's ear, and walked out.

"Have you ever been in Adel's house?"

"No," Amy started, before remembering that she had. "Yes, but . . . it was after."

"What's going to happen when they search your house?"

She shook her head. "Nothing."

"They're going to do it anyway, OK? Just to be sure. We've got three women dead and a neighbor with a bunch of paintings depicting the murders."

Amy nodded. "I understand."

"Who's that guy outside? Your boyfriend?"

"No. He's . . ." She shook her head. "He's a reporter." She then repeated the story she'd been telling since they'd sat down together. "He did a story about me on his blog, and then my studio was broken into, and then I called the police. Remember? I called *you*."

"I get it," he said. He shook his head. "I still have to check."

Amy spent the next few hours in a cell, slumped against a wall. She'd been arrested once, for marijuana possession when she was a teenager. Then, her father had picked her up and driven her home, lecturing her all the way about the dangers of drug use. Now, she realized, she had no one.

A different officer drove her home the next morning along with her paintings, which had been photographed and catalogued.

"It's not evidence," the officer said, handing them back to her. "But they still had to photograph them, just in case."

"In case of what?"

He shrugged. "You want a ride home or not?"

IT WAS JUST after sunrise when she got home, and Amy wanted nothing more than to go to bed. But the incident had been on the television news, and her phone was ringing just as she walked into the house. She let it go to the machine, but whoever it was hung up and called back.

When the phone rang for a third time, Amy answered.

"Amy, it's Mom."

It was Pete's mom.

"Your picture was on the news. You looked . . . crazy."

"Crazy?"

"Tired. You looked . . . tired."

"What did they say?"

"On the news? They said you were a suspicious neighbor, with suspicious paintings. I have half a mind to call Pete."

"What? And tell on me? I'm an adult, Meredith."

"You're being foolish, Amy."

"Good-bye, Meredith."

"Wait."

Amy took a breath. She waited.

"Why don't you come down and stay with me? Or go to Puerto Rico and stay with Pete?"

"I can't."

"Marriages are long and complicated, Amy. They're not these perfect love stories everybody likes to imagine. It's not like that."

"I know, Meredith, I know."

"Just don't throw the baby out with the bathwater," she said. And then: "I'm sorry. That was a poor choice of words."

"I understand what you're saying, Meredith. I just don't think he wants me anymore."

"I don't think *you* want you anymore."

Amy sighed into the phone and closed her eyes. "That's probably true."

When she got off the phone, Amy went outside to clean up the mess from the night before. There were flies swarming around plates of half-eaten masala, and a half bottle of good red, spoiling in the sunlight. She scraped the plates and washed the dishes, thinking about the supplies she'd have to replace, and of her last prestretched canvas, still in police custody, a knife's cut down its center. She *should* leave, she knew that. But she couldn't. To leave now would be to abandon them—Adel, the others, her work. She had spent too long doing nothing to leave just as her muse had returned.

BERNARD

THE ORIGINALS GATHERED INSIDE THE CLUBHOUSE rec room, along with others they had recruited into their group—elderly residents who had come to the neighborhood more recently. This time Cal Hendricks was at the center of the room, standing in front of a dry erase board, a marker in hand. He wrote:

Homeless guy
Pizza delivery guy
One of us
A drug addict
A drifter
Someone from Colored Town

"You can't say 'colored town' anymore," April interrupted him.

He rolled his eyes and erased it. In its place, he wrote: SOMEONE FROM WEST FORT LAUDERDALE.

"Still racist," she said.

He erased it and wrote AN OUTSIDER.

"So," he went on, "the police say it's not the homeless guy." He drew a line through HOMELESS GUY.

"They say they checked out the pizza delivery guy and it's not him either," Marty said.

Cal drew a line through PIZZA DELIVERY GUY.

"That leaves one of us, an outsider, a drug addict, or a drifter."

"That's pretty much everyone else!" Danny said.

"I'm trying to do something here. Trying to *narrow it down*, you know, *brainstorm*, think it out."

"What about the woman with the paintings? That's suspicious," Leslie said.

"I agree!" Marty said.

Cal wrote: WOMAN WITH PAINTINGS on the board.

"The police say she's innocent," April said.

Cal drew a line through WOMAN WITH PAINTINGS.

"This is getting us nowhere," Bernard said, frustrated.

"What would you rather," Cal started, "sit around and wait for this guy to get tired of it? Stop on his own accord?"

"I don't know," Bernard said, his shoulders slumped and head heavy. "To be honest, I'm tired of thinking about it." He looked around the room. "Maybe we should all just move."

"I *can't* move," Leslie said. "I took out a reverse mortgage when the market was going gangbusters."

"I did too!" Roberta said.

"Forget it," Bernard said. "It's not practical."

"If we just stay together . . ." Danny said.

Maryanne shook her head. "We can't do that forever."

Her remark dug at Bernard. Just that morning he had referred to her place as "home."

"Have you guys had a look at those paintings?" Marty asked. "They were in the paper—a big spread!" He handed a folded section of the newspaper to Cal.

"You're forgetting," Cal said as he opened the paper, "this woman is just making it up. It's not *real*. She doesn't know anything more than we do."

"They looked real to me!" Roberta said.

Cal turned the opened paper toward them so they could all see.

"It does look like the pizza delivery guy, doesn't it?" Maryanne said. "We saw him on TV this morning."

"Poor guy," April said.

"Maybe he has a twin!" Roberta said.

"If he did, don't you think the police would have looked into it?" Leslie said.

"This is all distracting!" Cal said, crumpling the newspaper. "The guy who's really doing this is probably having a good laugh."

"What we need is a plan to protect ourselves," Harry said. "Pairing up is probably not enough."

"You know what we need to do?" Marty said, looking at Bernard. "Arm ourselves, and contact that reporter and let him know that we have. If he—if everyone—does a story about it . . . that the fogies in Seven Springs are armed to the teeth . . . this guy will move on."

Cal nodded. "It's a good idea."

Everyone else in the room seemed to agree.

"Maybe we should all take a class," April said. "A self-defense class."

"I took one once," Leslie said.

"Do you remember anything about it?" April asked.

"Something about poking," she said, jabbing a finger in the air. "Maybe poking the guy in the eyes?"

"A self-defense class is a good idea," Harry said, an eye on his wife. "We'll look into it and let you all know."

AS THEY WALKED back to Maryanne's, Bernard said: "What would you do? If someone came into the house?"

She shook her head. "I don't know. I've thought about it, but really, I don't know."

"Do you have any weapons?"

"No. I mean, I have an old sword that belonged to my son. But . . . nothing I'd be comfortable using."

"Should probably get rid of that sword."

"I would never," she said, shaking her head.

He put a hand on her shoulder.

Her son had been killed during one of the later battles in Vietnam. He was nineteen, and, unlike the other boys of that era, was excited to go off to war—even volunteered. Neither of Bernard's boys went. They were too young—thank God—and by the time they were of age, there was no need, the war was over.

"Let's hide it well, then, OK? And maybe . . . get a Taser or something."

"Why not a gun?" she asked.

Bernard shrugged. "I'm not sure I'd be able to use one if I had to. I don't want to kill anybody."

"You're a lover not a fighter, ha-ha-ha," she said, unamused.

"I am," he said. "I'll show you."

"No thank you," she said, with a trace of a smile. Then: "A Taser's a good idea. And I'll go to the class with the other girls, to learn how to use it."

"Perfect," he said, then: "What's for dinner?"

"I don't know," she said. "Maybe you should take me out."

MADDIE

IT WAS A SLOW NIGHT AT The Smiling Pig, and there was not much else for Maddie to do but watch the door and wait for Charlie to walk through as he always had, taking his seat facing the window and twisting the cap off of his beer. But she knew that he wouldn't. He hadn't been at the intersection that evening, and Maddie wondered where he could have been—where else his life took him. There were likely streets she didn't know about. Libraries and benches and soup kitchens too. Charlie lived in a world that she couldn't even conjure, couldn't imagine if and when she tried.

She thought about the dream she had had—the blue hatchback, the running away—and decided it wasn't too far from reality. She had $1,600 saved for a car, and it was only the beginning of the summer. If she worked more, she could have a car in no time.

But where would she find Charlie?

Maddie closed her eyes to think about it. Where *was* he?

When she opened her eyes, Nate was in front of her.

"Sleeping on the job?" he asked.

"Oh hey," she said, forgetting for a second that she was still mad at him.

"Tired?"

"No. I'm fine."

"What are you doing later?"

Maddie shook her head. She wanted to give him an excuse, but she wasn't good at thinking up lies.

"Good," he said. "Come out with me."

She shook her head again. "I don't want to go to the parking lot."

"We'll go somewhere else, then. Somewhere better," he said.

"OK," she said quietly. Then: "You're my only customer. Can I get you something?"

"Sure," he said, climbing onto a barstool. "What's good here?"

With that, the night, such as it was, began. A few more people walked in, sat down, and ordered plates of barbecue. Each time the door opened, Maddie looked for Charlie, and each time it wasn't him, a balloon popped in her heart.

By the time she switched off the neon lights and settled out with Bob in the kitchen, Maddie felt completely deflated. When she saw Nate outside, idling in his truck, she nearly told him that she had changed her mind, and that she wanted to go home. But she didn't want to disappoint him twice in a row, so she climbed up into his truck and held her breath as he peeled wheels out of the parking lot.

At first, they didn't speak. A song Maddie didn't know played on the radio, and she focused on the lyrics, the story it told.

When Nate made a right onto Marina Mile Road, the surface street that ran adjacent to the interstate, Maddie looked over at him, asked where they were going.

"It's a surprise," he said, making a left onto a paved boat access trail. He parked in the boat lot and cut his lights.

They sat in the dark a moment and Maddie oriented herself. They were only about a mile outside Seven Springs, in a kind of nowhere land between there and Fort Lauderdale. Caroline had taken her kayaking once, and they dropped in there, or near there. Maddie remembered being amazed that you could simply walk up to a canal, push a kayak into the water, and be gone. But, it turned out, there wasn't really anywhere to go. They paddled alongside the highway, and then under it, until they came to a small patch of solitude.

"The wetlands," Caroline had said. "Such as they are."

Maddie was amazed by the place. It was empty and wild. There were birds and mangroves, and bugs bleating into the dusk.

"How did you know this was here?" Maddie asked.

"You can see it from the highway," Caroline said. "They can't build anything here, because of the airport, the planes—"

Just then, a plane passed low overhead, its roar drowning out her mother's voice, its dark, wide shadow briefly covering them.

"We should come here all the time," Maddie said, after they had turned and were paddling back toward home.

"We should," her mother agreed.

Maddie turned to Nate. "It smells like fish here."

"Let's get out, then," he said. "Go for a walk."

"Where?"

"Just follow me. I have an idea."

They walked along the canal, down to where the interstate's exit ramp met Highway 7. Nate climbed up over the pylon that separated the grassy area from the exit ramp and held out his hand.

"Wait," Maddie said. "Where are we going?"

He pointed up to the highway.

"The *highway*?" Maddie shook her head. "I don't think so."

"Relax," he said. "It's late; there're practically no cars on the road."

"It's not *that* late."

"It'll be fine," he said, and she let him take her hand.

Together, they walked up the exit ramp to the interstate.

As they walked along the shoulder, Maddie could feel the rush of the highway push against her. She could smell the exhaust, the oil, the plain grime of it.

Nate stopped, said, "Here. This is good," and boosted her up on a cement pylon.

They sat facing the highway. Maddie asked: "What are we doing here?"

"Look up," he said.

Maddie tilted her head all the way back, said, "I don't see anything."

He took her head in his hands and tilted it downward, until she was looking out just over the horizon, at the low lights of the airplanes as they drifted slowly to earth.

"Oh," she said.

"They have to slow down so much to land, you know. For a few seconds it looks like they're not moving."

"Yeah," Maddie said in a low whisper. She thought that she had never seen anything so beautiful as those lights, suspended momentarily in the sky, twinkling through the heat and smog. They were magical, otherworldly. She took a breath and relaxed against him.

Nate put his arm around her and pulled her into him. He took a pint of peppermint schnapps from his pocket, unscrewed the cap, and took a long pull from the bottle. "Here," he said. "Try this."

"What is it?" she asked him.

"Try it. You'll like it."

Maddie took a small sip from the bottle and found that she did like it. She took another sip and passed it back.

"Where'd you get it?"

"I bought it. My friend Duck made me an ID."

"Oh."

"Look," he said, pointing south, where an airplane dropped below the highway and out of sight.

"I've never been on an airplane," Maddie said. It seemed a terrible thing to confess, because what it meant was, *I've never been anywhere but here.*

"Never?"

"Nope." She frowned.

"Where would you go if you could?"

Maddie shrugged. "Everywhere."

They passed the bottle back and forth until it was almost gone. Maddie started to feel loose and happy and light. She stared up at the sky, at the stars and the hovering lights, beginning to love the moment, the landing airplanes, the *whoosh* of cars moving past. It occurred to her that South Florida only felt big. In fact, there weren't many places you could go via an east-west highway. In fewer than ten miles to the west, that very highway broke for north and south; beyond it was the ruined swamp, with its electric-green nitrogen blooms and pythons the size of ocean liners. Maddie had gone to the Everglades once with her environmental biology class, where she learned about both.

Maddie shivered and Nate held her closer. "Do you want to get out of here?" he asked.

"Yes," she said, but she realized that she didn't want to be anywhere that they could realistically go. She wanted to be out of there completely and never return. She wished she was in one of those cars headed down the highway, breaking north and driving through the Everglades. She imagined it out there, an empty highway cutting through the swamp.

"Come on," he said, jumping down and taking her hand.

They walked down the ramp and climbed back over the pylon. The grassy spot between the canal and the highway now seemed pretty to her, in comparison. "Let's wait," she said. "Let's stay here a little while." She walked to the edge of the canal and sat on the wide cement slab.

"Hold on," Nate said. "I'll get a blanket."

As he walked to his truck, Maddie watched the water slowly running east. There was a tree a bit farther down that leaned slightly into the canal, as though it were taking a drink. There were lights from nearby apartment buildings that she could see, and then not see, depending on how the breeze went through the thick hedge of areca palms that made this place seem isolated even though it wasn't. Maddie finished the schnapps and tossed the bottle into the canal, but immediately regretted it; she would grow up and move away and have babies and that bottle would still be there, the earth's muscle memory of this moment.

Maddie lay back on the cement and looked up at the stars. She couldn't tell which were stars, which were planets, and which were satellites. She imagined for a second that they were all satellites, swirling above her, keeping a record of everything, the way the earth did. She lifted a hand to them, waved. *This is me right now*, she thought. *Never going to happen again.*

When Nate returned, he suggested they go beneath the road, under the small, shallow bridge that the exit ramp made over the canal.

"It's gross under there," she protested.

"How do you know?"

Maddie shrugged and gave in, letting Nate take her hand and help her up.

They crouched to get under the bridge and Nate stood on his knees to spread the blanket. Once the blanket had been spread out, they lay together, kissing. After a while, she let him unbutton her pants and slide his hand down underneath her panties. "You're wet," he breathed, and pressed his hand deeper into her pants. With his free hand, Nate unbuttoned his pants and slid them down around his knees. He brought her pants down too, but not far enough, and she couldn't open her legs.

There was a moment where she realized she still had control over the situation. She could roll away from him and out from underneath the bridge. She could tell him to stop and he would pull up his pants and take her home. Or, she could just give in. And she wanted to give in. Wanted it now more than anything else.

Maddie kicked off a shoe and freed one of her legs from the confines of her pants. "Condom," she said, or thought she said. The moment was too hot, too humid, too filled with the smell of exhaust and saliva. She thought *condom*, but she pulled him close and he moved up into her and Maddie cried a bit at the suddenness of it, at the sheer and terrible pain it caused. But then the pain gave way to something else, and a feeling of release washed over her, and she breathed hotly in his ear and he in hers.

BY THE TIME Maddie got home, the neighborhood was completely dark. Maddie crept noiselessly around the house, not wanting to wake her brother. It was midnight and her father would be home soon. In the kitchen, Maddie made herself a sandwich, drank a glass of juice, and took a vitamin. She didn't feel any different—didn't feel the way she was sure most girls did after their first time. If anything, she felt smaller, more aware of herself physically in contrast to the size of the world around her. But that could have been the schnapps, or the way she had felt that night, like a trapped rat.

She was so tired that she didn't even want to brush her teeth or wash her face of the grime she'd surely collected on the highway. She went into her bedroom, collapsed into bed, and stared at the ceiling. She wasn't a virgin anymore. She was a sexually active woman—no—a sexually active *teen*. She always thought she'd lose her virginity when she was seventeen—it seemed like the right age to do it—but she had beaten herself by two years. She couldn't decide how she felt about it. Did she love Nate? No. But she did like him, sometimes. And she did like *it*—all of those things that they did together. So it was fine. It had to be. It was already done.

She decided to take a shower after all. When she stood to lower her blinds, she saw that her neighbor was standing at his fence, staring in at her. This was not the first time she had caught him looking in, and Maddie stared back for a moment, wondering what he knew about her, before dropping the blinds and getting undressed.

AMY

THE AIR-CONDITIONING CUT OFF WITH A click and the house fell silent. Amy turned off all but one light and sat on the sofa, Indian-style, with a cup of tea. She hardly ever sat on the sofa, and it was strange to see the house from that perspective; it looked larger, more perfect—everything in the kitchen tucked away in its place, nothing on the dining room table but a squat houseplant, a round cactus with a red flower. With the air-conditioning off, the house was quiet. She could hear bugs outside, but nothing else. Even the highway—with its omnipresent wash—had fallen silent. It occurred to her how rare such a quiet was. How precious. She thought she'd like to bottle it and keep it for the times that needed drowning out. Instead, she closed her eyes, and tried to capture a memory of it.

Driving though the neighborhood that night, she'd felt an almost overwhelming sense of alarm. It was quiet then too, but she had a feeling that it wouldn't last, that the quiet would snap like a stick. That someone would scream, call her name, draw a line in the earth. She felt that everything was about to change—that she was driving through a time, a feeling, a universe she could never return to.

All through the evening, she couldn't shake the feeling. She took a shower, cooked and ate dinner, and did the dishes, all with the feeling that she better tread lightly, as if afraid to trip some invisible wire that would set the change in motion. She had been too afraid to go into her studio that night. Too afraid to think about murders, and about the murderer, who had now likely been inside her studio. Who likely knew who she was. Who could be looking in through the window at her this very moment.

Then there was a break in the quiet. A key in the dead bolt.

Amy's pulse quickened, her palms dampened, her face and chest flashed with heat. She watched the doorknob turn, the door push open. Her heart raced.

Finally, she let out a sigh. It was Pete. He pulled a suitcase through the door, stuffed his keys into his pockets, and closed the door behind him.

When he turned and saw her, he jumped.

"Amy! Jesus!"

"Hi," she said, too shocked to say anything else.

"Hi." He came over and stood beside her, smiled. "How are you?"

She looked up at him, too in awe of him to say anything. Was he really there, or had she manifested him? She held up her hand to him and he squeezed it. His hand was warm. He was real.

He sat down next to her. "Aren't you surprised to see me?"

"Yes." She nodded, failing to suppress a smile.

"I thought I'd come home for the long weekend."

"Why didn't you call?"

"I wanted to surprise you."

She looked at his face, tried to gather the details of him. "I don't understand."

He seemed to study her, and Amy wondered what he saw. *Tired? Too thin? Suddenly old?*

"I'm worried about you," he said finally.

"Ah."

"What do you mean, 'Ah'?"

"You're not here for the long weekend. You're here to check on me."

"Is there something wrong with that?"

"I guess not," she said, turning to him. He looked tan and tired. The folds around his mouth and eyes seemed more definite. It had been only four months since he left, but it felt like longer. It felt like she'd lived a lifetime in that house by herself, waking up in the night to inspect noises, drinking too much out of habit or boredom, wasting time. He had told her that once. "You're wasting your time."

She wanted to touch his face, to press her thumbs into the creases around his eyes, to kiss him. To not kiss him seemed like a crime. Or, an admission of a crime. It said: I do not love you; you do not love me; we do not belong to each other. When, really, only one, maybe two of those were true.

Instead, she said: "Are you hungry? Can I get you anything?"

IN BED TOGETHER, they didn't touch, not immediately. She stayed solidly on her side and he on his. It was a brother and sister in bed, a pair of cousins, a couple after a relationship-ending fight. Then, her leg brushed his, or his hers. They left them there—finally skin to skin. They inched closer, she to him and he to her. Finally, he took her in his arms and breathed in. She was surprised at his strength, his gall. "I missed you," he said. And she started to cry.

In the morning, they fell into their routine, and she took a bath while he shaved. As she sat in the tub, she studied him, tan and fit in a pair of blue boxers, with hair that had grown long around his ears. She took in every possible detail. His long toes and narrow feet, the ropey muscles in his legs, the constellation of birthmarks on his back. She wanted to reach out to him, to caress the back of his knee, but she didn't dare. Even there, naked together in the bathroom, there was an unspoken discomfort. They'd barely said anything to each other that morning, embarrassed, maybe, or perhaps afraid to admit the mistake. Soon, they'd have to negotiate their day, to confront the reality of their lives together. Now, though, she didn't want to say anything, didn't want to spoil the peace. He tapped his razor on the sink, and she released the plug on the drain, and there was a moment—this waiting moment before the water was sucked through the drain—that to say nothing seemed almost a sin, a recognition at least, that they did not want to have to talk to each other.

In the kitchen, she scrambled eggs and made toast. She put on some music but then turned it off. She didn't know how to treat the day, didn't know what his intentions were. She made coffee and put the music back on; she needed the noise, the distraction.

"Smells great," he said, coming into the kitchen and kissing the top of her head. "What can I do?"

"To help? Nothing. Just have a seat."

He sat at the bar, and she poured their coffee and plated their food.

"So what are you up to today?" he asked.

"Me? I thought I'd do some work but . . . I have to get all new supplies. The studio was broken into, and—"

"I think you should stop that," he said while peppering his eggs, "the work that you're doing."

Amy shook her head, looked down into the dirtied pan.

"I can't."

"It's dangerous. You shouldn't have let that reporter write the article."

"You read it?"

"My mom sent me a link."

"So that's why you're here."

"I told you why I'm here. I'm worried about you."

"I understand why you think it's dangerous. But . . . I can't stop. I don't want to stop."

"Come back to San Juan with me. Paint there."

"It wouldn't be the same."

"What do you mean?"

"I can't explain it. But . . . it's happening here. I need to be here."

He pushed eggs around his plate. "You've always done this. This sanctimonious thing where you play with death."

"What are you talking about?"

"It's just like when you got cancer and you paid someone to *pray over you*," he said, referring to her Reiki treatments. "That's not how it works!"

"I didn't pay someone to pray over me."

"You know what I mean."

"You don't get to tell me what's good for me anymore, Pete. You left. You forfeited your vote."

"I left to work, Amy!"

"You didn't even ask me to come with you."

"I just did!"

"After the fact. It's not the same."

"You're right," he said with a sigh. "We needed a break. Truth is, I couldn't stand being around you."

"Great. Thanks."

"That doesn't mean I stopped loving you."

He reached across the counter, took her hand. "Let's talk about this rationally."

"I'm not being irrational."

"We can agree to disagree on that," he said.

"I don't think we can, Pete." She took her hand back and stood in the kitchen, eating eggs.

When she was finished, she left him with the dishes and went into her studio.

It was a mess. She hadn't been out there since the break-in, hadn't yet catalogued what she'd lost. She had told herself that she was too busy, but she was actually afraid—afraid to be out there, in the open, afraid that the murderer could take his knife and slice through her. Despite this, she didn't want to leave. For the first time in years, she didn't want to go or be anywhere else.

The crash she and Steven had heard was a stack of terra-cotta pots, which had gotten knocked over somehow, and smashed. There were rags and tools on the floor and open drawers that the intruder had dug into. He'd broken her easel by picking it up and smashing it against the floor, and so there were shards and scraps of wood everywhere. She picked up the easel and, deciding it was beyond repair, tossed it into the trash. She swept the terra-cotta and wood shards into a dustpan, and put away what had been tossed from the drawers. The intruder had taken all of her supplies. She would need to buy everything all over again—paint, brushes, a new easel, and new canvases.

"How about some help?" Pete said, appearing in the doorway.

She shook her head. "You don't want to help me."

"It's *all* I want to do."

He walked into the garage and took her hand. "Show me the paint-ings."

Minus the one she'd done of the murderer and the crude yellow and green landscape she'd initially painted, there were three—Adel and her murderer shocked-still, the bar of light dividing them; the murderer advancing, the teakettle glowing in the background; and the painting depicting the impact, which she'd only just completed the day before the break-in.

"I'm planning two more. In one, Adel is on the floor, dead or dying. Another is the taped outline of her body."

"They're . . . terrific," he said, letting out a breath.

"You really think so?"

"It's the best work you've ever done."

He paced around for a few seconds, ran his fingers through his hair. Finally, he said: "I understand why you don't want to leave."

"Thank you."

"It's just . . . I'm worried about you."

"I'm worried about me too," she said. "But if I don't do this, if I don't finish . . . it won't matter where I am."

"I don't know what to do with you, *for* you," he said.

"Why do you have to do anything?"

"I can't just leave this up to . . . *fate*. You working in plain sight of the guy who did this." He motioned to the paintings.

There were sirens in the distance, and they both stopped to listen.

"We need to talk," he said. "About this, and more."

"What do you mean, 'more'?"

The sirens were getting closer. It felt like they were right up on them.

He shook his head. Looked at her and away. "Maybe we should have lunch somewhere."

"We just had breakfast," she said, worried now.

He looked at her again, squarely in the eyes. "It's just that . . . I want to be honest with you. I want to be able to put this all behind us and start over. That is, if you want to."

Amy nodded, her eyes fixed squarely on him.

"The thing is," he said, looking at her and then down at the floor. "I had an affair."

When she didn't say anything, he continued. "I'm not in love with her. I was lonely, alone in Puerto Rico, and there was this woman, at work."

Amy could feel her heart beating. Her palms started to sweat. She figured that he was. That he had. She tried to be rational: "You left, Pete. It's not an affair after you leave."

"It felt like one." He sighed. "It still feels like one."

"What do you want, absolution?"

He ran a hand through his hair in frustration. "I want to hit *reverse*. I want to go back to us. To when I loved you and you loved me and everything was ahead of us."

"It's not, though," she said. "Everything's . . . around us."

"I know. I feel like I'm treading water here." He reached out for her but she would not let him take her hand.

"I hate you," she whispered.

"Amy." He sighed, and tried to reach out for her again.

"You shouldn't have left. Not the way you did. You were my best friend. And then you left and I had no one."

"We've made mistakes," he said.

"Did I?" she asked, incredulous. "Did I make a mistake?"

He shook his head. "That's not what I meant."

She held his gaze for a second. Was he waiting for her to say something? Do something? She wanted to reach out to him, to take him into her arms, to absolve him of everything. Instead, she left him there. She walked into the house, grabbed her keys off the hook by the door, got into her car, and backed quickly out of the driveway.

AMY DROVE OUT of the neighborhood, her head full of bees. She felt that boot on her chest again. Her throat was tight and sore. She wanted to cry but couldn't; wanted to think but couldn't. Her head was full of contradictions. He had had an affair . . . he loved her . . . he had an affair . . . he loved her. They were not mutually exclusive, but it felt like they were. She didn't know how to square the two realities. Didn't know whether to push him out or take him back.

She had meant to go to the art supply store, to replace what had been taken, but she ended up at the beach instead. She parked in the shadow of an abandoned motel and walked to the wide strip of sand that had been built back up since last summer's string of tropical storms had taken most of the sand back out to sea.

On the beach were crowds of families and groups of friends, just arriving to set up their encampments for the day—umbrellas and canopies that would knit a kind of tapestry on the sandy strip. There were boom boxes and coolers and the occasional early game of soccer or paddleball. There were the beach regulars, whose skin was like leather and who drank beer from cans at 11:00 a.m. Amy walked past them, dropping her purse in the sand, straight to the water's edge. She looked out to the horizon, which was dotted with cargo ships bound for the port. In the foreground, kids on Boogie boards were spit out by the sea, while athletic men and women stood on paddleboards, paddling against the current and riding the waves. The ocean sparkled in the strong morning sun.

Amy, who had worn a dress that day—dark pink with thin straps that crossed in the back—stepped into the water. She swam deep and far, past the Boogie boarders and stand-up paddlers, her dress rising up around her, amorphous as a jellyfish. The water was warm. It had its own secret rhythms that Amy tried to tune in to. She wanted to become a part of it, to be some fish or plankton, so she swam with the current, letting it pull her gently southward. She put her head underwater and opened her eyes. But there was nothing to see. Just salt and particulate, floating in the light, and the occasional strand of seaweed. She came up and looked out to an unrecognizable strip of beach.

At some point, she knew, the beach receded where the ocean liners and cargo ships entered the port and left again. Then there was the power plant, with its red and white towers that often emitted green smoke, and then the Dania Beach Pier, where people fished for snook and grouper. She and Pete had gone there once, just after she'd moved down. They were doing days full of what Pete called "touristy things" to get them out of the way. They paid a dollar apiece, walked to the end of the pier, and looked down into the water at the fish, who seemed completely unaware that they were being hunted.

While they were there, a lesbian couple pulled up a skate and everyone on the peer looked on, marveling at it. The skate, more annoyed than anything, pulled the hook from its mouth with its barb, and dropped back into the water in a single athletic triumph.

"Amazing," everyone said. "Incredible."

Pete had pulled Amy close and kissed the side of her head.

I want to hit reverse, she heard him say.

Amy felt like lead. She realized that this had been a bad idea—swimming out so far. She looked at the shoreline. At the families and their encampments. She didn't know what to do. Didn't know which way to go anymore. Should she swim farther out, let the ocean take her? Or should she swim to shore? It seemed an actual choice.

She heard Pete say, *play with death.*

Amy held herself there in the ocean, trying to keep her face above water. She did not want to go anywhere or be anywhere. She wanted simply to melt away, take on some other form. But she swam to shore anyway, struggling at first and then letting the waves bring her in, one little push at a time, until she was standing, and then walking, a sea creature in a dark pink sundress. The families in their encampments looked at her in bafflement.

Amy collapsed on the sand and stared back at the ocean, at the waves coming in and going out. The sun blazed down on her. Her hair and skin dried quickly in the heat, a film of salt crusting over her skin.

She watched a family arrive and set up their temporary home on the beach, arranging chairs under umbrellas. She watched as the mother slathered sunblock on her young son, while the father slid plastic floaties onto his daughter's arms. When his mother was finished with him, the boy, who was old enough to walk but still so young that he did so precariously, tottered toward Amy.

"Hi," he said, putting his hand on her arm, to steady himself.

Amy felt solid under the clammy weight of him, as though his presence brought her back into her body.

"I'm a princess!" his sister said, bounding after him.

Before Amy knew it, the children were climbing onto her, making a jungle gym of her body, and their father was rushing over, spouting apologies. He scooped the children into his arms and carried them down to the water. Amy watched as he stepped into the surf, a child on each arm, and glided them over the surface, smooth and steady as a ship.

Amy looked around for her purse, as though forgetting her long swim south. Realizing her mistake, she lay back in the sand, done with it. She was thirsty, hot, and tired. She wished that Pete would appear and pick her up and carry her away. Together, she imagined, they would walk into the past and do it all again. In reality, she'd have to walk down the beach to find her purse. She'd have to go home and face him alone.

WHEN SHE GOT home, Pete was not there. Amy quickly showered and dressed, but skipped her ritual with the cream, telling herself it didn't matter anymore how her scars looked. Still, she ran a comb through her hair and misted it with some spray gel, a step she rarely bothered to take. She thought about mascara but didn't bother. The raccoon eyes she might get later from crying wouldn't suit her. She was staring at her reflection when she heard a sound come from the garage. She wondered if she had bothered to lock the front door, and thought about locking herself in the bathroom, just to be safe. Instead, she picked up Pete's safety razor and held it out in front of her as she crept toward the front door.

She found that the door was locked and she pressed her face against the window, to see what she could see. She thought of the 9-1-1 operator, ridiculing her for calling because of a noise, and decided to see for herself. She opened the front door, listened for noise coming from the garage, but heard nothing. She crept slowly toward the garage, opened the side door, and jabbed at the air with the safety razor and screamed. The garage was empty, but the large barn-style doors were open.

Amy stared blankly into the room and at her paintings, which had been undisturbed.

"Amy?"

She swung around with a growl and jabbed the air with the razor.

"Jesus," Pete said, jumping back. And then, "Is that my razor?"

Amy let her shoulders go slack. "I heard a noise."

"It was me."

"I see that."

He shook his head. "You can't stay here."

"I'll be fine."

"Like hell you will."

"What are you doing anyway?"

"Just pulling out the grill. I thought we'd barbecue. It is a holiday, after all."

"I'm not feeling very festive." She turned around to go back into the house.

"Amy," he said, calling after her, "we have to work this out."

THAT NIGHT, PETE grilled steaks and they sat outside together, eating but not talking. They could hear parties in the other yards, people with their people, and here they were together, struggling to connect over steak and potato salad.

"Remember that party where we met?" Pete asked.

"Of course."

"What ever happened to that? People that we knew, having parties?"

She shrugged. "They had kids."

"So what, then, no more parties?"

"They probably still have them," Amy said, thinking of the group of friends they used to be close with, who were now spread throughout the tri-county area. They were likely part of new groups now, bland groups formed because they had children on the same street, or in the same school. "We're just not invited."

"That's not true."

"Of course it is. We're in social purgatory—between one stage and the next."

He seemed to consider this.

"Do you still want kids?" he asked.

There was a time when she was obsessed with adoption, and he knew it. She would look at adoptable kids on the computer, turn the screen to him, and say, "What about this one?"

"I don't know what I want," she said finally.

"I'm trying here," he said, taking her hand.

"I don't want you to try," she said. And then, "Would you be happy with her? That woman from work?"

He shook his head, sat back in his seat, but didn't say anything.

"Because I think that, if you were, if you could be, you should just . . . be with her instead. You could have babies with her and be invited to parties again."

"Amy," he said with an incredulous frown.

"I'm serious."

Their neighbor lit a firecracker and it made a single *POP*.

She continued: "I know I said I hate you but I don't. I love you and I want you to be happy."

"I love you too," he said, and rushed to take her hand.

That should have been it, then. It should have satisfied her, but it didn't. She swiped her hand away and snapped at him.

"Then why did you leave?"

He sat back in his chair, frustrated. "I left to work!"

"But you left *me*. To, to . . . waste away here. In *your* house."

"Amy . . . Come on. Is this really the issue?"

She shook her head. It all felt tangled, like wires or scar tissue.

"I don't know," she said.

She looked up at Adel's house, wondered what Adel would be doing if she was alive and at home. Wondered if Adel's husband had ever had an affair, and if so, how Adel had handled it.

"Is the woman . . . is she still there? Working with you, I mean?"

"Well I can't exactly fire her."

"Right," Amy said. And then: "What was it like?"

"Oh God, Amy, don't do this."

"What was it like?" she asked again, insistent.

"It was . . . great," he said sharply. "It was really, really great. I felt alive."

"That's great, Pete. I'm *so* happy for you. I think you should go back there. I think you should go tonight."

"Come on, Amy. What did you want me to say?"

"I don't want to be like this anymore. The person that I am when I'm with you. The grief of it all."

"But it doesn't have to be like this," he said, exasperated.

"I don't know how to make it any other way."

"Fine," he said. He stood up from the table and walked away.

Amy sat outside as the night grew dark, drinking glass after glass of red. When the fireworks started, she couldn't bear to watch, so she went inside. Pete was packed and on the phone with his mother. When he hung up, he said, "I'm going to stay in Miami tonight."

"Fine," she said.

"Tell me not to go," he said.

Amy shrugged. She pushed past him and disappeared into the bathroom, locking the door behind her.

"Amy," he said through the door. "I'm afraid if I leave here I'll never see you again."

Amy lay down in the empty tub, listening to the cacophony of fireworks outside and watching the window as it flashed with light.

She wanted him to stay, but she didn't know how to say so, didn't know how to be with him now that she had been without him.

She leaned her head back and closed her eyes. She hated that she was drunk. Hated to *be* drunk. After a few minutes, she called his name, but not loud enough. Then, she called him again. "Pete?"

When Amy got up to look for him, he was gone.

BERNARD

"I DON'T THINK THIS IS A good idea," Bernard said, trailing Maryanne. They were walking down the street on their way to Cal Hendricks's Fourth of July barbecue, Maryanne carrying a salad, Bernard a bottle of Canadian Club.

"Why is that?" she asked.

"What if something happens?"

"What do you mean? Everybody will be there."

"Well, then, what if . . ." he started, but couldn't think of anything. There was no *real* reason not to go—just that he didn't like Cal and Cal didn't like him and that particular backyard held a certain heartache that he preferred not to remember.

When they arrived, the party was in full swing, though there was nothing of the bombast these parties had once been. It was just a bunch of old people standing around a kidney-shaped pool, in the shade of palms and live oaks. Bernard couldn't help but try to remember the way that things had been. He felt as though he could squint and see them all—his kids doing cannonballs into the pool, Adel and Irene clucking away in a pair of chaise lounges, Danny by the bar, mixing drinks.

IT WAS 1964 and Pam had stripped down to her underwear and jumped into the deep end.

"Pam!" Bernard called, and "Irene!" when the girl ignored him.

"She's fine Ber*nard*," Irene said, annoyed with him. "She's *had* swimming lessons."

"It's not that, Irene. She's naked as a jaybird!"

"Come here, Pammy," Irene called. "Get your suit on."

With that, the girl shot out of the pool and ran, dripping wet, to her mother.

Bernard made his way to the liquor, which had been arranged on a table near the house. There were rows of bottles—Tanqueray and Wolfschmidt and Canadian Club—all lined up with their appropriate mixers. Bernard found a cooler of ice under the table and opened the Tanqueray, pouring himself a good dose of it before leveling it off with tonic. He was just about to take his first sip when Cal Hendricks came up from behind him. "How ya doing there, buddy? Name's Cal," he said, offering his hand for Bernard to shake.

"Bernard," he said, awkwardly giving Cal his left hand, his drink in his right. "Nice, um, nice place."

"Thanks!" Cal boomed. "Think I'll have one too," Cal said, looking at the drink in Bernard's hand. "What's that?"

"Gin."

"Don't have much of a taste for gin," he said, scrutinizing Bernard. "The wife likes it, though." He looked out into the yard. "Quite the brood you've got over there."

"Yeah." Bernard sighed.

"Ours are still off at camp. They haven't even seen the place yet. Gonna move them in just before school starts. Hey, where do your kids go?"

"The little one stays home. The other two go to Seminole."

"That private, Seminole?"

"No, public."

"I'd like to put my kids in private school, but I don't think they have any in this backwater."

"I don't know," Bernard said. "Maybe talk to one of the girls."

Each surveyed the yard for a bit, sipping their drinks, before Cal made his excuses and went out to greet the Trawlers and the Smiths, newly arrived with broods of their own.

Bernard made a drink for Irene, who had settled into a lounge and was watching the kids jump into the pool over and over again.

"We should put in a pool," she said, after he was seated beside her.

"Probably cost ten grand," he said.

"Look at how happy the kids are."

"Today they're happy, tomorrow they're drowning."

"Oh, Ber*nard*."

"They're a lot of maintenance."

"We can get somebody for it."

"And who's going to pay for *that*?"

He settled into the chair and looked around. The yard was a pretty good size, but the pool took up too much space. He didn't know how half the neighborhood was going to fit back there, or why the Hendrickses had invited everyone anyway. Still, the families kept coming, the food table swelling with the standard backyard fare. He was hungry but didn't want to eat. He didn't want to be distracted or have bad breath. He hadn't seen Vera in weeks. Her house was dark every night; he wasn't invited. He had hoped to see her there ever since he heard about the party. For a week it was all he had.

"Why don't you go get us a plate?" Irene said after a while.

"What do you want?" Bernard said.

"I don't know," she said, annoyed. "Whatever's over there."

Then, when he was at the table, scooping macaroni salad onto a paper plate, he saw her. She was headed right for the table, a plate of cookies in her hands. When she saw him, she gave the cookies to her husband and walked toward the house instead. Bernard started to shake as her husband approached. He didn't even know the man's name, had never seen him before, but there he was—tall and handsome and important-looking. He dropped the cookies on the table, and picked up a plate of his own.

"Great they're doing this," he said to Bernard.

His southern accent surprised, and then horrified, Bernard. Of course he would sound exactly like Vera. Of course he would.

"Name's Steve," he said, offering his free hand to Bernard, who shook it, looking down.

"Bernard."

"You live close by, I think," Steve said.

"I do?"

"I've seen you," Steve said.

"Well, welcome, then," Bernard said before grabbing a pair of forks and walking away.

"Why'd you get so much macaroni salad?" Irene wanted to know.

"What?" Bernard asked, and then, "I don't know."

They split the plate, sharing a lounge chair because the other had been taken.

"Fun party," she said. And when he didn't respond: "What's the matter with you?"

"Nothing. You want another drink?"

"No," she said, and added sarcastically, "you get drunk, I'll watch our children."

Bernard went back to the booze table and poured himself another gin, and on a whim, made one for Vera. He set out to look for her, negotiating the crowded party with the drinks in his hands. When it became apparent that he wouldn't find her, he finished his drink and started on hers. Then, he went into the house and started searching room by room. Maybe, he thought, she had a headache and was lying down. Maybe he'd find her and they'd lie down together, a refuge against the boring chaos of the party. But he didn't find her. Instead, he finished her drink and used the bathroom.

When he made his way outside again, he saw her. She was talking to someone he didn't know. She had that look on her face, like she was telling a joke. She looked entirely radiant. Not like the other mothers, who had—it seemed to him—become old overnight.

He moved toward her, tried to catch her eye, but she wouldn't look at him. Then, she left the conversation she was in and walked toward the back of the yard, near the shed. "Vera," he called, trying to catch up with her. But she was walking too fast. "Vera!"

"Stop following me," she hissed.

He caught up to her and pulled her behind the shed.

"Why are you ignoring me?" he asked once they were face-to-face.

"Why are you following me around a crowded party?" she spat.

"Because you won't talk to me. You won't even *look* at me. You don't even leave your light on anymore."

"It's over, Bernard, OK?" she said gently.

"It's just *starting*," he said, pulling her into him.

"It's not," she said, looking steadily at him.

"Why?"

"If I tell you, will you leave me alone?"

"No promises," he said, shaking his head.

She looked down and back up at him. She seemed to be steeling herself against him. "I'm pregnant."

"But that's *wonderful*," he said. "It's just what we need."

He went to embrace her, and she tried to back away, but he pinned her against the wall of the shed and kissed her. Her lips were stiff. She smelled of Coppertone.

That's when Adel came upon them. She was holding a naked child on one arm, a diaper bag on the other. Bernard will never forget her look of shock, and then horror.

"Not *you too*," she said.

Though he had always thought she'd said, "Not *you two*."

That's when everything changed for him. And not just Vera but also Irene, who found out from Adel not ten seconds later, and let out a wail so loud everyone at the party stopped what they were doing and looked at her. And then they looked at Bernard, who stood next to the shed alongside a flushed and petulant Vera.

He didn't want to remember the rest—how two weeks later Vera took a lethal overdose while her kids were at school; how her kids sat wild-eyed on their front porch while her body was carried away, and her husband stood in their front yard with his face buried in his hands. It was all there for everyone to see, and so they watched. Even Bernard stood in the street that night, slack-jawed, as the body of the woman he loved, and the body of his unborn child inside of her, was carried out on a gurney. Irene stood next to him and watched his face as he took in the scene. That night, she was kinder to him than he deserved, and as they lay in bed together, she stroked his hair and back as he cried. Whatever she was thinking, she kept it to herself.

BERNARD BLINKED AWAY tears and walked out from behind the pool shed. He had been at the party for a while now but was still carrying the bottle of Canadian Club. He hadn't said hello to anyone, just found his way behind the shed and took a swig or two of the whiskey, wondering how it was that he got there. It was 2009, but in his mind and in his heart it was still 1964. The decades that stacked up between now and then were nothing like the ones that had come before. Everything had been sped up, like a carnival ride. It made him dizzy.

He made his way over to the drinks table and finally set the bottle down. Then he shrugged and poured two fingers into a plastic cup.

"How ya doing there, White?"

"Cal," Bernard said, almost more as a reminder for himself than a greeting.

"Did you hear the news?"

"What news? What happened?"

"About Danny and Roberta."

"Are they OK?" he asked, alarmed.

"Better than OK. They're shacking up permanently. Getting married."

"What?"

"I take it you *hadn't* heard," Cal said, bemused.

"Why would anyone . . ."

"What? Marry Roberta?"

"Get married at all! He's got to be . . . Well he's older than I am!"

"He's young at heart!" Cal boomed.

Bernard searched the party for Danny but couldn't find him. Some of the women were gossiping about it in the kitchen. Bernard overheard Leslie call it "scandalous." *Weird, maybe*, Bernard wanted to add but didn't.

Bernard found Danny outside. He had hiked his pant legs up and was sitting on the edge of the pool, his feet dangling into the water. Bernard wanted to do the same, but he was afraid if he sat down he wouldn't be able to get back up. So he stood, casting a shadow over Danny in the strong patio lights.

"Heya, Danny. What's going on?"

"Not much, my friend," Danny said, turning to look up at him, "how are you?"

"How am I? I'm shocked, that's how I am."

"Why? What happened?"

"You're marrying Roberta, that's what happened."

"Oh, that."

"Why on God's earth?"

"Why not?" Danny shrugged. "We have fun together."

"Well I have fun with you," Bernard said, "but I'm not going to marry you."

"Why don't you sit down instead of lording over me?" Danny said.

Bernard sighed and took pains to sit down next to Danny, crouching and then leaning back on his hands. He hiked his pants up one leg at a time, and dangled his feet over the edge of the pool.

"There, are you happy?" Bernard said. "I don't know how I'm gonna get up."

"Who said you have to? You have a drink, the sun's gone down, there's this beautiful old pool . . . I say we sit here forever."

"Might have to," Bernard said, easing a little.

"So where have you been?" Danny asked. "Haven't seen you since I got here."

"Just wandering around, thinking about old times."

"You shouldn't think so much."

"Why's that?"

"Because life doesn't happen in the head," Danny said, tapping his temple.

Bernard looked up at the sky. A few neighbors had been shooting off fireworks all day. Now that it was dusk you could finally see a few.

"So when is this happening? This wedding?"

"Saturday."

"Saturday? *This* Saturday?" Bernard asked, incredulous. "Why so soon?"

"I'm eighty-one! No sense in a long engagement."

"Is it the money? Does she have any?"

"No!" Danny said, feigning disgust. "I like being with her. It's nice to have someone."

"I thought you liked being alone," Bernard said.

"I thought so too."

There was a pause. Danny looked down at the water. Bernard looked up at the sky as a few fireworks crackled and fizzed.

"Got any whiskey in that cup?" Danny asked.

"No," Bernard frowned. "I drank it all."

"You know what that means . . ."

"What?"

"Time to get up!" Danny said, lifting his feet out of the pool and slopping away.

Bernard leaned back on his hands, and drew his feet out of the water, but he was drunk and tired, and wasn't sure if he could get back up. So he stayed, put his feet back in the water, and watched the party from a distance. It seemed to be winding down now, early for a Fourth of July but late for this crowd. He watched a few women practice their self-defense moves in the light of the porch. Though she had taken the class, Maryanne was not among them. He started to wonder where she was, even started to worry about her, when she came up beside him.

"You look like you could use this," she said, handing him a bottle of water.

"Thanks," he said. "Wanna sit with me?"

"Actually I was thinking about leaving."

"OK," he said, and started to panic at the prospect of getting out of the pool in front of her.

"Need a hand?" she asked after a while.

"Please," he said, and lifted his arm to her, and Maryanne, stronger than she looked, pulled him to his feet.

AT HOME, SHE made tea and they sat together on the screened-in porch. The air was thick with sulfur. They could see the occasional firework light up the sky along the horizon.

"Did you have fun at the party?" he asked.

"Not really. You?"

Bernard shrugged. "I can't believe it about Danny and Roberta. Getting married."

"I can't either!" she said conspiratorially.

He looked over at her. "Would you ever want to, again?"

"Me? No. I miss Gerry but . . . I'm happy now. I like that my time is my own."

"'I like that my time is my own,'" he mused. "I never really thought of it like that."

"What would you do differently, if you did?"

"Get *married*?" Bernard shrugged. "Everything. But . . . I'm too old. What would be the point?"

"Companionship, I imagine. But even that's overrated. No offense."

"You're going to give me a complex."

"I said no offense!" she said, laughing.

Her laughter lit him up inside, made him feel years younger. He wondered if she really did want to be rid of him, and what he would do if he went home, how he would live.

He reached over and took her hand, and she let him hold it for a few seconds before pulling away.

As she pulled away, he moved toward her, bringing his face to hers and attempting a kiss.

Maryanne stiffened and backed away.

"This isn't . . ." She shook her head. "We're not . . ."

"But we could be," he said, and took her hand again.

Maryanne pulled her hand away and backed away from him.

"I think you better go."

"Go?" he asked.

"Home, Bernard. You better go home."

"But . . . the . . . how will you . . ."

"I'll be OK," she said.

"You're serious?" he asked. His heart was breaking. God, he hated the Fourth of July.

"Please," she said. "Go now."

And so Bernard packed his things and walked home through clouds of sulfur.

MADDIE

TO PREPARE FOR NATE'S PARTY, MADDIE took sixty dollars from her savings, rode the bus to Target, and bought a pair of cutoffs, a sleeveless top, and a bikini that came together with strings at the hips and the neck. In the dressing room, she evaluated her scars under the fluorescent light. Some were pink, some were white, but they were all terrible. She considered what she would say if someone asked her about them. "Surgery," she might say, or "cat." Both excuses seemed implausible, so she went to the makeup aisle and bought waterproof concealer.

On the day of the party, she took a shower, applied sunscreen to her entire body, and lipstick to her lips and cheeks. She covered her scars with the concealer, but they only looked worse—an obvious cover-up of some horrible thing, so she washed the concealer off and decided that she wouldn't go swimming so that she could keep her shorts on. She tied the strings of her bikini bottoms and stepped into them, and tied the strings of her bikini top around her back and neck, and evaluated her appearance. Although she had seen herself in the dressing room she was still surprised at how good it looked on her. She turned around and around in front of the mirror, modeling for herself. She pretended to laugh at somebody's joke, and practiced a few lines about herself. "I'm still in high school." "Environmental science, maybe?" "Libra."

She stepped into the cutoffs, pulled on a soft blue sleeveless tee, and modeled for herself once more, tucking in the shirt, pulling it out, and finally deciding on a half-tuck. She mussed her hair, tucked it behind her ears, and mussed it again. She put a hand on her hip, looked at herself a final time, and left the house.

Nate lived only a few miles away, so she dug her bike out of the garage and sailed out of the neighborhood, her perfectly mussed hair flying out behind her. She was nervous, and the loud bangs and pops from fireworks you couldn't yet see, but that people set off nonetheless, put her even more on edge. She had only ever been to a house party once, and she'd never gone to a party alone. But she had seen dozens on television and in movies and knew she simply had to step in and pretend like she belonged.

When she arrived, the house was quiet. It didn't seem like there was a party going on at all. She pulled her bike inside the wrought iron enclosure that separated the patio from the front yard, and rang the bell. Nate didn't answer. A tall boy with a bit of a belly did. "Hi," she said. "I'm Maddie."

"Nate!" the boy called, opening the door farther. "Your girl's here."

Maddie stepped in and saw that the house was filled with boys. Boys lounging on a leather sectional, playing video games. Boys in the kitchen, making macaroni and cheese. Boys on the deck, comparing their individual caches of fireworks. Boys in the pool. She didn't see Nate anywhere.

"Where is he?" she asked the boy who opened the door.

"Don't know," he said. "Around here somewhere."

"Where should I put my bike?" she asked him.

"How should I know?" He shrugged, and walked away.

She chained her bike to the wrought iron enclosure and took herself on a tour of the house.

The house was neatly kept. Or *had* been neatly kept. There were plush towels and fancy soaps shaped like seashells in one bathroom. In another bathroom, a pile of wet towels was swamped in a puddle on the floor. The bathroom smelled like shaving cream and urine, almost exactly like the bathroom her father and brother shared at home. There were razors and toothbrushes on the sink. A pair of blue swim trunks hung, dripping, from the shower rod. The shower itself had not been turned off all the way, so the faucet dripped too. Maddie turned the knob to cut the flow of water, and moved on, into the bedrooms—first, Nate's mother's, which had pink-and-green-striped wallpaper, white enamel dressers, and a walk-in closet; then, a guest room, which was plain and neat with tan and blue nautical accents. Maddie walked into a third bedroom expecting to find Nate but found a couple instead, the girl bent over, the boy coming at her from behind. "Hey!" the boy barked, and Maddie quickly backed out, closing the door with an unintended slam and practically ran back into the living room, her heart racing.

She found Nate outside, hitting a can of propane with a wrench. "Hi," she said, standing above him. "What are you doing?"

"Fucking can's rusted in place. Can't get it off to switch it out."

"Oh."

"How are you?" he said, pulling himself up.

"I'm OK."

"Just OK?"

"Yeah," she said, hugging herself, as if from cold.

"Why don't you go sit by the pool? I've got to figure this out."

"I could help."

"How are you gonna help me with this?" he asked, frowning.

Maddie shrugged. "Do you have any WD-40?"

"Uh, probably."

Maddie waited for him by the grill as Nate went to get the WD-40. In the pool, a couple of guys wrestled over a football, and another, in a lounge, played a game on his phone. Maddie felt like she had stumbled on a frat house, or a summer camp for young, shiftless men. So far, the only other girl there was in a sexual position. She felt foolish and out of place. She didn't know what she had been expecting, but it wasn't this.

When Nate returned, she told him to spray the rusted joint, wait a few minutes, and knock the can gently with his wrench. "How do you know all this?" he asked.

Maddie shrugged. "From my dad, I guess."

Nate did as she suggested, and tried to turn the can. It wouldn't budge.

"Now what?"

"Spray it down again. Wait a few minutes, and try again."

This time, the can easily slid loose from the rusted threads.

"Yay," Maddie said in a hush, softly clapping her hands. "Can we hang out now?"

"I've got to put this new can on and start the grill. Gonna cook up some hamburgers."

"Oh." Maddie frowned.

"But go ahead down to the pool," Nate said.

"I . . . I'm shy," she said finally.

"I'll walk down with you."

Nate took her hand and walked down the stairs to the pool. One boy, whose name Nate said was Duck, looked up from his video game. The others were still chucking a ball back and forth in the pool and did not seem to notice them.

"This is Maddie," Nate said. "Maddie, Duck."

"Doug?"

"Nope," he said, putting down the video game. "It's Duck. Don't ask."

"OK," Maddie said, smiling.

"That's Marc and Diego," Nate said, pointing to the pair in the pool. "Hey, guys, this is Maddie."

Maddie waved and the boys nodded in her direction before returning to their game.

"You OK hanging out here while I deal with the grill?" Nate asked.

"I guess so."

"Don't worry," Duck said. "We'll keep her entertained."

Maddie settled onto the lounge next to Duck. She took her T-shirt off but kept her shorts on. She sat back and closed her eyes. She hadn't thought to bring a book or even a towel. She hadn't thought she'd be so alone there, left to her own devices. Maddie also thought, she realized, that there would be more girls. More people to talk to.

Maddie felt foolish. This wasn't a party, it was just . . . hanging out with strangers. And she wasn't even *with* them, aside from Duck, who had already returned to his video game. She thought about sneaking around to the front, getting on her bike, and going home. But it would be too obvious now. Too obvious that she was uncomfortable. That she did not belong.

The midday sun was brutally hot and there was very little shade by the pool. Maddie thought about the fact that she did not have a towel. She thought about the plush peach-colored towels she saw in one of the bathrooms that were clearly not meant for the pool. Then she thought about the boys seeing her in her bikini, seeing her scars. Even now, in her shorts and bikini top, she felt exposed. If she took off her shorts, she'd be practically naked. Nate was over on the deck, grilling burgers. She looked over at him, and he waved.

The day grew hotter. The boys who had been comparing fireworks when she arrived had started shooting them off, in a kind of call-and-response with the neighbors. From this point on, the day was marked with staccatos—*bang, pop*, nothing, *bang, pop*, nothing. The air was thick with clouds of smoke from the fireworks and the grill. Maddie felt like she might evaporate, the water in her body steaming off her skin. In front of her, the pool sparkled like a mirage.

She thought of her scars, how they had looked in the mirror that morning, pink and tough and disgusting. If she took off her shorts, would the boys see them from the pool? Would they know? She could feel herself sweating beneath her shorts, sweat pooling at the small of her back, and the space where her legs met her torso. Did she even care if they saw her scars? What they thought of her?

Without another thought, Maddie stood up and shimmied out of her shorts. Somewhere, somebody whistled. She looked up at the deck, thinking it must have been Nate, but he had opened a beer and was talking to someone, his back turned toward her. The boys in the pool, she noticed, had stopped their game to watch her.

Maddie walked to the shallow end of the pool and dipped a toe into the water. The water was cool, but not cold, and she stepped in without reluctance, happy to have her body concealed beneath the water's surface. The boys tossed the football out of the pool but kept themselves to a corner of the deep end, so Maddie had room to glide from one end of the pool to the other, cooling off.

She was not in the pool long, but long enough for the party to change direction. The couple that had been in the bedroom came down in their swimsuits and got in the water. The boys who were making macaroni when she arrived came down too. Someone carried a cooler out, and cans of beer were popped and chugged. Maddie looked up and watched the beer-commercial camaraderie of it all. She wondered if any of them would even be friends if they hadn't all grown up in the same neighborhood and gone to the same school. She thought about herself, and why it was she didn't have any friends, other than Stacia. She didn't feel comfortable in social situations. She never had, and she definitely didn't now. Maybe *she* should drink a beer, relax a bit. But no one offered her one; instead, they seemed to go on like she wasn't there, making jokes she either couldn't hear or didn't understand. What she did want was a towel, and one of those burgers Nate was cooking. She hadn't realized how hungry she was.

A game had started without her knowing it, and one of the boys swam over to her and tugged on the string on her bikini bottoms. Maddie pushed away with her legs and tied the side of her bottoms that had come undone. Then another one did it, swimming over to her and pulling the strings on the other side of her bikini. He grabbed hard and did not immediately let go. Maddie yanked the strings back and kicked him. She retied the bottoms fast as she could, moving to the stepladder as she tied them. Then, two more boys jumped into the pool—Maddie saw the shadows and heard the simultaneous splashes, felt the weight of them as they displaced the water. Soon, one of them was behind her, untying her bikini top, where the strings came together under her shoulder blades. Loose, the top floated around her like a necklace. Maddie tried to reach back and join the two sides together again, when someone pulled the strings on either side of her bottoms, and her bottoms fell away. The boys laughed, and Maddie whipped around to retrieve them and started to scream. When she did, one or two of them forced her underwater and held her there.

Maddie struggled to regain control. Her arms were held behind her and someone was pushing her head. She had no breath to hold, so she screamed underwater, blue bubbles rising from her mouth. She was caught in a tangle of arms and legs and bodies. She tried to kick them but couldn't get any leverage; they were rocks and she was sand.

Her bikini top slipped away, and she was completely naked. She felt her nakedness as their hands were on her bare skin, touching her breasts and her butt, pushing themselves against her, keeping her underwater. She tried to claw at them, to poke them with her fingers or pull their leg hair, but there were too many of them, and soon, she stopped struggling. *I'll drown*, she thought, *I'll drown*. Then, she felt a splash, and there was a brawl above her, and suddenly she was above water, sucking air into her lungs.

Nate had jumped into the pool with his clothes on, and was now telling his friends to get the fuck out of the pool, the fuck out of his house. He took off his T-shirt and gave it to her. It was sopping wet but Maddie put it on and climbed out of the pool, noticing the girl she had walked in on earlier staring coolly at her. She watched as Nate fought with his friends, shoving one, and telling them all to get the fuck out. She watched as her bikini floated on the surface of the water, its newness and beauty mocking her. She watched as Nate's friends gathered their things and left in a sea of cusses and half-assed apologies.

When everyone was gone, Nate walked over to her and asked if she was OK. Maddie said nothing, but frowned and looked down into the pool. She felt so small, so diminished, like she might just slip into the shadows and disappear. "Let's go inside," Nate said, and Maddie nodded, letting him lead the way.

In the house, he gave her a towel and asked if she wanted him to take her home. She shook her head, and he asked if she wanted to take a shower. "OK," she said, and he let her use the shower in his mom's room, which had shampoo and conditioner that smelled like coconuts and a clock radio tuned to a classical station. She flipped it on and off, facing the mirror but not looking at herself. She took a shower, turning the hot water up all the way, and the shower massager to its strongest setting, so that, when she emerged, her skin was red and battered. Maddie was still shaking as she ran his mom's comb through her hair.

She wanted to hurt herself. Just one little pinprick—something to take away the feeling of heaviness and stupidity that was swallowing her. Maddie rummaged through the drawers of the sink cabinet. She found his mother's flat iron, his mother's hair dryer, his mother's tampons. The medicine cabinet was full of makeup and teeth-whitening strips and moisturizers. Everything dull and ordinary. She thought about plugging in the flat iron and sticking her hand in it, but she didn't want that kind of pain, that kind of scar. She rummaged through the drawers once more and found a manicure kit with a pair of cuticle scissors. She couldn't find any peroxide, so she ran the scissors under hot water, and sat on the edge of the tub with them. She made a fist around the scissors, spread her legs, and stabbed the soft fat of her inner thigh. But the scissors were bent at the tip and did not penetrate her skin. She turned them around in her hand and tried again, but felt nothing. She looked at the manicure kit, and particularly at the nail file, which was chalky with nail dust and could not be properly sterilized. She took to the cabinets once more, going deeper into the drawers. Finally, she found a small sewing kit, the kind that might be sold at a dollar store. Inside were three different sewing needles and three straight pins, the kind with little plastic balls on top.

Maddie sat on the ledge of the tub again, took one of the needles, and pressed it into her thigh. Pain radiated up into her groin and down her leg. But it was a small and useless pain, one that would not last beyond the moment. Then, she remembered something she had read in a book. She took the needle and pressed the tip of it beneath her thumbnail. She took a breath, and drove the needle down underneath the nail, squeezing her eyes closed and biting her lip as she did it. Here was a wrenching, searing, lasting pain. Her thumb throbbed and bled. Pain traveled in waves up the small appendage. Maddie was certain that she would feel it all night.

Nate had laid a pair of his cotton drawstring shorts and a T-shirt for her on his mother's bed. The clothes were huge on her, but she put them on and walked out to the kitchen, where Nate was cleaning up after his friends.

"Hi," he said when he saw her. "How do you feel?"

Maddie shrugged.

"Are you hungry?"

She nodded.

"All the burgers were ruined. How about I go and get us a pizza?"

"Do you have to go?"

"We could get one delivered. What do you want on it?"

"I don't care."

"I'm really sorry that happened. My friends are stupid fuckwits."

"I don't want to talk about it," Maddie said.

So they didn't talk about it. They ordered pizza and watched movies as the day grew long and tired. Outside, the sound of firecrackers built to a two-hour finale, as night fell and people in backyards all over Seven Springs were finally able to see the results of their small explosions.

THE NEXT MORNING, Maddie's thumb throbbed. Her neck ached. She had slept, she discovered, curled into a ball on the end of the sectional, her head on the armrest. She remembered everything from the day before in quick succession, starting with her thumb and going back to the pool, back to her bike ride, and the way she had felt that morning, like she was about to become something new. Now, in the cool quiet of Nate's living room, all she felt was shame. She wanted to get out of there, and she never wanted to see Nate, or any of them, ever again.

She rose quietly so as not to disturb Nate, who had slept on the floor below her, and tiptoed around, looking for her things. But she couldn't find anything—not even her shoes. It was all still outside, by the pool. She slid the sliding door open slowly, and closed it behind her. From the deck, she saw that her bikini was still floating in the pool, and was immediately embarrassed by it, as though she had done something wrong by wearing it, or by getting into the pool, as though she had invited the thing that had happened. Maddie took a deep, sad breath and descended the stairs to the patio below. She found her things and stuffed her shorts and top into her backpack and slipped on her flip-flops. She considered retrieving her bikini from the pool with the bug skimmer, but only stared at it a second—the strings reaching out in all directions, the small blue flowers that matched the color of the swimming pool—before deciding to let it go. She was just about to leave when Nate appeared on the deck.

"Hey there," he said. "Whatcha up to?"

"I have to go," she said, not looking at him.

"Can I make you some breakfast or something? I have this pancake batter that comes in a can."

"No," she said, still looking down, and added, looking up at him, "that sounds disgusting."

"I guess it kind of does." He shrugged. "I could make you something else."

"I have to go."

"I could drive you."

"I have my bike."

"What are you doing later?"

"I have to work."

"How about after?"

She shrugged. "I'll probably just go home, watch TV with my brother."

"OK. Well, if you decide you want to do something . . ." his voice trailed.

"OK," Maddie said, and left through the gate.

She walked around to the front of the house, to where she'd left her bike, but discovered that it was gone. The cable lock had been cut, the bike stolen. The lock itself dangled off the wrought iron patio enclosure, useless. Maddie picked it up and examined the spot where it had been severed. Her palms felt hot, her chest heavy. She wanted to scream, but she knew that it was pointless. The bike was gone. *Her* bike was gone, taken, she assumed, by one of Nate's friends. She looked back at the house but couldn't bring herself to knock on the door and tell Nate what had happened. She left the cable where it was and walked home.

The walk was long and her flip-flops inadequate. As she walked she thought of her mother, of how much she wanted her. Maddie imagined rounding the corner of her street and seeing her mom's car in the driveway. She would run up to her and cry into her chest. She would tell her what had happened. She would forgive her mother of everything, so long as she stayed. And her mother would forgive Maddie too, for everything she'd done—going to the party, losing her virginity, cutting herself. But when she rounded the corner of her street, it was only her father's truck in the driveway. And everything was as it had been the day before.

By the time she got home, Maddie had cuts on the top of her feet, from where the flip-flop straps rubbed her skin. She felt sweaty and tired. She had to be at work in an hour. She had a plan: take a shower, get dressed for work, make a sandwich, and eat it on the way. But her plan was thwarted by her father, who was not in bed after his shift as he usually was this time of day, but was sitting at the kitchen table, his eyes bloodshot, his face weary.

"Where in the hell have you been?" he asked.

"I . . ." Maddie said.

"I was about to call the police!"

"I'm sorry," she said.

"Why didn't you answer your phone?"

"It died."

"Whose clothes are you wearing?"

Maddie looked down at herself, at the men's gym shorts and T-shirt. What could she tell him? That she had gone to a pool party and was held underwater? That these were the clothes of her nineteen-year-old boyfriend? That she was sorry? What *was* she sorry for exactly? Nothing. Everything.

"I'm sorry. I should have called."

"Whose clothes are you wearing?" he asked again.

"Stacia's brother's. I forgot to bring a change of clothes, and mine got wet, so Stacia lent me these."

"Why not just wear Stacia's clothes?"

"Because Stacia's, like, a size zero," Maddie said, thinking fast now.

"I thought Stacia was in New York for the summer."

"She is. She just . . . came home for the holiday."

Her father shook his head. "If you're lying, I'll find out."

"I'm not lying."

Maddie tried to walk past him, but he grabbed her arm. "Stop," she said, and shook her arm free.

"I thought you were dead," he said, his bloodshot eyes looking down on her.

"Well, I'm not."

"What's gotten into you?"

"Nothing, I'm just . . . tired. And I have to be at work in an hour."

"I want to talk later. To figure out a punishment."

"Don't you think that mom being gone is punishment enough?"

"You can't use that as an excuse for everything, Maddie. You used to be good. I need you to be good again."

Maddie wanted to scream. She felt alight with frustration and anger. If she opened her mouth, she didn't know what would come out. Instead, she held his gaze, waited him out.

Finally, he said, "Did you have breakfast?"

"No."

"I'll make you something."

"I have to go to work," she said, and he let her turn into the hallway and escape into her room.

AMY

AMY WOKE THE MORNING AFTER PETE left to the sounds of someone in the kitchen. She lay awake, thinking of the night before, of Pete disappearing after their argument. He must have come back. Maybe his mother convinced him, or maybe it was true—he did still love her. He wanted to try.

Amy rubbed her eyes. Her head pounded. There had been too much wine and too much fighting and too much of the past creeping in to ruin their delicate present, like ink to lace.

She resolved to be better. To do better. To try and make it work.

In the bathroom, she washed her face and brushed her teeth. Her lips were stained from the wine and she scrubbed them with her toothbrush. She combed her hair and squeezed her cheeks to give her face some color. She pulled on her robe and walked out toward the kitchen.

But it wasn't Pete standing in the kitchen, squeezing juice from an orange. It was a stranger.

"Can I help you?" she asked, shocked-still.

"I think so," he said.

He stirred something in a bowl and then poured batter into a hot pan.

Amy clenched her fists. She thought of the Maglite beside her bed, and of the razor that Pete had likely packed up and taken with him.

"Who are you?" she shouted. "What do you want?"

"You know my mother almost never made breakfast for us? It was always cereal. Cold cereal. Never pancakes, never sausage, never eggs."

"Who are you?"

"You know who I am," he said.

"I've already called the police."

"I doubt that," he said, flipping a pancake.

Amy took several steps back, toward the bedroom. She meant to reach down and grab the Maglite, but she didn't see it.

"If you're looking for your flashlight, I have it. I also have your phones," he said, holding up both her cordless and her cell and giving them a wave.

"What do you want?" she asked.

"Why don't you sit down? I made coffee. You take it black, right?"

"How do you know that?"

"You take your wine red and your coffee black. You take your husband for granted and yourself too seriously."

"What do you want?"

"For starters, I'd like you to *sit down* and have some coffee. Then I'd like you to have breakfast with me. And then I'd like you to help me with something."

He piled three pancakes onto a plate and held up the plate for her. "Come, come."

Amy took the plate from him and sat down at the counter.

"Is this a joke?" she asked. "Are you a friend of Steven's?"

"I assure you, I am no friend of Steven's. And this is not a joke."

"So, what, then? You're the murderer? Did you poison the pancakes?"

"Up to you. Yes. And no."

Amy froze, looking up at him.

"I'm not what you pictured."

"No," she said. He was small, thin, and balding. He was a little sad-looking, but not the angry, aggressive killer from her dreams.

"I had a laugh about your 'visions.'"

"What do you want?"

"Eat up! It's getting cold."

Amy cut the pancakes with the side of her fork. She looked up at him.

"They're not poisoned. That's not exactly my MO."

Amy sighed, thinking of his MO. She took a bite.

"Good, good," he said. "Here's some syrup. Here's some juice."

Once she started eating, he ate too, standing at the counter where she had stood the day before, eating eggs while arguing with Pete. She'd do anything to have him back now. To have had the day go any other way than how it had.

He must have read her mind, because he said: "I wasn't sure we'd have the opportunity to do this, what with your husband coming home. But the way you fought last night, I'm guessing he won't be back."

"What do you want?" she asked again.

He put his fork down and wiped the corners of his mouth with a napkin. "I want you to paint my portrait."

She looked up at him—his small, unfamiliar face. "Why?"

He shrugged. "Why not? You're *so* good. Everybody thinks so. And the poor pizza deliveryman. Boy you got that wrong!"

"I'm not a clairvoyant."

"No," he said, shaking his head. "You're a dreamer of dreams, a seer of visions!"

Then, he said:

"I want you to paint my portrait, Amy. I want you to get it right."

"Then what?"

"Then at least people will know."

"Know what exactly?"

"Have some more coffee, Amy."

He poured her the rest of the coffee from the pot and started to fill the sink with water.

"People need to know that I did this, why I did it."

"Why did you do it?"

"Later," he said. "I'll tell you later. Now I need you to get ready. We have work to do."

"Can I take a shower?" she asked.

"No time for that," he said. "Just put on your painting clothes. We're going for a walk."

"A walk," she said.

"Yes, a walk. You use your legs." He mimed walking with his fingers.

IN HER BEDROOM, Amy dressed quickly and looked for a weapon to use, a way to escape. But her closet was full of clothes and sensible shoes, nothing that could be even remotely weaponized. She put on her sneakers and considered the jalousie windows. She had heard that they were unsafe and could be easily broken into. But could they be easily broken out of?

She examined her bedroom window. There was a screen that could be pushed out, and twelve-inch panes that she might be able to fit through. The window would require a push before she could crank it open, these old windows always did, and that would make a bit of noise. Amy listened for a second to the sounds coming from the kitchen. The sink was going; he was doing the dishes.

Confident that he would not hear her, Amy pushed the window and cranked it open, far as it would go. She climbed onto her dresser, and gazed across the yard. The view was the same from here as it was from her kitchen window—the royal poinciana, still bright with orange blooms, and, beyond it, Adel's house. It was hot already. The cumulus clouds were high overhead. Amy stuck her head out the window, and leaned out, looking down at the ground four feet below. She pushed herself out farther, worming through the opening an inch at a time until her entire torso was outside.

"Amy!" she heard him call. "Let's shake a leg!"

She heard him open her bedroom door and pushed herself off the dresser, a second too late. He grabbed her by the ankle and then by the waist, and pulled her backward through the window, her chin and then back of her head hitting the metal window frame along the way.

"Stupid woman," he said, throwing her onto the bed. She was surprised by his strength. Her head rang with pain. "Get up," he said. "Let's go."

So she left with him. They left through the front door and walked down the street, as normal as anything. As they walked, she looked at the houses, expecting to see somebody, expecting to be able to communicate her alarm. But nobody was out. The day was hot and still smoky from the night before. Many of her neighbors, she thought, would be inside, keeping cool in the air-conditioning and nursing hangovers. Glen and Carlos were away that weekend—they'd gone with Steven and Kenny to Bimini. She knew because they'd asked her to watch their house.

They turned down a side street, and again on a street that ran parallel to her own. This street appeared to have been hit harder by the housing crash. Every third house, it seemed, was empty or overrun with bushes or vines. Amy was reminded of what people always said about Hurricane Andrew: some homes were completely destroyed while others were left untouched. On this street there were four houses that appeared to be abandoned. He led her to one of them.

"You live here?" she asked as they climbed the porch.

"I live here," he said.

He pushed open the door and led her in.

Inside, the windows were covered with heavy brown kraft paper. It was dark, and he did not turn on a light. As her eyes adjusted, she could see that the house was mostly empty. In the center of the room, there was an easel set up across from a heavy industrial drafting stool.

"I have your brushes," he said. "You can use them. And I got some paint."

He sat down on the stool and looked at her expectantly.

"You want me to paint your portrait right now?"

"Well I didn't bring you here to play Yahtzee."

"What if I don't?" she asked.

"I'll kill you."

A chill ran through her. "And if I do?" she asked.

"Then we'll see, won't we?"

She looked around the room. If there was no way of getting out of her own house, there was certainly no way of getting out of here. The windows were covered, the doors locked. "OK," she said, "but I'll need some things, a sketchbook and a pencil. You said you have my brushes?"

"Here," he said, handing her a plastic bag full of things—her brushes and pencils, palette and palette knife, all taken from her studio. She considered the palette knife for a second. It was diamond-shaped and dull from use.

"I usually do a sketch first," she said. "And then transfer the sketch to the canvas."

"That's fine," he said.

"So I need my sketchbook," she said.

He sighed and looked around a minute before tearing a large square of paper from the top corner of the window, which allowed a square of light to stream in.

"Will this do?" he asked, handing it to her.

"Yes," she said. "Do you have a book or something for me to lean on?"

"Do I have a book or something?" he said, looking around. "Probably not."

He came back with a framed picture of the Virgin Mary and handed it to her.

"It came with the house," he said with a shrug.

Amy recognized the picture from art history. It depicted Mary ascending to heaven while angels surrounded her and God and Jesus waited on thrones above her.

"Can I sit?" Amy asked.

"Whatever you need," he said, throwing up his arms in exasperation.

Amy sat on the futon and he on the stool. The light was terrible. The paper on the windows gave the room a dark, amber glow, and she wasn't sure how she'd paint him, much less sketch him. "Would you mind moving back a few feet? Into the light?"

He begrudgingly complied, pushing his stool back into the square of light. This illuminated one side of his face, and cast soft shadows over the other.

"Good," Amy said, and began sketching him, puzzling over his face, how unfamiliar it was. She'd never seen him anywhere. He was an outsider, coming in.

"I'm from Ohio," Amy said, thinking she might get him talking. "How about you?"

"Originally from Georgia," he said. "But I grew up here. Lost my accent."

"I've never been to Georgia. I mean, I drove through, on my way down, but I never spent any time there."

"No small talk. I don't want you to get distracted."

So she sketched him in silence. His thin eyebrows, thin lips, slender nose. He was a blank of a person. There was nothing distinct about him. If she saw him in public, she wouldn't give him a second look. Maybe that's why he did this. Or how he got away with it.

When she was finished with the sketch, she handed it to him. "Is that OK?"

"It's fine," he said, handing it back to her.

She stood and began transferring the sketch to the canvas while he watched. She thought about the easel, the weapon it created in combination with the large, wood-backed canvas board. Would he use it against her? Could she use it against him?

"You said you have paint?" she asked.

"Right," he said. "I'll get it."

He came back with a paper bag from Utrecht. She opened it and examined the colors, deciding how she would combine them to match his flesh and lips and eyes. She wondered where her own paint was, what he had done with it, but didn't dare ask.

"There's no blue here," she said, looking back into the bag. "What do you want me to do for your eyes?"

"Oh," he said, irritated. "I just grabbed a bunch of things. What can you use instead?"

"I can use brown for your eyes. Is that OK?"

"Fine," he said, "fine," but he seemed disappointed. Then: "Can you do black for my eyes? Did I get any of that?"

"Yeah, I can do black."

"I like this," he said, "making things up as you go. Maybe I should have been an artist. But then, I like to plan things. I like everything in its place."

Amy was surprised that he, a man who walked into houses and

selected murder weapons at random, considered himself a planner. She wanted to say so, to know more, but she didn't dare ask him.

She took out her palette and stuck her thumb through the worn wooden hole, happy to have it back. She was just about to start mixing paint, when she thought about the smell, the fumes.

"I usually have the windows open," she said. "For the smell."

"Sorry," he said, shaking his head, "no-can-do."

"Just a crack," she said, "for ventilation. And maybe a fan."

"What do you think this is?" he asked. "Obviously I have to keep the windows covered."

"But nobody knows you're here."

"Because the windows are covered."

"Fine," she said. There was no turpentine to thin the paint. Turpentine usually made the fumes much worse.

Amy started mixing the colors. She would paint his skin as it was under the shadows, and would use black, with a bit of red, for his eyes. As she mixed the paint, she considered her palette knife, how she might jab it into his stomach if she had to, and how much force she'd have to use if she did.

Once she had the colors mixed, she put the palette knife on the edge of the easel, and began painting him, moving quickly but deliberately. The oil paint had a strong smell and she tried to keep her mouth closed, and her face away from it, so as not to breathe it in, but this was impossible. The air-conditioning was on. This dispersed the fumes but circulated them around the house, so that, soon, the fumes were everywhere. After a while, Amy felt light-headed. She wanted to ask for a glass of water, but didn't want to test his patience again. She wanted to paint his portrait and get out of there. Her chin was bleeding slightly and she wondered when she'd last had a tetanus shot. Her head throbbed.

"I should tell you why I did this," he said.

Amy nodded, thinking it couldn't hurt to keep him talking.

"I'm sorry I broke into your studio," he continued. "I wasn't thinking right. I was trying to scare you into stopping. But . . . it's much better this way. People need to understand why."

Amy continued painting. She was going too fast, and it was all wrong. The shadows were harsh, his features muddled and unspecific.

"Here," he said, reaching into his pocket. He handed her a photograph. "That's my mother, my brothers, and me."

Amy looked down at the picture. "Your mother is beautiful," she said, handing it back to him.

"*Was*," he said. "She *was* beautiful. But the women in this neighborhood . . . They taunted her. Gossiped about her. I was only a kid but I remember it, the whispers, the rumors."

Amy stopped painting and looked over the canvas at him. "That's why you did it? Because these women were *mean* to your mother?" She couldn't help her tone.

"My mother *killed* herself. And these women . . . they drove her to it!"

Amy thought of Adel, taunting one of her peers into suicide the way some schoolgirls did nowadays. It didn't make sense. She put her paintbrush down and steadied herself against the easel. The fumes were so strong that she thought she might faint.

"Why are you stopping?" he asked nervously. And then yelled: *"Why are you stopping?"*

Amy thought she might fall back. She held on to the canvas for support.

He grabbed her wrist and pulled her toward him. "You cannot stop!"

AMY WAS TWELVE when her mother was diagnosed with cancer, and fifteen when she died. Those three years should have been spent in a kind of preparation for the inevitable, but Amy never believed that her mother's death *was* inevitable. She never believed that it would happen. Even as her aunt took her aside and told her to prepare for the worst, even when she got the call that her mom was leaving the hospital and going into hospice care, suspending treatment because of an infection that had come on due to chemotherapy, even as that infection spread into her lungs and kidneys and spleen, even as she was told it would only be a matter of days, Amy was certain that her mother would return home, healthy, happy, cured. Why and how this would happen, Amy didn't know. But the movies she watched, and the books she read, confirmed that bad things did not happen to good people. That, in the end, after a challenge or heartbreak or even an illness, health and happiness were restored, the world was righted, and the characters moved on. And so, Amy was not with her mother when she died. She was at a house party after her high school's homecoming dance. She was wearing a blue taffeta dress, dropping acid and losing her virginity in the bedroom of a classmate.

That night, when her date brought her home, the house was lit up like an explosion. Her date dropped her off at the curb, and Amy walked up to the house alone, approaching it slowly, the acid still working on her so that the light streamed from the house like rays of sunshine, and the lawn that bookended the long cement walkway was like a dark, green ocean, churning toward the house. When she walked in and saw her sister, home suddenly from college, Amy knew that something was wrong.

Everything moved in slow motion as Amy's eyes moved from her sister, to her aunt, to her father. They looked like fun house versions of themselves—Amy's father taller than usual, her sister and aunt shorter and fatter. Her sister looked up at her but did not move. Her aunt reached out an arm and said, "Come here, dear."

Amy did as she was told and allowed herself to be pulled down onto her aunt's lap. It was an awkward position for a fifteen-year-old girl in a taffeta dress, and Amy suppressed a giggle.

"Amy," her aunt began.

"Mom's dead," her sister said, and it was like all the lights went out at once.

AMY WOKE UP on the floor, the murderer hovering over her.

"You fainted," he said. "I caught you."

Amy held her breath, unsure what to say or do. She was sure that he was going to kill her, that this was the end.

"Do you want me to help you up?"

"No," she said. "Just . . . give me a minute." He watched her, an attentive nurse, and she propped herself up on her elbows. "Can I have a glass of water?" she asked. "And can you please crack a window?"

"Fine," he said.

In the kitchen, he pulled the paper from the bottom of the window and rolled it up several inches so that he could open the window. He did the same in the dining and living rooms, rolling the paper a few inches from the bottoms of the windows and cracking them open. He brought her a glass of water, and Amy sat up to receive it.

"I can see if there's a fan around here. Maybe in the garage," he said.

"Thank you." Amy nodded, drinking the water down.

She sat facing the canvas. It was not her best work. Instinctively, she thought about how she might correct it, what she might do differently. In the corner of the easel, she noticed, he had placed the photograph.

Amy reached over and grabbed it. She studied it, particularly the beautiful woman at the center, who did not look like the type to crumble under the weight of neighborhood gossip. She turned the photograph over. On the back, it said, SEVEN SPRINGS, 1964. THOM (9), DAVID (6), AND ANDREW (4). Amy looked at the picture again, and tried to figure out which of the boys was standing there now. She looked at the painting, and back at the photograph. It was Thom (9). Plain as day.

"Thom?" she asked.

"Yes?"

"Tell me everything."

BERNARD

BEFORE HIS ARGUMENT WITH MARYANNE, BERNARD had not been home in a month. He had gotten so used to being with her that he had forgotten what it was like to be alone. Had it not been for the fireworks, which went on all night in endless cacophony, he might have enjoyed the silence. But each boom and blast only amplified his loneliness. Still drunk from the party, Bernard eased himself into his Barcalounger and alternately cried and dozed. His life had come down to all that was in front of him: a darkened television set, dingy curtains, a front door that only opened when he came and went.

It was the middle of the night when Bernard woke again. The whole world was quiet until, in his living room, Vera put on a record.

"I always loved this song," she said, standing in front of the record player, swinging her hips. "Why don't you get up and dance with me?"

Bernard started to stand but found that he couldn't, not right away. He had seen somewhere—on television, maybe—a Barcalounger that ejected you with the touch of a button and made a mental note to look into it.

"Come on," she said, taking his wrist and pulling him toward her. She put her arms around his neck and sang as they swayed back and forth.

"I was crazy about you," he said.

"So, what? You're not anymore?"

He thought about it. What was it about her? What had it been?

"I was in love with you," he said finally.

"Not me," she said, shaking her beautiful head. "Some idea you had."

The song ended and the needle went around and around, tracing the record as it popped and hissed.

"It wasn't your baby anyhow. You know that, right?"

Bernard nodded. He hadn't known it, not until just then, but he nodded anyway.

"Whose was it?"

"I don't know," she said, and put her head on his shoulder.

Just then, Irene called from the kitchen to say that his eggs were ready.

"But it's the middle of the night!" he called back.

"Don't you want them?"

He turned to her, and it was 1959. They had just moved into the house they had built with their eminent domain money. "You look pretty," he said to her.

"Thank you." She smiled, her hand on her hip. "It's a new house."

They ate together, and sipped coffee and held hands.

"Don't forget to take your medication," she said.

"Medication?"

She picked up a bottle, rattled it.

"Oh, that."

He swallowed his pills with his coffee and slipped his arm through the electronic blood pressure monitor at Irene's urging. It was sky-high, off the charts.

"You've been forgetting your medication," she said, and suddenly she was old—bald and jaundiced.

"What do you remember of the end?" he asked her.

"Of life?" She sat back, thought about it. "I remember feeling like I was being erased. Like one day I would open my eyes, and the rest of me wouldn't be there."

◆　　◆　　◆

THERE WERE YEARS of cancer—either going through treatment or getting over it—but in the end, it was six weeks that he remembered, the six weeks after they realized that there wouldn't be another recovery, another remission. By then it had spread to her liver and nothing was working. Her skin turned yellow and she was hot and cold, like a child with a fever. She was in almost constant pain—which is why the marijuana. They smoked it together, sitting up in bed and watching television until Irene would pass out again and Bernard would go into the kitchen to make grilled cheese or to cry.

He called the kids one after the other, starting with Pam, then John, then Dan. He didn't want them there—didn't want them crowding the house—but he knew they had a right to their mother's last days. Pam came immediately. John too. It took Dan almost a week, and a pleading phone call from Pam, to get him to come down from Connecticut. But he came. And soon they were all there—no kids, no spouses—just the five of them, together in the house, the way it used to be.

The first night they were all there, Pam cooked dinner and they sat around the table together, the five of them, and everything—the table, the room—felt absurdly small. It was as though the house had shrunk without them, and when they returned, it was not large enough to fit them. Bernard remembers Dan's knees, bumping up against the underside of the table, water sloshing out of their glasses. Irene joked that the house never felt so small and so full all at once.

"Just imagine if we'd brought the kids," Pam said.

"I wish you had," Irene said. "I want to see them."

And then there was silence, because what could anyone do?

"Tell them I'll haunt them," Irene said with a wan grin.

John wanted to plan. Wanted to talk about "after"—right then and there, with his mother at the table.

"What are you going to do, Dad?" he'd said, as though he were talking about job prospects or retirement.

"Do?" Bernard asked.

"After," John said.

"After *dinner*," Pam said, taking Bernard's hand and eyeing her brother, "we'll all watch a movie."

Pam focused the family, settling them into a steady routine. She took care of bathing her mother, of calling the doctors, filling prescriptions, and coordinating with the hospice nurse. She told the boys what to do—yard work, mostly, but also shopping, also getting Bernard out of the house. They went bowling one night, Bernard and the boys, somewhat strangers in rented shoes. Bernard didn't know what to do out of the house, didn't know how to be. Also, he realized, he didn't know his sons. Irene spoke to them over the phone. She knew all their kids' birthdays and what their sizes were and the things they liked. She knew how things were going at work for the boys, how they were getting on. Bernard knew them through her, but in a way not at all.

So when John sat beside him, beer in hand, and said, "So can we talk now? Talk about after?"

"After what?" Bernard said, honestly confused.

"After Mom dies."

Bernard was aghast. "We'll have a funeral, of course. We'll bury her."

"No, Dad," he said. "What will *you* do when you're by yourself?"

Bernard looked up at the ceiling, toward the scoreboard. Dan was winning, but not by much.

Bernard said, into the air, and then, a second time, to John, "I'm not going to do anything."

"OK," John said, nodding.

That night, the kids had an argument. Bernard was in the bedroom with Irene, smoking, and the kids were in the kitchen, talking, then shouting.

"What's that?" Irene asked. "The kids?"

"The television," Bernard said. "I'll ask them to turn it down."

Bernard walked into the kitchen just as John was about to deck Dan.

"What's happening?" Bernard asked, his voice a strong whisper.

"We want to sell the house," Dan said. "Get you a condo somewhere."

"*Dan* wants to sell the house," John said. "Dan does."

"Dad," Dan said. "Do you know what's going on with the market now? Do you know what this house is worth?"

They turned to Bernard, waiting under the fluorescent light.

Did he know what was going on? It seemed to be a test. Were they testing his cognition? His ability to live by himself?

He shook his head. "I'm not selling this house." And then, because he wasn't sure they understood, "Your mother is dying. She's in that room, right now, breathing her final breaths. You're here. For her. *Be* here for her." He looked at John, pointed a finger. "No more talk of after." And at Dan. "No more talk of selling."

He turned around and walked out of the house. But there was nowhere to go, no one left in his life to comfort him.

The next day, Dan said good-bye to his mother and flew home. He had work, he said, couldn't drop everything forever. A few days later, John drove back to Jacksonville with a promise that he'd return as soon as he could.

Irene held on for three more weeks. They watched home movies, looked at photographs, and reminisced, everything tinged with what they were not saying, which was that things could have been better. If only Bernard hadn't broken her heart.

"I hated you for a long time," Pam said to him one night under the glow of the porch light. They were drinking gin and listening to the bugs.

"Everybody hated me," he said.

"Mom didn't. She just didn't understand you."

"I didn't understand myself," he said, looking down at his shoes.

"You were just unhappy."

"I had no right to be unhappy."

She took his hand. "That's not how it works."

"And what about you?" he asked, looking up at his daughter. "Are you happy?"

"Well," she said. "I love my kids, and I love my husband, most of the time. But sometimes no. I'm not."

"It's probably my fault," he said, taking a sip, the ice cubes clinking inside his glass. "I've just always had this feeling that things could have turned out differently, you know?"

"I do," she said, now through tears. "But I don't know how."

"I feel like I should say something," he said, "something to settle things between your mother and me."

"Haven't you already?"

"No. We've always just . . . ignored it."

"Were there others?"

"Other what?"

"Other women?"

"No," he said, looking out over the lawn. The trees had grown tall and dense; the grass was mostly dead for lack of light. "But Vera never went away for us—for me. And . . . I think that your mother is dying because of it. That the cancer is somehow my fault. That she held it in, and . . ."

"It's not your fault, Dad. Come on."

"You don't know."

"You don't know either," she said, standing. "I'm going to check on Mom."

IRENE DIED ON a Thursday. John was on his way down from Jacksonville, and Pam was walking back from The Smiling Pig after picking up their dinner order. There was still light in the house, the type of dim evening light that persists after the sun goes down. Irene slept in Bernard's arms, thin as a whisper, and he listened for the space between her breaths, panicking a bit when it got longer. His heart was beating stronger, and hers was weakening. He said, "I love you." He said, "I'm sorry."

And then he felt her leave him. Felt her there, and then not there. In pain, and not in pain. He stroked her face, her hair.

He said, "I love you, I'm sorry, I love you, I'm sorry."

BY FRIDAY, BERNARD decided that being in the house was no good for him. There were too many memories there, too many regrets. Maybe he should have left when the boys suggested it, should have sold the house when the market was up and bought a condo near the beach. But that was just another regret. And what good were regrets?

He left the house to run his errands. He had clothes at the dry cleaner's that he'd never picked up, and a whole pile to drop off to be laundered. He had to figure out what to wear to Danny's wedding the next day. "Danny's wedding." He said it aloud, but it still sounded absurd.

When he was young and all of his friends started getting married after high school, coupling up, buying houses and having babies, it all felt too soon, like it was happening too fast. And now, on the other side of his life, he was experiencing it again. He was out of rhythm with the rest of his generation. He didn't know he was supposed to go on living.

MADDIE

AT 11:00 A.M., THE SMILING PIG was empty. Maddie had walked through the restaurant a half hour before, filling the ice bin and the napkin holders, stacking the red soda tumblers and the small side plates. At a minute before eleven, she switched on the neon signs and unlocked the front door. But *tick*, no one walked through the door. *Tock*, the restaurant remained empty. She put her apron on and filled her pockets with wet wipes and straws. She poured herself a Coke. She watched the door.

She did not have a book with her. That summer, she was supposed to read three novels: *Blu's Hanging*, *American Rust*, and *The Solitude of Prime Numbers*, all novels the summer AP reading list said "presented starkly different views of young life," but she had yet to buy them, or even think about buying them. She was too caught up in her own young life. But now she wished she had something to read, something to busy her mind. She checked behind the bar for the stack of magazines that had been left by patrons and saved by bored waitresses, but there were only three: *Salt Water Sportsman*, *Consumer Reports*, and *People*. Maddie had already flipped through the copy of *People*, and didn't care anyway about the crumbling marriage of reality stars or the teenage pregnancy of a politician's daughter. She threw out the magazines and sat at the bar with her Coke, hoping the bubbles would settle her stomach—she was filled with a kind of anxious dread that morning, and the scents wafting from the kitchen only made her feel worse.

Bored, Maddie took out the small pad she used to write down orders. At the top of a fresh piece of paper, she wrote, *Dear Mom*, and crossed it out. Then she wrote, *Mom*, crossed it out, and then wrote: *Caroline*, using her mother's beautiful name. "Caroline," she whispered to herself, and wrote below it, *I miss you*. She looked down at the words and up at the empty restaurant. "I miss you," she said aloud, and wrote, *I hate you for leaving. I wish you'd come back, but if you did, I'm afraid of what you'd think of me. Of the things that I've done.* She paused then, took a sip of her Coke. *I am not a good sister to Brian*, she wrote. *I don't do enough for him. And I hate Dad for driving you away. Is that what happened?* Then, a confession: *I heard you fighting one night. It was late and I was supposed to be asleep, but I crept into the hallway to listen. You said 'things weren't supposed to be like this,' but how were they supposed to be? How am I supposed to grow up without you? How am I supposed to be?* Maddie looked up at the empty restaurant, and down at the page. She said aloud, "How am I supposed to be?"

She shook her head, closed the small notebook, and stuffed it in her apron pocket. Just as she did, her pocket buzzed to life, a text message coming through on the screen. In the movies, the text would be from her mom, telepathically aware of her daughter's questions and ready to answer them. But it was Nate, asking how she was. Maddie pictured herself snapping her phone in half by way of response. Instead, she turned off her phone and placed it back in her pocket.

She felt a wave of nausea come over her and thought about replacing her Coke with ginger ale, which The Smiling Pig did not have. When she was sick to her stomach, her mother would make ginger tea and sit with her, telling her stories about what her life was like when she was young. Caroline had a brother who died when he was ten, so most of her stories took place before that, and included both Caroline and Teddy, off on some adventure together, swinging on vines or doing cannonballs into one of Ocala's many spring-fed lakes. It was no wonder Teddy died, Maddie always thought, the way they carried on, treating the forest like their backyard, feeling safe in a truly unsafe place.

The door swung open and a customer entered.

"Hi," Maddie said. "Have a seat anywhere."

"I wanted to get some takeout," he said.

"Do you know what you want?"

Maddie took his order and packaged it a few minutes later, putting the ribs in tinfoil and Styrofoam, the coleslaw and potato salad in small plastic cups. The smell of the ribs made her want to vomit—what was with her today?

She handed the package over to the man, and he gave her a nice tip. "Have a great weekend," he said, and she smiled wanly, trying to hide her urge to vomit. The moment he left she ran into the bathroom, but the urge had left her.

It was nerves, Maddie told herself—a reaction to what had happened in the pool, and then the fight with her father, her anger over it all. After her shift, she would go to Walgreens and buy some ginger ale and go home and get in bed. She would wake up in the morning and it would all be one more day behind her.

She waited on a light lunchtime crowd, biding her time, her letter to her mother tucked neatly in her pocket. She felt better for having written it, for giving her problems a voice. Maybe she'd buy a journal. Maybe she'd start writing instead of cutting. Maybe, she thought, there was more than one way to let yourself bleed.

AFTER HER SHIFT, Maddie walked to Walgreens to buy the ginger ale and to try to find a suitable journal. She chose one with a plain, purple canvas cover and college-ruled lines, and splurged on a nice pen, a six-dollar Zebra. When she left the store with her purchases in hand, Charlie was standing outside.

"Charlie," she said, surprising herself by how easily his name rolled off her tongue.

"Hi," he said, maybe somewhat embarrassed.

"How are you?"

"Just getting some air-conditioning," he said.

"Air-conditioning?"

"From the store. Here," he said, putting his hands on her shoulders and positioning her in front of the twin doors that slid open whenever a customer entered or exited the store. "Stand right here."

Sure enough, Maddie received a blast of cold air each time the doors slid open, a momentary bit of relief from the ninety-degree summer heat.

"Are you OK?" she asked, looking at him. His face was grimy. He smelled particularly ripe.

"In what sense?" he asked.

"I don't know," she said with a shrug, and, feeling the urge to vomit, said, "I should get going."

"Do you have any money?" he asked.

She had made twenty-one dollars in tips that day. She'd spent fourteen of it in Walgreens just then, splurging on the notebook and pen. But she reached into her pocket and gave him what she had.

"Can I ask you a question?" she asked.

"Sure," he said.

She wasn't sure how to start, how to ask him what needed asking. Finally, she said, "Do you know where I live?"

Charlie shook his head and shrugged, unconvincingly.

"My house was broken into. Some things were stolen—some money. I never said anything to anyone because I didn't want to get you in trouble."

"Why would you assume it was me?"

"I don't know," she said, then: "I don't know anyone else who would need it."

"Yeah, well . . . I know lots of people. Besides, I'm not a criminal."

"No," she said, shaking her head, "I didn't say you were—I just asked."

"I'm saving for a bus ticket," he said. "Can't get a fair shake here."

Maddie wondered if he could get a fair shake anywhere, but asked: "Where will you go?"

"North. New Orleans, maybe."

"Huh," Maddie said.

"Huh?"

"I never thought about New Orleans—as a place to live, I mean."

"Most people don't nowadays," he said with a smile. "But it's still warm, and that's the thing. Need a place that doesn't get too cold."

"Right," Maddie said. She stood there for a moment as the automatic doors opened and closed.

"Well, good luck," she said after a while, "and . . . thank you. For not breaking into my house."

"Somebody did, though," he said, an eyebrow raised.

"Right," Maddie said. She thought of Nate and his friends, her stolen bike. "Somebody did."

"Good luck to you," he said, straightening.

"Good luck to you too," she said, bowing slightly because it seemed like the right thing to do.

AT HOME, SHE took a shower and drank her ginger ale, suddenly feeling better, as though this was the thing she needed all along. She watched a movie with Brian, having resolved, at some point during that day, to be a better sister. It rained. Maddie listened to the thunder come in and the sound of rain on the roof and the patio outside. She imagined her mother walking through the door, soaked through with rain. She imagined her mother saying "I got lost" or "The traffic was terrible" or "What should we do for dinner?" She imagined Charlie, still standing outside of the Walgreens, waiting out the rain. She imagined a future without them. It was blank as a page.

When the movie was over, Maddie made grilled cheese sandwiches for herself and Brian but was unable to eat hers, the smell of cheese too strong. "What's the matter?" Brian asked, when Maddie covered her mouth and nose with her hand.

"I'm just not feeling well," she said.

"Can I have your sandwich?" he asked.

Maddie went to bed early, but woke at 4:00 a.m., the moon so bright it was as though someone was shining a light into her room. She thought again of her mother and wished that she hadn't. Wished that she could get her out of her head, that she could have one waking moment where she wasn't missing someone who was no longer there.

She took out her new notebook and pen and looked down at the blank page. She wanted to write *I hate you, I hate you, I hate you*, but also didn't want to write that, didn't want to put that down. And so she wrote nothing and let the hate course through her, a disease of the blood. She wanted to cut herself but also didn't want to. She was tired of hurting herself, tired of the bleeding and the scars. Instead she turned on her computer and googled "alternatives to cutting." She found a long and somewhat ridiculous list that included: "viciously stab an orange," "throw an apple against a wall," and "scream very loudly." Farther down the list it said, "Go for a run." Maddie thought about this, her sneakers in her closet, the strong moonlight outside.

She got up from her desk and pulled on a pair of gym shorts, a sports bra, and her mother's Pretenders T-shirt, but waited until she was outside to put her shoes on, not wanting to wake her dad or brother.

Outside, she stretched her quads, hamstrings, and triceps. It felt good to stretch and she took her time, breathing through the discomfort. When she was ready, she walked quietly down the stairs and jogged away from the house.

Soon, she was running hard and fast. Her lungs burned and her heart pounded, she was so unused to strenuous activity. But it felt good to move, to feel her legs stride out in front of her, her stomach tighten, her fists punch the air. She wasn't even scared. Not of being out in the middle of the night, or encountering any would-be murderers.

She ran the entire perimeter of the golf course, colliding with the occasional spider's web, and dodging the occasional toad. She heard the bugs in the trees and focused on the music they made, the low hum of night, and the sound of her own breath. At some point, she realized, she did feel better. Not cured, but on her way.

She curved toward the highway but stopped herself from running out to the space where Charlie begged. Instead, she watched the median from the side of the road. The lights from the firehouse flashing on the dark and empty street. Nowhere else to go, Maddie turned and ran home, taking the same way she always had, ducking down the street that ran parallel to her own, a shortcut of sorts. When she passed the house that sat directly behind hers, the man who lived there—the one she often caught watching her at night—was sitting on his porch. Seeing her, he called, "Hey!" and took off after her.

"Hey!" he screamed, running after her. "Where is it?"

Maddie's stomach lurched; she felt her arms and legs go to jelly but didn't dare stop. Instead, she picked up her pace, not turning down her street, but going straight, running faster, pushing harder. *Where was what?*

"Where's the money?" he called, still chasing her.

The money. Maddie ran as fast as she could, thinking: *The money, the money, the money.* Then she remembered: the money from her room. Her tips. It was him. Not Charlie, or Brian, or Nate, but him. She ran and ran until she had the nerve to slow down and look behind her. He was gone, but she didn't stop—didn't dare turn back toward home. Maddie ran all the way out to Manan Boulevard, and all the way up to Publix, which was just opening for the day. She was exhausted and thirsty but didn't have any money, so she sat on the curb in front of the supermarket and waited for daylight.

AMY

WITH THE PAPER ROLLED UP AND the windows open, Amy could breathe. The afternoon light and air warmed the room. She looked down at the photograph and felt the possibilities open up around her.

"Thom?" she asked.

"Yes."

"Tell me everything."

"What do you want to know?"

"What do you want people to know?"

"That I'm not a monster. That my mother wasn't a slut."

"Why would they think that? About your mother?"

He shook his head. "They said things about her. There was gossip, talk—even after she was gone. It was the kind of thing where you enter a room and everyone stops talking. Where people's faces go crooked with pity every time they see you—'poor child,' I heard someone say once, 'poor children.' But what did they know?"

"What else is there to know?" she asked tentatively.

Thom shrugged. "I don't know what to tell you."

"Maybe start at the beginning."

So he told her about his mother. As he did, Amy sketched him anew, turning over the paper she'd done the first sketch on and carefully replicating the details of his face, the strain of worry and grief that passed over him as he recounted his story, his mother's story.

• • •

HER NAME WAS Barbara but after they moved to Florida, she insisted on being called Vera, preferring it to the cutesier "Bobbie," a nickname that had followed her from adolescence. She wore swing dresses and high heels, even to mop the floor or do the laundry, and even after women switched to wearing shift dresses and even pants. "It was as though she were playing a role, or waiting to be discovered," Thom said, shaking his head as he mused: "My mother in the kitchen in high heels."

She even made her children call her Vera. "She couldn't stand being called 'Mom,' 'Mommy,' or 'Mama,'" Thom said.

"That must have made you feel horrible."

"No," he said, blinking. "Why?"

Amy shrugged, thinking back to her own mother, who liked to be called "Mommy" even when the girls were older and refused.

"I loved her," Thom said. And, as though he were being challenged, "I still love her."

"Can you sit back in the chair?" Amy asked. "And hold the photo out in front of you, like this?" She held the sketch in front of her stomach to demonstrate.

"What are you doing?" he asked.

"You want people to know," she said. "This is how they'll know."

He sat back in the chair and held the photo out in front of him, as she had asked. Just like that, there was a change in the room, a shift in power, like when two weather systems converge. She sketched him, and he talked to her, and she felt somehow safe, like she might survive.

"When we moved here," Thom told her, "we'd spend all of our days outside, finding and killing snakes and geckos and anything else we could get our hands on. We were brutal. It was mercilessly hot outside, but when she wanted to be alone, Vera would lock the door. So we learned how to break into other people's houses, just for the chance to be inside for a little while, to drink Sprite and watch television. We knew what houses had the biggest TVs, the best food. We knew who was home and who was working, and how to get in and out. There was one house, a couple blocks away, with a great swimming pool and water slide. We'd spend hours there until we heard a car in the driveway, and then we'd be gone so fast, out of the pool and over the fence, dripping wet as we slipped between fences, moving from backyard to backyard.

"At home, we'd sit on the front stoop until she'd let us in. She was happier in the evenings and would sing songs with us while she cooked us dinner and gave us baths. She'd pick up Andy and turn around and around with him, dancing. He threw up once all over her dress. God, she was mad," he said with a smile and laugh that seemed to betray him, the person he had become.

"She was the first person I ever knew who died. We had killed snakes and lizards, but when we did, there were always more; they were like water, there was an endless supply. But when Vera was gone, she was just gone . . . I'd wake up in the mornings and run into her bedroom expecting to see her. Once, I ran into her room and pulled the covers off the bed, thinking I'd find her, but it was only my father, in bed alone, and he jumped up and came after me, angry because I'd woken him.

"It's different when you're sick," he said. "When *a person* is sick, I should say. You expect them to go. Some part of you does, anyway. But . . . she wasn't sick! She was fine!" The weather changed again and Amy was scared. At one point he would be cool and calm, the next, hostile or erratic, the wind whipping up before a storm.

Still, she couldn't help but ask: "Why now?"

"What do you mean?" he said.

"Why avenge your mother's death now? It was forty-five years ago."

"So I should just get over it?" he said, an edge of hostility in his voice.

Amy shook her head. "That's not what I meant."

He was quiet for a moment. He tapped his index finger on his thigh, a restless or nervous tick.

"I lost my job last year, after the crash. I didn't have anywhere else to go so I came here, to stay with my dad."

"Your dad still lives here?"

"In Fort Lauderdale. He and his wife usually go up to Maine for the summer, but they didn't this year. They didn't want to leave me alone in their house. People with money never want you to have any of it, you know?"

Amy didn't respond, and he went on. "So I told them I'd found another job in New Jersey, which is where I'd been living. And I left. Or," he said, leaning forward, "I was about to leave.

"I decided to come through here one last time. The neighborhood's changed," he said somewhat wistfully. "The houses are old and falling down. Some of them empty, abandoned, like this one. I thought: I wonder if I can go home. So I did. Or I tried." He looked down at the floor. "There's a family there now. They have a swimming pool. There's a cabana in the back with twinkling lights. It's a place for *fun*," he said, his eyes darkening. "My mom died there," he said slowly, "but you'd never know it."

He continued to stare at the floor. He looked confused, bewildered, as though he was trying to draw a line for himself between then and now.

"I drove away and thought I'd never come back. I was going to go somewhere, as far as the gas in my car would take me. But I stopped first, at the Publix here in town, to get lunch before heading out. And . . . I saw Adel in line at checkout," he said. "I hadn't thought of her in years, but I saw her—standing there, *alive*—and . . ." He shook his head, his face was gray. "I just wanted to hurt her. To kill her. To make her go away." He looked over at Amy from across the easel. His eyes glinted as he spoke.

"So I moved in here, and watched her. When the time was right I walked into her house and killed her." His face was dark and wild. "It felt good, like I was taking the power away from her. After that I decided to find the others and kill them too."

Amy ran the pencil again and again over his face, to capture the darkness, the emotion. She finished the sketch and handed it to him.

He looked down at it, seemed to consider it, and passed it back to her.

"It's fine," he said, a trace of sadness in his voice. "It's good."

"I need different colors," Amy said finally. "If we're going to do this right."

"What do you need?"

"Ultramarine and Phthalo Blue, Titanium and Flake White, Raw Umber, Vermillion, Cadmium Yellow, and Yellow Ochre," she said, surprising herself by how quickly she could rattle off a palette, as though color were a language she'd only just learned to speak.

"Can't you mix something?"

"I can, but I need those colors. They're the ingredients."

"What are you suggesting?"

"We could go to the store together."

"No." He shook his head. He looked around the room, and then at the front door. "I'll go. You can stay here."

He took her into a bedroom and handcuffed her wrist to a metal bed frame.

"Don't make a sound," he said, leaning in close to her face. He closed the door behind him and shut her in.

THE ROOM SHE was in had once been a child's room. The walls were painted a deep, cheerful orange. There was a giraffe decal on a wall with measurements growing up its neck and a few notes in Sharpie indicating where a child had grown, the last of which read CARLY, AGE 6. There were nail holes and scuff marks on the walls, where, she assumed, pictures and furniture had once been hastily removed. Other than the bed, which, Amy assumed, Thom had brought in, the room was empty. She thought about the family who had lived there, and about Thom's family too—about how quickly things could change.

In the living room, she heard him close and re-cover the windows. She lay back in the bed, thinking of what he had told her. She pictured him as a boy, killing snakes, and then as a man, killing women. Maybe he was going to kill her too. She listened to his car start up and pull away. She was alone. Amy thought about screaming, about pounding on the walls or pushing the bed over to a window and crying for help. The paper-covered windows gave the room a sinister appearance, a dark orange glow. Outside, the street was quiet. She couldn't even hear birds squawking, the typical music of the neighborhood.

Amy thought of the woman in the photograph, her red hair and lips, her practiced smile, and then of Adel and the others—all young once, all gone now. She thought about Pete and wondered where he was. She thought of the child they would never have. He had been OK with it from the beginning, she realized now. It was only Amy who felt the need to atone, to repent for some failing of hers, to repair what could not be repaired by painting herself out of the picture. She thought about what her mother-in-law had said to her about marriage being long, and she supposed that it was, if you allowed it to be.

Amy knew what she would do. She would finish the painting. She would find a way out. She would call Pete and then the police. Thom would be arrested and she would be free. Maybe the world could not be righted. But she could start again.

THOM WAS GONE for an hour, maybe more. When he returned, he released her from the handcuffs and led her back into the living room. He brought the paints she had asked for, a pizza, and a bottle of wine.

"I figured you might be hungry," he said.

"I am," she said. It was already late, five or six or seven, she didn't know.

He poured some wine into her water glass and handed it to her.

"The wine will make me too tired to paint," she said, refusing it.

"Maybe stop for the day," he said, "come to it fresh tomorrow."

"I can go home?" she asked in disbelief.

"No," he said with a bit of a laugh, "of course not."

She thought about Pete, in Miami at his mom's. He would have to come back up to Fort Lauderdale to fly out. She would miss him.

"Fine," she said, and grabbed a slice of pizza and accepted the wine he handed her.

He seemed calm and happy enough, not irritated or hostile, and she steered clear of questions, of talk about his mother and the others.

At one point he said, "I like what you're doing with the picture. What you're going to do." And she didn't respond because what could she say? It wasn't as though she had a choice. But of course she did— she could have left the original painting stand and wait to see what would come next, whether he would kill her or let her go.

That night he let her shower and brush her teeth, and chained her to the bed again. Alone and in the dark, she turned her thoughts to the painting, to how good it could be—the true penultimate of the series, the *raison d'être* for everything that had come before.

The street was quiet, the house noiseless but for the occasional *whirr* of the air-conditioning. Amy wondered how the electricity could even be on—surely Thom couldn't get bills here, a house that wasn't his. She wondered how many other houses in the neighborhood were occupied by squatters, and thought of all the families who had lived there just a year or two ago, before the housing market crashed and they were forced out. Finally, she slept, a heavy, dark, underwater kind of sleep. In the night, she woke to the sound of someone shouting "Hey!" and she thought of Pete, but it wasn't his voice, and two blocks may as well have been two miles.

THE NEXT DAY, she woke slowly, hesitantly. She was dehydrated and head-achy. She had a knot on the back of her head where she'd hit the window frame the day before, and an impending feeling of doom. She wasn't sure how the day would end. Would he simply let her walk away?

She had to pee and looked up to where her arm was cuffed to the bed frame. Her wrist was red, her arm sore from hanging. Should she call out for him? The house was still. Was he asleep, or had he gone out?

Finally, there was a slight knock on her door. He called her name.

"Amy?"

"Yes."

"Ready?"

"Yes."

He uncuffed her.

"I got breakfast," he said. "Bagels and coffee."

"I have to use the bathroom," she said.

"Of course."

In the living room, she stood in front of the fresh canvas he'd purchased the day before, and the sketch she'd pinned to it, thinking of the work ahead of her. She was torn between wanting the painting to be very, very good and wanting it to be done. She wanted the thing that was going to happen to happen already, to be free, no matter the outcome.

After breakfast, he sat for her, holding the photograph out in front of him, a slight bit of armor, and she transferred the sketch, making a life-size copy of him as he was that morning, steady and resolute. When it was time to paint, she urged him to open the windows and he complied, rolling up the paper, and cranking the windows completely open. The light in the room was a revelation. She didn't know how dark it had been until there was light again. She could hear birds outside and she thought briefly of screaming. But who would hear her, and what would they do?

Thom seemed to know what she was thinking.

"Don't bother," he said. "I'll cut your throat."

"I wasn't going to," she said, and fought the urge to touch her throat.

She took the paints from the bag and thought about how she'd use them. The blue she had asked him to buy was the same shade she'd used to paint Adel's teakettle and skirt in the previous paintings. Here, she would use it for his shirt, lightening it to the color of faded denim, and for his eyes, which would be, like the skirt and kettle, deepest blue.

He was quiet as she worked, and she wondered what was happening with him, where he had gone inside his mind. She worked on his skin first, combining Vermillion, Yellow Ochre, Ultramarine, and Flake White to achieve a basic flesh tone, and combining Raw Umber with Titanium White to create the palette of grays that she would use to lighten the flesh. It was difficult to capture his emotion, because, unlike the day before, he did not wear it on his face, so she relied on the sketch, moving her eyes between the sketch and his face, creating a version of him, a composite. Under ordinary circumstances, a painting like this would take a week or more, and she wished she had the time to stay on his face, to achieve the depth of grief and madness she had seen on him the day before, but she moved on to his neck and ears and wrists and hands, deciding that it was better to be finished than perfect.

Once she had his face and neck, wrists and hands, she mixed a palette for the faded Kodachrome photograph he held between his thumb and forefinger, working with hues of red and blue and ochre for their clothes, and combining the yellows and blues to create shades of green for the tropical landscape behind them. Amy had seen a documentary once on public television about Nixon's Florida, and this photograph reminded her of it—middle-class white Americans coming to Florida to live the good life in the land of swimming pools and cheap real estate. She painted the 1960s versions of Thom, his mother, and brothers. She wondered what had happened to his brothers, but she didn't dare to ask. Probably Thom was the family outcast, the family pariah. The brothers were likely off living their own versions of normal somewhere while Thom was here, squatting in their old neighborhood, avenging his mother's suicide, using a nine-year-old's memory for guidance.

Maybe, she thought, he would have always been a killer, no matter what had happened to his mother. Didn't Jeffrey Dahmer kill baby squirrels and bury them in his backyard? Hadn't Thom killed the harmless blacksnakes that had once been so plentiful around here? Amy thought of the snake that had taken up residence in Adel's yard, and a chill ran up her arms. Her hand cramped. She put down the paintbrush and massaged her hand.

"Need a break?" he asked.

"I think so," she said.

"Can I see?" he asked.

Amy shrugged. Obviously he could do whatever he wanted. She turned the canvas to face him.

"It's good," he said, nodding. "Very, very good. You have an eye, Amy."

"Thank you."

"It's a shame," he said.

"A shame?" she asked carefully.

"This is all going to end soon," he said.

Amy turned the canvas back toward her. "I'd like to continue," she said, "if you're ready."

"I'm ready," he said.

Amy continued, her hand shaking. Before she could stop herself, she was asking the question: "How does it end?"

"I shouldn't tell you," he said.

"Why is that?" she asked, looking up at him.

"I don't want to spoil it for you."

They were coming close to something. She was standing on a cliff with him. His hand was on her back.

"Go ahead," she said. "Spoil it."

"Finish the painting, Amy."

Amy put the paintbrush down, challenging him.

He took a breath, looked off into a corner.

"Do you really want to know?" he asked.

"Yes," she said.

He looked directly at her, his eyes dark and narrowing. "You're going to be found dead. They're going to find you, and this painting. They're going to connect it with all the others. They're going to say, 'She was a foolish, foolish woman.'"

Just then, Thom looked over her shoulder, at something beyond her. She turned around and saw a girl, staring wide-eyed into the room.

BERNARD

AT THE COUNTRY CLUB, ROWS OF seats had been arranged on the terrace overlooking the ninth green. Just inside the double sliding doors was the rec center, which had been decorated for the reception with white paper streamers and tablecloths. Bernard took a peek in to see what they might be eating—there was a deli tray, a few salads, and a sheet cake. On another table were large glass carafes filled with water and iced tea. This brightened him. There was going to be a party. He sat down next to Maryanne, who barely acknowledged him.

"You look nice," he said to her.

"Thank you," she said, crossing her legs at the ankles, and looking straight ahead.

After a while, Danny emerged from the rec room with his son alongside him, and gave a little wave to the guests. Bernard noticed how excited he seemed, and how happy. He still couldn't shake how odd it was to be at a wedding of old people, but he was happy for his friend. Someone brought out an old boom box, placed it near the front, and pressed PLAY on the CD player. A piano version of "Here Comes the Bride" started playing, and everyone stood and turned to watch Roberta walk down the makeshift aisle in a long yellow dress. When she arrived at the front, someone shut off the music, and the officiant—who wore a long, New Agey robe—started up, talking about the luck of the Irish and how everyone seated there today were each other's soul mates.

"There is a reason you have all found each other in this life. Just as there is a reason Daniel and Roberta have found one another. You are each other's keepers, each other's friends, each other's soul mates." Then, Danny and Roberta exchanged vows and rings. They kissed, and everyone clapped. Everyone except for Bernard, who hadn't eaten anything since breakfast and was already singularly focused on the roast beef and Swiss sandwich he planned to make himself.

After the ceremony, Bernard jumped up to make a beeline for the deli tray, but Cal and Harry intercepted him and pulled him aside.

"Leslie and April are missing," Harry said.

"What do you mean they're missing?" Bernard asked.

"Well, they're not here," Harry said.

"Were they invited?" Bernard asked.

"Well, I *assume*..." Harry said. "It'd be pretty rude to exclude them."

Bernard shrugged. His stomach growled. "Let me ask Danny."

Inside, Bernard made himself a sandwich of roast beef, Swiss, mayo, mustard, and pickles. He took a bite of it but found it hard to savor, thinking of the two missing girls. He found Danny and Roberta, posing for pictures in front of the ninth green. When they were finished, he took Danny aside.

"Leslie and April are missing. Were they invited?"

"Well of course they were invited," he said. Then he called over to Roberta and asked her.

"They're probably protesting," she said. "You should have seen the look on Leslie's face when I told them we were getting married."

"Probably," Bernard agreed, but his stomach was already sour with worry. "Listen, congratulations, you guys. And thanks for"—he held up his sandwich—"thanks."

He backed away from them and found Cal and Harry out on the terrace. "They should be here. Roberta thinks they're protesting."

"What do you think?" Cal asked.

Bernard shrugged, looked at his sandwich. He wasn't hungry anymore. "We should probably go check on them."

"Give me a few minutes to go and get my gun," Cal said.

Bernard sighed. The idea of going anywhere with Cal was unsettling. But going somewhere with Cal and his gun? He'd rather not. "Tell ya what. You stay here. I'll go check on them."

"Fair enough!" Cal said. "I've got my phone on if you need me."

"Sure," Bernard said and swiftly left the party, walking through the clubhouse and out through the large gates.

AT FIRST, BERNARD couldn't remember whose house the two were staying in, or even where either of them lived, but he just kept walking, and his feet eventually carried him to the right place. By that time, he was carrying his jacket and had soaked through his dress shirt. Sweat dripped into his eyes and down his neck. He tried to think of happy things, like Maryanne in her breezy purple dress, and the notion of them all being soul mates, but he was too worried. He kept imagining what might have happened to April and Leslie, kept imagining himself walking in on a grisly scene, like the kind they show on TV nowadays—blood everywhere, bodies strewn.

He knocked on the front door, and waited.

He knocked again, this time walking between the house and the shrubbery to get a look inside, but the curtains were drawn. He had a feeling of déjà vu. He had done this before, not two months ago. He knocked a third time.

This time, April answered the door. She was wearing a yellow robe. There were splotches of makeup dried on her face. She looked stunned. "She's dead," she whispered.

"What?"

"She's dead," she said again. "Leslie's dead."

She pulled Bernard into the house and walked him down the long hallway.

"All morning she had been saying she was feeling weak. I told her she was probably just tired. Then, we were getting ready in the bathroom together—I was putting on my makeup and she was taking out her curlers and"—April's voice cracked—"she stumbled and fell back."

She stood aside so he could see. Leslie was slumped against the bathroom tile, her hair still partially in curlers.

"Are you sure she's dead? Did you check her pulse?"

"Of course I checked her pulse! I tried to give her mouth-to-mouth. But she's gone. Look." April crouched beside Leslie and lifted and dropped her hand.

"Did you call an ambulance?"

"No. I've been sitting here with her, holding her hand." April started to cry. "She was my best friend. My *only* friend." She turned to Bernard and he watched her crumble.

"It's OK," he said, and reached out for her. "Don't hold it in. Let it out." And she let him embrace her and cried against his chest, while Leslie lay beneath them, her mouth slack, her eyes dark.

Bernard couldn't help but think about what the wedding officiant had said about them being each other's soul mates. A more cynical version of him would have countered that they had simply lived in the same place, at the same time, but he didn't know what difference it made. *Sure, fine,* he thought. *We're soul mates.*

"What should we do?" April asked, looking up at him through teary, tired eyes.

"Call her son," he said.

"He's out of state."

"Does she have anyone else?"

"No," April said. "Just us."

"OK," Bernard said, looking down at Leslie's body. "Do you think we should move her?"

"I don't know," April said. "What if somebody thinks I killed her? That I'm the . . . killer."

"Nobody's going to think that," he said.

April looked down at her friend. "I'll get her a pillow."

"I'll call 9-1-1," Bernard said. "See what they say."

After calling 9-1-1, Bernard called Cal with the help of the list of neighbors' phone numbers taped to the refrigerator. Before long, he was receiving wedding guests at Leslie's front door, including Danny and Roberta, who stepped through the threshold hand in hand, and Maryanne, who followed them.

"It's awful," Maryanne said, hugging him.

But they both knew that it could be worse.

THE ORIGINALS STAYED there for the rest of the day and held vigil around Leslie's body. They carried chairs into the hallway so they could sit with her before the ambulance came and took her away. Someone said a prayer. Another told a story about Leslie and her husband, Avery. "They walked around the neighborhood every evening holding hands. They didn't even have a dog. They were just walking, talking, enjoying each other's company."

"She missed him so much," April said, staring blankly ahead.

"They're together now," Maryanne said, taking April's hand.

"Do you really believe that?" April asked.

"No," Maryanne said after a while, shaking her head, and the two women broke into hysterics, which surprised Bernard—he'd never seen Maryanne laugh so hard.

After the ambulance came and took Leslie away, April decided that she wanted to stay. "I'll stay here with you," Bernard said.

"No," April said. "I'll lock the doors. I'll be OK. Besides, Leslie's son will be here tomorrow. I want to be here when he arrives."

And so he left Leslie's house several hours after he arrived, trickling out with the rest of the originals—tired, hungry, spent. Bernard hugged Danny and Roberta. He said good night to Cal and Harry. He started down the street, headed home, the strong July light an antidote to his blue mood. The next thing he knew Maryanne was next to him, slipping her hand into his. "Can you come back with me?" she asked. "I don't want to be alone."

MADDIE

MADDIE SPENT THE MORNING WITH HER blinds drawn, pacing nervously. She found, counted, and rehid her money, thinking of all the times she had blamed her brother for her missing tips. After the man was arrested, Maddie decided, she would take her brother out and do something nice for him, maybe take him to the movies or out to lunch, something they used to do with their mother. When her father woke, she would tell him about the break-in, about the man who had chased her. Together, they would call the police. Now, though, she showered and dressed, and, feeling exhausted, got back into bed.

She didn't wake again until her phone buzzed later that afternoon. It was Nate, texting her to see if she wanted to hang out. She didn't, but didn't have the heart to write "no" either, so she ignored him, turning off her phone and pulling the covers up over her head. But she knew she couldn't stay in bed. It was already after three. Her father would be leaving for work soon. After a few moments' hesitation, Maddie got up to talk to him.

In the kitchen, Brian had his face in the refrigerator.

"Where's Dad?" Maddie asked.

"Work," Brian said. "Where else?"

"He left already?"

"Yup."

"Dammit."

"You need to apologize, huh?"

"Apologize?" Maddie asked, and remembering how she'd behaved the day before said, "I guess."

"There's nothing to eat here," he said, slamming the refrigerator closed.

"Do you want to go out? We can walk somewhere."

"Like where?" he asked, perking up.

She shrugged. Besides The Smiling Pig, there wasn't much. There was a Checkers on the other block, and a bad pizza shop next to the drive-thru liquor store.

"Checkers or the Pig," she asked.

"Checkers!" he said with a smile.

"All right." She shrugged. "Get a hat so you don't get sunburned."

Before they could leave there was a knock on the door. It was Nate, and when Maddie opened the door, he rushed in.

His hair was messy, his eyes wild.

"Where've you been?" he asked, walking into the house and sitting on the couch.

"We're on our way out," Maddie said, still standing by the door. "I'm taking my brother to lunch."

"How about pizza?" he said, not standing up. "We could order in, my treat."

Maddie turned to Brian, who had emerged from his bedroom in sneakers and a hat, ready to go.

"Pizza?" she asked with pleading eyes.

"Fine," he said with a shrug and turned back toward his bedroom.

"What do you want on it?" Nate asked.

"Half plain, half pepperoni and sausage," Maddie said, rattling off her family's typical order.

Nate called and ordered the pizza and Maddie sat in the living room, watching him. She realized that this was only the third time she had seen him in daylight. He was taller than she remembered, larger. She was grateful then to have missed her father. If he were home, he would want to know what this man was doing in their living room.

Nate stuffed his phone in his pocket and leaned forward, his elbows on his knees.

"I was wondering if it would be cool if I stayed here for a few days."

"What? No," Maddie said, shaking her head, "definitely not cool."

"Well can I at least park my truck in your backyard?"

"Why?" she asked.

"My dad wants to take it away. We got in a fight."

"I thought your parents were out of town."

"They were. They returned last night, but I didn't know they were coming, so I hadn't cleaned up yet. Anyway, it's such bullshit—him suddenly appearing back in our lives and laying down the law."

Maddie thought about this. She would love it if her mother reappeared. If she laid down the law.

"Well you can't keep it here. My dad . . . doesn't even know about you."

"Why not?" he asked, looking directly at her, challenging her.

Maddie shook her head, changed the subject. "Remember when I told you that someone broke into my room? I think I know who it is. I was going to call the police, but—"

"Don't call the police," he said, jumping up.

"Why not?"

"I—I just don't want you to, OK?"

Brian came back into the room. She looked at him and then back at Nate. "What's going on?" she asked Nate.

Just then, there was a knock at the door, strong and quick.

"Don't get it," Nate said, panicked.

"Why?"

"You have to hide me."

"I'm not hiding you," Maddie said, incredulous.

Nate looked around the house and to the back door. "Forget it," he said, and attempted to open the back door, which always stuck in the summertime, the jamb swelling around it.

The knock came again, harder. A voice called out and said, "Open up. Police."

"What's going on?" Maddie asked. "What did you do?"

"Nothing," he said, pulling harder at the door.

But it was too late. The police were in the house. Nate was trapped. Three officers rushed to him and pinned him against the door. One put him in handcuffs and began reading him his rights.

Maddie heard: Rape. Lillian Flores. Remain. Silent. Against. Law.

Wait, Maddie thought, *wait*. Nate wasn't a rapist. Maybe one of his friends, but not him. She *knew* him. This was all a mistake. And then she remembered: the night before. Being chased.

"Wait!" Maddie yelled. "He didn't do anything—he couldn't have! The man who lives behind me . . . He broke into my room. He stole things. Last night! Last night he chased me! He *watches* me." She was panicked—everything she was saying coming at once, bleeding together in a kind of word salad. But nobody even seemed to notice that she was talking. They carted Nate out and he looked at her with the most pathetic baby face, like he was either going to cry or laugh and wasn't sure which.

Maddie said again, "Wait! It wasn't him! *I'm telling you!*" But they dragged Nate out the front door and down the walk, and stuffed him in the back of a patrol car.

Brian, who had let the police in, was standing in the living room, watching.

"What's happening?"

"I don't know," Maddie said, staring back at him. It was as though a curtain had been pulled and another world revealed.

"What did he do?"

"Nothing. I mean, I'm not sure." Then: "Do you remember when my room was broken into, and I accused you?"

"Yeah."

"OK, so, last night I went out for a run and a man chased me. He said, 'Where is the money?'"

"What money?"

"The money that was stolen from my room. I used to keep my tips in my drawer, but they kept getting stolen, so I hid them."

"OK..." Brian said. "What does that have to do with your boyfriend?"

"I'm not sure . . . But . . . I went out for a run last night and I was chased—he chased me."

"The man who lives back there?" Brian said, pointing with his thumb.

"Yes."

"I still don't understand what it has to do with—"

"They're saying Nate raped someone! Rape! He couldn't have! But that man," she said again, pointing toward the back of the house, "I bet you he did it." She was nodding now, emphatic. "I have to find him," Maddie said, pacing. "To get him to confess."

"Maddie . . ."

She stopped pacing and looked at him. "What would you do?"

"Tell Dad."

"But Dad's not here."

"Call the police, then."

"Did you see what just happened?" she asked, yelling now. "They wouldn't listen to me!"

"Let's call Dad at work," he said, pulling his cell phone from his pocket.

Maddie watched as Brian waited for someone to pick up. "Can I talk to George Lowe, please? It's his son. OK, thank you." Brian looked up at her. "They're paging him."

Maddie watched Brian and he watched her. It was as though everything depended on whether their father picked up, and what he said and did after.

"Oh, OK. Thank you. No, no message." Brian put the phone back in his pocket. "They said they couldn't find him."

"OK," Maddie said with a sigh. "Go to your room and stay there."

"Just call the police, Maddie. Call the police right now. Here, I will." Brian took his phone back out of his pocket and dialed.

"What do I say?" he asked her.

"Say that a man in this neighborhood chased me last night and that he might have raped her."

"Who?"

"The girl! Lillian Flores!" Maddie said, repeating the name the police had used.

"Hi . . . This is Brian Lowe at 4590 SW Seventh. My sister says she was chased last night by a man who might be a rapist. No, it's . . ." He started. "It's not an emergency, it's just . . . my sister's boyfriend was just arrested and she thinks it was a mistake. For rape. Yes."

Brian looked up at her. "They want to know his name."

"Nate's?"

"No, the guy who chased you."

"I don't know his name, just where he lives."

"She doesn't know his name, just where he lives." He looked up at her. "What's his address?"

Maddie shook her head. "I don't know."

"We know where his house is. Not his address. If you come we can show you." When he got off the phone, Brian said, "They said they were too busy right now to send a car. That because it wasn't an emergency they would have to call us back."

"I can't believe this," Maddie said, falling backward into the couch.

"They'll call back," he said, sitting next to her and taking her hand.

"But what if he rapes somebody else, and what if it's my fault because I didn't call the police last night?"

"It's not your fault. You don't even know if it's really him. Besides . . . What about your boyfriend? What about what just happened?"

"I don't know but . . . I know that he's not a rapist. That he couldn't have done something like that because . . ." Maddie looked up at the ceiling. The truth was, she *didn't* know that Nate didn't do it. She didn't know anything.

She looked at Brian.

"I'm going to go for a walk," she said. "Stay here."

"Where are you going?"

"I just want to see what his address is. So I can call again and give it to them."

"Let me come with you."

"No," she said, getting up. "Stay here and lock the door."

In the garage, Maddie looked for something heavy to protect herself with and found her father's baseball bat from when he played in college. Then, she took off and walked down the street.

Her legs felt like jelly. Her heart pounded. She was more nervous than she had ever been, more even than when she was being chased. She thought about Nate's pleading face. Did he say that he didn't do it? That it was a mistake? Maddie couldn't remember. She thought of coming home to find her room ransacked. She thought of the day her mother stopped coming home, and all the days after.

Before she knew it, she was standing in front of his house. It was an exact copy of her house, except that hers was green and his was blue and badly in need of repair. There was no house number. Not on the garage or mailbox or by the front door. She ran around to the back of the house to make sure that it was his. She saw his yard, and then her yard, separated by a chain-link fence. She saw her bedroom window and understood how easy it would be to look into it at night, to watch her.

Chilled, Maddie walked back around to the front. She climbed the porch steps, her heart pounding. On the porch, she looked into the window and saw him.

She saw the image of him first, on a poster-size painting, and it seemed to be a joke or a dream. A woman was painting him and he sat behind it, not a bad guy but an aristocrat, somebody from a novel.

Maddie locked eyes with him and then with the woman, who gave her a sick, pleading look. The woman yelled: "Call the police! Hurry!"

AMY

THOM ADVANCED TOWARD HER, AND AMY let out a full-throated scream. She picked up the painting and attached easel and hit Thom across the ribs with it, hard as she could. Thom reeled back but didn't fall. He turned and picked up the heavy industrial stool that he had been sitting on and swung it wildly toward her, the steel legs hitting her roughly across the face. Amy fell back in a shock of pain. Then, there was another person in the room—the girl. She came from behind her and hit him with something, hard across the ribs. Thom groaned and reeled backward but came toward the girl, swinging the stool. She hit him once more across the ribs and Thom dropped the stool and fell back. Amy struggled to her feet, grabbed the stool, and hit him with it as hard as she could, the heavy steel back contacting his head. From the floor, Thom lunged at Amy, grabbing her ankle, and Amy hit him again, harder. This time he fell back hard against the floor.

"Run!" Amy told the girl. "Get the neighbors." But the girl just stood there, watching him. "Go!" Amy said.

Amy thought that Thom would rise at any moment, angry and powerful, like in the movies. But he didn't move, and she saw blood start to spread under his head, blooming large and bright, like a rose. His eyes were open, dark and vacant. He was dead. Amy looked at the painting, resting beside him. *You foolish, foolish woman*, she heard him say.

Soon, the girl returned with a man.

"The police are on their way," she said.

"What happened?" the man asked.

"He was going to kill me," Amy said, looking up at them. "And then she came." She pointed at the girl.

"Are you OK?" he asked Amy.

"I don't know," she said. She reached up to touch her face, thinking that she might be bleeding. Her head rang like a bell.

"Are *you* OK?" Amy asked the girl, whose arm was bleeding, and the girl burst into tears.

Soon, the police were there and Amy was in the back of an ambulance, the girl beside her.

"How did you know to come?" Amy asked.

"I didn't," she said, as though in a daze.

In the ambulance, an EMT gave her ice, took her vital signs, and asked her to squeeze his fingers and count backward from ten. At the hospital, they took her vitals again and asked her if she felt up to filling out some forms.

"Not really," she said. "Can I just give you my insurance card and do the rest later?"

"Sure," the nurse said, looking at a chart. "Just tell us who your emergency contact is, so we can let them know you're here."

"My husband's out of the country. Call my mother-in-law, Meredith Espinosa. Her number's in my phone . . ." Amy looked around for her purse and realized that she didn't have it, and that, even if she did, her phone wouldn't be there. "I don't know her number."

"We can look it up. Does she live in the area?"

"Miami."

"No problem. I'm sure there aren't many Espinosas in Miami," the nurse said with a wink.

"I'll have to call you later with my insurance information. I don't have anything with me."

"That's fine. Let's get you ready for your CT. Any chance you're pregnant?"

"No."

"OK. An orderly will be here shortly to take you to radiology."

After her scan, a doctor came in and took her vitals once again.

"Eyes look clear," he said. "How's your head?"

"It fucking hurts."

"Good. That's how it should feel. I'll send a nurse in with some ibuprofen. Now let's look at these films," he said, sliding a film from her CT scan against the light.

"OK, so you see this area right here?" he said, circling the back of his pen around her right cheekbone. "It's what's called a zygomatic fracture. It's a fracture of the cheekbone. The good news is that your fracture is extremely light. See this line?" He asked, turning to look at her.

"Like a crack," Amy said.

"Yes. You're very lucky. It hasn't shattered, and there are no clots. That means you probably won't require surgery. It'll get better on its own.

"Now, I want to keep you here for observation," he said, "just to make sure that you don't have a concussion. Is your family here?"

"I don't think so."

"OK, well, I'll talk to them when they arrive."

"Thank you," Amy said. Then: "Do you know anything about the girl who came in with me? If she's OK?"

"I'm not sure," he said. "Is she family?"

"No," Amy said, looking down into her lap.

"Unfortunately, then, I can't tell you. HIPAA regulations."

Amy sat back in the bed, thinking about what had happened. It was as though the girl had heard the scream that hadn't left her throat.

MADDIE

MADDIE'S ARM HAD BEEN CUT, BLUNTLY, by the stool. At the hospital, a nurse cleaned the cut and stitched it closed. Then, she asked Maddie to bend her arm at her elbow, and asked Maddie to press her hand against the nurse's.

"That hurt?" the nurse asked.

"Yes," Maddie said. "A little."

"I don't think it's broken but I'm going to recommend an X-ray anyway, just to be safe. Any chance you're pregnant?"

"No," Maddie said. "Wait . . ." She hesitated. "Maybe."

"Maybe?" the nurse said, an eyebrow raised.

It hadn't occurred to Maddie until then that she might be, that the constant nausea she'd experienced since yesterday could be anything other than nerves.

"But . . . probably not."

The nurse sighed. "I'll order up a test for you."

"I don't want to take a test . . . I mean, I don't want anyone to know."

"Anyone like?"

"My father, my brother, anyone . . ."

The nurse looked at her chart. "You're fifteen? I'll see what I can do."

The nurse returned a few minutes later with a cup and instructed Maddie to take it into the bathroom to give her a urine sample.

In the bathroom, Maddie paced back and forth, holding the empty cup out in front of her, as though it contained something lethal. Statistically, Maddie thought, the odds were in her favor. She had had sex once. With a condom. Or . . . *probably* with a condom, she couldn't be certain. She looked at herself in the mirror. She barely recognized the person looking back. It was like a dream she couldn't wake from.

Finally, she did it. She peed in the cup. She wiped the cup off with paper towels, washed her hands, and walked back to her room, which was more like a cubby with a curtain.

"I'll take that," the nurse said, and carried the sample away.

Then, as though on cue, her father arrived.

"What happened?" he wanted to know.

Maddie started at the beginning. She told him about the break-in, and about her fears all summer, building up, about not wanting to get anyone in trouble—Charlie or Nate. She was going a mile a minute, the words connecting in a stream that made sense only to her. "When the police came for Nate I was sure they were wrong. That they had the wrong guy. And then I thought about the man who chased me, who always watched me—did I tell you about that? At night, he watched me—I thought that if anyone was a rapist, it must have been him. So I went to his house, to get his address and give it to the police, and . . ." She looked up at her father and saw the darkness on his face, the confusion, and started to cry.

"Who is Charlie?" he asked. "Who is Nate?"

But before she could answer, the nurse appeared in the doorway.

"I brought you a sling," she said, coming in and putting the sling around Maddie's neck and gently tucking her arm into it. "There," she said, "is that comfortable?"

"It's OK," Maddie said.

"Now," the nurse said, looking intently at her, "you're going to be able to go home. Take Tylenol for the pain, but not more than six a day."

"So," Maddie said, "no X-ray?"

"No," the nurse said. "No X-ray."

"Are you sure she's going to be OK?" George asked.

"She should follow up with her general practitioner within a day or so."

"Now, for the stitches . . ." the nurse said, continuing with her instructions.

BACK AT HOME, Maddie was visited by a police officer who took her statement, and an attorney that the airport employees' labor union sent over at her father's request. Then, she took a shower, making sure to cover her bandaged arm with a bag, and got into bed. She closed her eyes and heard the nurse's voice saying "No X-ray," which Maddie took to mean that she was, in fact, pregnant. It felt like the most impossible thing ever.

The next morning, Maddie stayed in her room, the door locked and the curtains drawn, the Planned Parenthood website on the screen in front of her. She read about the abortion pill and what they called "in-clinic" abortions, which, she knew, were like a vacuum sucking up the baby, which she did not want to do. But the pill sounded OK. And, she reasoned, if something could be dislodged with a pill, it wasn't a baby yet, but a cluster of cells, a bacterium or a virus that would ruin her life. She looked down at her stomach. It didn't look different. She held her stomach in her hand. It didn't *feel* different. She decided that she would go out that day to buy a pregnancy test, to be sure. She cleared her browsing history, put her hair in a ponytail, and joined her father and brother in the kitchen.

"How's your arm?" George asked.

"It hurts," she said.

"How'd you sleep?"

She shook her head. "How much trouble am I in?"

"You're not in any trouble, so far as I know."

"But the break-in. I didn't call the police."

"That was stupid but . . . not a crime."

"Oh," Maddie said, dumbfounded but not relieved.

Her father took her hand. "There was no way you could have known."

"He killed two people after that."

"And he almost killed a third," George said. "But because you did another stupid thing . . . he didn't."

"It *was* stupid," she admitted.

He squeezed her hand and let it go. "We all do stupid things."

"Do you?" she asked, searching his face.

"Oh yes," he said.

In the dining room, Maddie mussed Brian's hair. "You're quiet," she said.

"What do you want me to say?"

"I don't know. How about, 'I'm glad you didn't die yesterday'?"

He looked at her wearily. "This wouldn't have happened if you hadn't left the house."

"I know," she said. "But . . . the woman. He was going to kill her."

"You didn't know that," Brian said.

"You're right."

He looked up at her, tears in his eyes. "If anything bad happened to you . . ." He shook his head. "It would be, like, the worst thing ever."

"I know."

"Did you see the news?" he asked.

"No."

"Do you want to know?"

She shook her head. "Not right now."

After breakfast she took a shower, grabbed her backpack, and walked to Walgreens to buy a pregnancy test. She was half expecting to see Charlie standing out front, waiting for a burst of cool air, but he was nowhere to be seen, and she wondered if he had bought a bus ticket, if he was really gone.

Inside Walgreens, she stood in the fertility aisle, looking at the pink and blue boxes. She couldn't believe how expensive the tests were. She'd have to wait on four tables at The Smiling Pig to make up the cost. She thought about stealing one, stuffing it deep into her backpack, and walking out, but there was no way she could get caught stealing a pregnancy test—then, even if she wasn't pregnant, her dad would know what she had done. Finally, she selected one at random and walked up to the front and stood in the back of the long line. She kept wondering what to say to the clerk—an old lady with dyed red hair and drawn-on eyebrows, who, Maddie was sure, would offer up a lecture.

But when it was her turn, the clerk scanned and bagged her box, not even looking at her as Maddie shakily handed over a twenty-dollar bill and received her change. Before leaving the store, Maddie stuffed the box under the change of clothes she always kept with her to change into after work. Then, she walked home.

Safe inside her bathroom, she dug into the bottom of her backpack for the pregnancy test. She tore it open and read the instructions. She stopped when she got to the words "first morning's urine," and turned on the computer to google the phrase. She wanted to get this right. She didn't want to have to buy another fourteen-dollar pregnancy test. She found a page that explained that pregnancy hormones are most concentrated after they have built up in the urine over a period of time. "That makes sense," she said to the screen. She thought of the test she had taken in the hospital, in the middle of the day, and decided that it could have been flawed.

At 5:00 a.m., and after a sleepless night, Maddie went into the bathroom and unwrapped the thin white stick, and peed on it, just like the instructions said. She waited three minutes, watching color move into the results screen, her heart beating so hard that she felt a pulsing in her temples and down her arms. She closed her eyes and prayed, deciding that she would believe in God again if he could just get her out of this. *Please, God, please*, she thought.

After what seemed like three minutes had passed, she looked down at the test, which showed a clear, strong, pink plus sign. Positive. She sighed deeply and began to cry.

"I WANT TO know what happened," she said to Brian in the morning. "Tell me what was on the news."

"You mean what your boyfriend did?"

"Yes."

And then he burst forth with the news. It was as though he had been holding water in his mouth. The moment she asked, he gushed.

"He was at a party with his friends. There was a girl who was drunk and . . ." He paused then and looked up at her.

"Go on," she said.

"They raped her," he whispered, as though he were afraid of the word.

"I don't believe it," Maddie said, shaking her head. "I mean his friends, yes, but . . . not Nate. I know him." But even as she said it she started to doubt herself.

"Dad wants to go to Ocala," he said.

"He does?"

"He's in the garage now, getting the truck ready."

"Really?" she asked, craning her neck to peek through the blinds.

"I don't want to go," he said. "Do you?"

"Not really," she said. "Reminds me too much—"

"Of Mom," he said, finishing her sentence.

Just then, her father came through the door. "You're up," he said to her. "Someone's here to see you."

It was the woman, the painter. She stepped inside and handed Maddie a box of something. "It's pastries," she said. "I wanted to thank you." She shook her head. "I know that a box of puff pastries is inadequate, but . . ."

"It's fine," Maddie said. "Thank you." She put the box on the table and stood to greet the woman. Maddie could tell that she had been pretty, but that her face was bruised and swollen.

"My name is Amy," she said, extending her hand. "Amy Unger."

"Maddie Lowe."

"Here!" Brian said, jumping up, a young gentleman. "You can sit here."

Amy took Brian's seat and Maddie sat back down.

"Are you OK?" Maddie asked.

"Healing," she said. "I have a hairline fracture." She touched her face, tracing her cheek with her index finger. "A crack nobody can see."

"How about you?" Amy asked.

"Um . . ." Maddie said. "My arm is fine. I mean, it hurts, but. It's going to heal."

"So you won't have a scar, then?"

"I don't know." Maddie shrugged. "I didn't ask."

They were silent for a minute. Maddie realized that her father and brother were just standing there, staring at them.

"Anyway," Amy said, pushing up to her feet, "I just wanted to say thank you. If you ever need anything . . ."

Maddie stood up with her. "I'll walk you out," she said.

They walked down the driveway together, awkwardly, saying nothing, and it felt to Maddie like the longest walk ever. At the end of the driveway, they hugged, but when it was time to let go, Maddie found that she couldn't. Instead of releasing the hug, Maddie held it tighter, allowing herself to collapse against Amy, as though Amy were a raft, and Maddie had been swimming a long time. Amy hugged her harder, and Maddie began to cry.

"Are you OK?" Amy whispered.

"No," she whispered back.

AMY

AMY PULLED BACK AND LOOKED AT her, trying to understand what was happening. She felt a sudden responsibility for this girl. A sudden pull toward her.

"Do you want to talk?"

"Yes," Maddie said tentatively.

"Now?" Amy asked, imploringly.

"Yes," Maddie said, her eyes wild. "Let me tell my dad."

She ran up to the house and back. "OK," she said, "I have an hour."

They walked out to the golf course. At first, Maddie said nothing, and Amy realized that she was afraid. So Amy started talking.

"I googled your name," she said. "I read about your mom."

"What about her?"

"Just that there was a search, and that the police decided that she had left on her own accord."

"Oh," Maddie said blankly. There were tears streaming down her face and Amy noticed that she was tensing and releasing her hand.

Amy took her hand and rubbed it.

"My mom died when I was fifteen. So . . . In a way I know what it's like."

"I just want to know where she is," Maddie said. "What happened to her."

"I'm sure," Amy said.

They walked the path around the golf course, hand in hand, a strange new couple. Amy waited for her to say more, but the girl remained quiet and Amy resisted the urge to make small talk.

She had spent the day before at her mother-in-law's, who preached, among other things, the gospel of patience.

"Peter loves you," Meredith had said. This time it was her hands on Amy's, clasping them together, as if in prayer. "We all love you."

They had been sitting together in Meredith's Coral Gables kitchen, two cups of tea steaming between them.

"I wish you would let me make an appointment with my doctor," Meredith had said. "She could help."

Amy shook her head. "The hormones again?"

"Menopause is like *climate change* for the body. Everything goes haywire. The hormones help."

Amy shook her head. "It's unnatural."

"All of this is unnatural! I should be bouncing my grandchild on my knee right now!"

Amy cringed; her eyes welled with tears.

"I'm sorry, I'm sorry, I'm sorry," Meredith whispered, petting Amy's hair with her large and wrinkled hand.

"Peter loves you," she said again. "We all love you."

"Thank you," Amy said softly.

"He'll come back to you when he's ready. But you've got to give him something to come back to. You've got to try to be you again."

This time Amy took Meredith's hand and squeezed it. "Thank you, Meredith."

"For God's sake, Amy, call me Mom."

On the golf course, Maddie said, "I have a secret. It's really bad and I don't know what to do about it."

"OK," Amy said tentatively.

"I found out . . . at the hospital . . . that I'm . . ."

Maddie started to cry. She stopped walking and blinked through the tears. "I'm pregnant," she whispered.

"Oh God," Amy said, horrified for her. She took the girl in her arms again and held her as she sobbed.

"It says on the Planned Parenthood website that I could take a pill and have an abortion, but that I have to get my father's permission first." She sobbed and sobbed.

"It's OK," Amy whispered, rubbing her back. "It's OK."

"I don't know what I'm going to do," Maddie said.

Amy pulled back, looked at her. "Are you afraid of your father?"

"No," Maddie shook her head. "I'm just afraid of him finding out."

"OK," Amy said. She looked at her watch. They only had thirty minutes left. "Do you want to sit down somewhere and talk it out?"

"OK." Maddie nodded.

They walked back to Amy's house and Amy put the kettle on for tea. "We don't have a lot of time. Do you think you could call your dad and tell him that you're here?"

"He wants to get on the road. To take us to Ocala. I don't even know for how long," she said. "Maybe even the rest of the summer."

"Do you know how far along you are?"

"Far along?"

"In the pregnancy."

Maddie shook her head. "No."

"When was your last missed period?"

Maddie shook her head. "I never missed a period."

"Are you sure you're pregnant?"

"They gave me a test at the hospital. The nurse wanted to see if I could get an X-ray. I took another one yesterday."

"And it was positive."

"Yes."

"OK," Amy said, nodding. Her thoughts were racing. "You're probably going to have to tell your father. But you don't have to do it right away. You're probably not very far along."

"OK," Maddie said, sniffling. "Do you have a tissue?"

As Amy walked Maddie back home, she was surprised to discover that she was worried about Maddie as though Maddie were her own child. She wanted to keep her, protect her. She thought about what she would do if she were fifteen and pregnant.

"Don't worry about this right now. Go to Ocala, get some rest. You can tell your dad when you're ready. And . . ." She stopped, she wanted to say something, but she wanted to be careful. "Make sure you know all your options. There are a lot of people out there who would love to adopt and raise your baby."

"Really?" Maddie asked.

"Probably hundreds. Maybe thousands."

"My dad would definitely have to know, then."

"He's definitely going to know anyway," Amy said. "No matter what you decide."

They exchanged numbers, hugged good-bye, and Amy walked home by herself.

When Amy got home, she washed their teacups, her head spinning.

AMY TOOK FOUR Advil and climbed into bed with an ice pack. Her face was purple and terribly swollen. She'd barely slept the last two nights, the first at the hospital, the second at her mother-in-law's, in Pete's childhood bed. In a day, she'd googled everything she could about everyone involved: Thom, Vera, Maddie, Maddie's mother. Adel Minor, Angela Greene, and Helen Johnson, whom, it seemed, Thom had mistakenly targeted; she had moved to the neighborhood in the past decade and couldn't have, as Thom said, taunted his mother in the 1960s. She thought about the family who lived in the house where Thom had squatted. She'd googled the address and saw that the family had been foreclosed on and forcibly removed the summer before, the house sitting empty until Thom moved in. The *Miami Herald* reported that police had found several instances of disturbed earth in the house's backyard and various things that Thom had buried—bloodied clothes and shoes, and three identical pairs of gloves—in shallow holes in and around an overgrown flower bed. Investigators were currently testing the pieces of evidence for DNA. "Even without DNA," the Seven Springs Police Department's information officer told the *Herald*, "the case is pretty solid. It's been a tough summer, but we're pretty confident that we've got our guy."

"It's been a tough summer," Amy repeated over and over after she'd read the line. It was an understatement, to be sure, but she couldn't blame the information officer for not having appropriate words. Sometimes, she thought, there are no words.

When she woke again, the house was dark. Amy was alarmed. *What time was it?* she wondered. *Had she locked the door?* She pictured Thom in her kitchen, pouring batter into a hot pan. But of course he wasn't. He had been killed and carted away, like the women before him.

She sat up in bed and waited for her eyes to adjust to the light. It was 1:00 a.m. Somewhere in San Juan, her husband was sleeping; she wondered how soundly. She wondered why he hadn't called. What he must be thinking.

THE NEXT DAY she returned to her studio. There were three paintings in total, not including the one she had done of Thom, which, she hoped, she would get to keep once the investigation was over. She had spoken to a lawyer while in the hospital, who told her that the police were unlikely to bring charges against her—she had killed Thom in self-defense and the girl had corroborated the story. It was clean. The lawyer had said that: "clean." He might as well have said, "This is easy money for me."

Amy sat in the garage, staring at the paintings. She wasn't sure what she would do with them. It felt wrong to try to sell them, to try to use them as a springboard into her art career. But they were the best work she'd ever done. It felt equally wrong that they be wasted.

She had always planned two more, one with Adel on the floor, dead or dying, and another of the taped outline of Adel's body in the empty room, the afternoon light. But Amy was tired. She had lost the momentum she had had in the beginning, having been seduced by the story, the mystery of it. Still, she felt she had to see it through. And so she spent the next week sitting on her patio, sketching Adel. As she did, she got to know the woman, a pseudofictional version of her, anyway, the Adel from her imagination coming sharply into focus. She gave her thick calves and ankles; bony, wrinkled hands; a bruised and bloodied face. Amy decided that she would paint Adel's face as though it had been muddled, like crushed berries, adding an impressionist's blur to the otherwise realist series.

A week later, Amy was in her studio, transferring the sketch to canvas, when Maddie walked in.

"Hi," she said, surprised to see her. "How are you?"

"Much better," Maddie said.

"Did you tell your father?"

"Not yet," Maddie said.

"And yet you feel better?" Amy asked, surprised.

"I told my grandma," Maddie said. "She told me she'd stand by me no matter what."

"That's great," Amy said.

"It feels funny, like there's this great big balloon over me, waiting to pop."

"Really?" Amy asked, considering her.

"Is that weird?"

"That's probably how I would feel," Amy said.

"Why don't you have kids?" Maddie asked.

"Why don't I have kids?" Amy repeated. "It's, um . . . it's complicated."

"I'm sorry," Maddie said. She seemed to look past Amy, to the sketch. "I'm bothering you. I'm sorry. I'll go."

"No," Amy said, shaking her head. "Don't go. Do you want to come in for some tea or something?"

"OK," Maddie said. "No caffeine, though."

Inside, they sat together at Amy's dining room table.

"My grandma told me a story about my parents that I didn't know," Maddie said. "My mom was still in high school when she got pregnant with me. I knew they were young, but I didn't know that. You don't really think of your parents as people, you know?"

"Totally," Amy said, looking across the table at her. It occurred to Amy that Maddie's mother would be close to her age. It seemed alien to think that she could have a teenage daughter.

"Anyway, it was a scandal. My dad's a few years older than my mom. And when you're a teenager, a few years is a lot. It made me realize that my dad can't be mad at me. Or ... he *can* be mad but, if he thinks about it, I'm just like my mom was. And he loves my mom, so ..."

Maddie looked down into her tea. Amy's heart broke for her. She thought, *Don't have that baby, don't become your mom.* But of course it was more complicated than that. Everything is.

"I was thinking that I might give the baby up for adoption," Maddie said, and Amy felt something in her lift.

BERNARD

THE NIGHT OF LESLIE'S FUNERAL, BERNARD returned home with Maryanne and sat with her on her screened-in porch. It had been a hard day, the fourth in the string of funerals they'd attended that summer, and he was exhausted from the emotional weight. There was a part of him that wanted to go home and melt into his Barcalounger and get drunk on television and cheap burritos, as he always had. But there were too many memories at home and he was tired of his memories. It occurred to him, sitting there with Maryanne, nursing a cup of tea and staring out at her yard as the dusk settled into the garden, that he didn't have to go back. He could sell his house. He could move in with her. They could be together, if only for companionship.

As if reading his mind, Maryanne said, "You can stay here as long as you like. You don't have to go right away."

"OK," he said, and he reached over to take her hand, which she let him squeeze. He wanted to say more. He wanted to say "thank you" and he wanted to tell her that he felt like he'd aged a thousand years that summer. He wanted to tell her about the ghosts that lived in his house, Irene and Vera and now, maybe, Vera's son too. Instead, he said, "I feel like it's my fault, what happened."

"What do you mean?"

"If you trace this summer back a long way, it leads to me."

"And a lot of other men."

"Thanks for reminding me," he said, taking his hand away.

"What I mean is, it's not your fault. It's not even Vera's fault. And that's as charitable as I'll ever be toward her. Plus," she said, "if this summer hadn't happened, Leslie would have died alone."

"That's cold comfort," he said.

"Yes," Maryanne admitted. "Yes, it is."

Leslie had had a stroke, they later found. There were warning signs, but April didn't recognize them. At the funeral, she'd fretted over this, wringing her hands, saying, "I didn't know, I didn't know, I didn't know." What difference does it make? Bernard wanted to say but didn't. Because, of course, it made a big difference to April.

"Well," Maryanne said, slowly getting up from her chair, "I'm going to bed."

"OK," he said. "I'm going to stay out here for a while. Enjoy the view."

"Don't forget to lock the door when you come in."

"Of course," he said. If they had learned anything that summer, it was that.

He thought again about the prospect of going home. He wondered what Irene would think about him staying there. About him finding someone else to spend his life with. He thought about the night they were married. The dark church and both of their families, how afraid he was, standing at the altar, waiting for her. And how pretty Irene looked with little plastic pearls in her hair, a veil over her face. That night, after they made love, he helped her take the pearls out, one by one, collecting them in the hotel ashtray. Everything she did that night amazed him—the pearls in her hair, the almost too-delicate lace of her slip, revealed to him piece by piece, moment by moment as her wedding gown dropped to her knees and he lifted her out of it; the light in her eyes as she turned around to him and whispered "husband."

But God, he was a louse. Didn't deserve her. Didn't deserve anyone. But what now? What about Maryanne? She had said something about leaving. Going home. He didn't ever want to go home, didn't want to go back to all his memories. He wanted to stay here, with her. He wanted to listen to Gershwin on her iPod and make zucchini pie.

He wanted to twirl her around the room in her pretty purple dress. He wanted for the two of them to be together the way that he and Irene might have been together if she hadn't died.

It was decided: in the morning, he would ask Maryanne to marry him.

WHEN HE WOKE the next morning, Bernard was still tired. He didn't hear Maryanne, or smell breakfast cooking in the other room, but he was sure it was late, and that he should be up. He moved slowly, stiffly. There must be something wrong with him, he thought. His limbs were cement, his head fog.

He found Maryanne outside, cutting cat palms with a pair of shears. She smiled at him, asked how he was feeling.

He hadn't realized until then that his hands were shaking. He was sick or nervous. He said: "Fine, I'm fine."

She smiled at him and went back to her work.

"Maryanne," he heard himself say.

She looked up at him, blinking, her sun hat casting a shadow over her face.

"I wonder . . ." He was trembling, he felt himself fall to his knees. "If you might like for me to stay here . . . permanently. If you might," he continued, "like to marry me."

She frowned, and reached out to take his hand, but couldn't reach him, and didn't move to try. "I'm sorry," she said, frowning. "But I like my life. I like being alone."

"OK," he heard himself say. He was still on his knees and would need help getting up. He fell forward onto his hands to try to leverage himself back to standing.

"Here," she said, "let me help you."

Maryanne put one hand on his back and one under his armpit and heaved him up.

"You're stronger than you look," he said.

"And you're heavier than you look."

The moment called for laughter, but he couldn't laugh. He felt awkward, defeated. "I should probably go."

"I meant it when I said you could stay longer. It's been a hard summer. There's no need to return to normal right away."

Bernard nodded but said nothing. He was embarrassed, his stomach sour. He wanted her normal to be his normal too. But there was no need to say it.

"I am fond of you," she said. It was a kindness, a consolation prize.

"I should go," he said.

"OK," she said, and looked down at the cat palms she had collected. "Thank you for staying here with me. Thank you for everything. Bernard?"

She was waiting for him to look at her, but he couldn't. He didn't want her to see that he was crying, but it was too late. Tears were streaming down his face.

MARYANNE OFFERED TO drive him home, but he told her he preferred to walk. He collected his things in a knapsack, stuffing even his suit into the bag. He made up the bed he had been sleeping in; the result was sloppy, though he had tried to make it look nice. He knew that she would come behind him anyway and strip the bed and wash the sheets, so his work was futile, but he wanted to do it—wanted to prove that he could make things the way that she would like them.

They said an awkward good-bye, and she hugged him, patting his back as she would a cousin or a brother, a friend.

He shouldn't have asked her what he asked her. He didn't know what had gotten into him—desperation, stupidity, or maybe even senility. He was almost eighty—his birthday was less than a month away—maybe he really was going senile, saying things he didn't or couldn't mean. Truth was, he didn't want another wife. One was enough.

The day was overcast. There was thunder rolling in from somewhere, making every step he took seem more and more ominous.

But, he realized, there was nothing bad that could happen to him. Everything had already happened. The rest was just the credits rolling on his life. And as he walked, he imagined the other pseudocouples that had formed that summer also separating, going off into separate houses to live separate lives once again.

He made it home before the rain began, and sat in the tub while his house was bathed in small, silver raindrops, the back of his head resting on the cold blue tile. He closed his eyes and saw Leslie, lying on her bathroom floor. He saw Helen, Angela, Adel, and Vera too. He saw Thom Johnson—the old photo of him they'd been using on the news. He looked more like his father than his mother. And if Bernard had seen him on the street this summer, he hadn't recognized him. And if he *had* recognized him, he wouldn't have said hello.

ON THE DAY before his birthday, Bernard never got out of bed. He was too weak, too tired. It was here, finally. He opened and closed his eyes, nodding in and out, dreaming of black-and-white movies and theaters that had long ago burned to the ground. The hemline of a woman's dress. His wife's neck, long and white. Snow cones. And his kids on the days they were born, pink and screaming and ready for the world.

He was ready for the next world. Whatever it was. Whatever hell or joy or nothingness. He could taste it—like metal on his tongue.

Bernard took a few quick, desperate breaths, and released.

AMY

AMY WORKED FURIOUSLY THOSE NEXT SEVERAL weeks, eager to finish the series and start the next, which, she decided, would be scenes from her mother's death. Just that week, she sketched from her memory, and drew the scene from her childhood living room from the night her mother died. Sketching her sister, father, and aunt the way she remembered them then, not as she had seen them that night, as LSD-fueled fun house versions of themselves. She sketched herself at fifteen, sitting on her aunt's lap in a big taffeta dress. The scene was her origin story, just as the photograph was Thom's.

But she put the project aside in order to finish *The Murder of Adel Minor*, which would culminate, as planned, with the taped outline of Adel's body. At one point, Amy thought she might paint herself into the last image, lying next to Adel's outline as she had the day she broke into Adel's house, but she decided against it. It wasn't her story, after all, and she no longer felt a kinship with Adel. She was alive, for one. And at the beginning of her life. At the beginning of the next step, anyway, which would be the best yet.

She had had calls from gallerists from as far away as Zurich who were interested in representing her. But she took their names and numbers down and told them she would call them when the series was complete. For now, she spent nights and weekends in her studio, her hands stained with the palette of Adel's living room.

She was in her studio one Saturday, putting the final touches on the final painting, when Glen walked through her open studio doors.

"Knock, knock," he said.

"Hi," she said, not looking up. In the weeks since the kidnapping, Glen had become like a brother—checking in on her and even bringing her food.

"Kenny and Steven are on their way over. We're taking Kenny's boss's boat out. We thought you might need a distraction."

"I don't need a distraction," she said, but thought about the deep blue water and the sunlight on her skin.

"We *all* need a distraction, Amy," he said.

"I want to get this finished before Pete comes home."

He stood in front of the canvas beside her.

"You've been living in this moment too long. You're alive. It's time to move on."

"I am moving on," she said, a little hurt.

"Come with us. I won't take no for an answer."

Amy sighed. "Fine. Yes."

AN HOUR LATER, they were motoring down the Intracoastal Waterway, past Port Everglades, and into open ocean. The waterways were clogged with boats—good-size yachts, like the one they were on, and small sailboats and motorboats, majestic catamarans, and powerboats destined to race one another the moment they got far enough from shore. There were throngs of women on the bows of almost all of them—tanned, bikini-clad women who existed, it seemed, to drape like seaweed on the bows of boats. Amy wished that Pete was there. She'd like to put her arm around his waist and lean into him, pointing out everything she saw. But she still had another week without him. After that, he'd be home for good, and they'd try to start over again.

"So, Amy, where would you like to go?" Kenny was asking in his smooth baritone.

Go? She thought they were already there. "I don't know," she said, turning around, "Africa?"

"Not Puerto Rico? Arrive like pirates, kidnap your wayward husband."

"He's not wayward. He's working."

"I still say he should have come back right away," Steven said.

"He wanted to and I told him not to. I don't want to be babied. His project's almost over. He'll come home then."

Carlos emerged from the hull with a bottle and five glasses.

"Veuve Clicquot!" Glen exclaimed, comically affecting a French accent.

Carlos peeled back the foil and it glinted in the light.

"What are we celebrating?" Amy asked.

"Everything all the time," Glen said.

Thirty minutes later, they dropped anchor. The guys each took their shirts off and, one by one, cannonballed into the ocean. "Come on, Amy!" they called, treading water in the shadow of the boat. Amy wanted more than anything to be the type of person who could dive off a boat and into open ocean. She wanted, if only for a day, to be like one of those boat women, so comfortable that the structures that held them would not give out.

She shielded her eyes and felt the sun on her shoulders, the salt spray on her face. Amy climbed up on the bow and looked down at the water glinting in the sunlight, each glint and sparkle saying *yes, yes, yes.* She took a running leap and jumped, arms and legs running in slow motion as she was, for a brief moment, suspended in air.

THE FOLLOWING WEEK, Amy was in her studio again, this time scrubbing her palette clean after having finished the series that morning, when a cab pulled into the driveway. Amy looked up to see Pete emerge from the car. Her hands started to shake and she wiped them off as best she could, and walked out to the driveway to greet him.

"I thought your flight didn't get in 'til tomorrow," she said.

"I couldn't wait."

He took her into his arms and kissed her. Then, he pulled back to look at her face.

"Does it still hurt?"

"Yes, but not as bad as before."

"My mom said you looked like a plum. I'd say you're more a green apple."

"You missed my plum days," she said.

They kissed again and the cab pulled away.

"You smell so good," he said.

"I smell like turpentine."

"Right," he said. "So good."

She hugged him again. "I'm glad you're here. I'm sorry for . . . everything."

"*I'm* sorry for everything," he said.

"What do you have going on in there?" he asked, looking over her shoulder and into the garage.

"Cleaning up," she said. "Finished the last one today."

"I don't want to interrupt you."

"Please," she said, "I'm not gonna let you out of my sight."

LATER, AFTER AMY had finished scrubbing the paint out of her cuticles, Maddie came by. They were supposed to have dinner together that night, but she was early.

"You just missed Pete," Amy said. "He came back a day early. He just ran to the store to pick up ingredients for dinner."

"Oh!" Maddie said. "We can do dinner another time, then. I'm sure you guys want to be alone."

"We can be alone another time," Amy said. "I want him to meet you."

"OK," Maddie said. "I want to meet him too."

"Do you want some tea?" Amy asked.

"I was actually wondering if you wanted to go for a walk with me. My neighbor died. They're having a yard sale."

"What kind of stuff do they have over there?"

Maddie shrugged. "Mostly old stuff."

"Who was it? That died, I mean."

"His name was Bernard. He was nice but, you know, old."

"How did he die?"

Maddie shrugged, looked at Amy with a face that seemed to say, *duh*. "He was old."

"Right," Amy said, smiling. "Let me get my keys."

They walked around the block to Bernard's. There were a few people picking through what had been arranged on card tables—table linens and place settings, stacks of dishes, and a pile of milk glass serving bowls. There was clothing on racks, but nothing anybody would want. There was a large ceramic planter filled with ancient gardening tools, an Exercycle, and a half dozen fishing poles. There were old avocado-colored kitchen appliances—a KitchenAid mixer, and a Silex coffee percolator. There was a set of walkie-talkies and an old IBM electric typewriter. There was a silver wig on top of a Styrofoam head. Amy wondered if these people were kidding themselves—who would want all this old crap? But one by one, things were disappearing, and Amy watched as a boy who looked about twelve paid a dollar for an old cap gun.

"Look," Maddie said, taking her wrist and pulling her over to a pair of vintage bicycles. One was silver, the other white. "We should get them," Maddie said.

Maddie had a good eye. The bikes were probably the best things there. "How much?"

"Doesn't say."

Amy found the man who looked to be running things. He was in his fifties and was probably Bernard's son. "How much for the bikes?" Amy asked.

"Those?" He shook his head. "I don't know. Twenty?"

"Twenty," Amy called back to Maddie.

Maddie looked at the bikes, seemed to work it over in her mind, and then ran across the street to her house.

"I'm getting the white one," Maddie said when she returned.

"OK," Amy said. "I'll get the silver one."

"It's a boy's bike," Maddie told her.

"That's OK," Amy said. "Maybe I'll give it to a boy."

They purchased the bikes and inflated the tires with the manual pump that was also for sale. "Let's take them for a spin," Amy said.

They rode out to the golf course, and Amy noticed how the strong afternoon sunlight seemed to fill every available space. It filled the canopies of trees, the cracks in the street, the spaces between blades of grass and the impossibly thin slivers of palm. It illuminated the messy tendrils of the laurel oaks, making the tops of the trees look almost white, almost on fire. Light spilled over the outstretched arms of the araucaria pines, filling the space between each needle with whitest light. Amy was overwhelmed by it—at once elated and crushed. She wanted to capture it. To fill cups with it to paint, or swallow. To absorb it, and reflect it out again.

Amy shook her head and swallowed hard. She thought: the beauty of the world will break your heart, and put it back together again.

THE END

ACKNOWLEDGMENTS

I WANT TO THANK BARBARA POELLE, Brita Lundberg, and everyone at IGLA for their enthusiasm and support; and Tara Parsons, Isabella Betita, Shelly Perron, and everyone at Touchstone for their editorial insight.

Special thanks to my early readers, Sarah Doyle, Diane Mooney, Jennifer Monteaux, Athena Ponushis, Stephanie Woolley-Larrea, Meredith Tucker, and especially Elizabeth Vondrak, who pulls double duty as my best friend and best reader.

Thanks to Lynne Barrett for sharing her brilliance with me, and everyone at the creative writing program at FIU, for simply being there.

My deepest gratitude to my mom, my first ever reader and editor, and my oldest friend; and to my grandparents, Elaine and Herb MacLellan, who let me come live with them when I was finishing my master's thesis and who will recognize at least one detail from Bernard's life; and my father, for his love and support.

And to my dear husband, Chris, my brightest light. Thank you.

ABOUT THE AUTHOR

LAUREN DOYLE OWENS is originally from Maryland. She is a graduate of Florida International University's MFA program, and lives near Fort Lauderdale, Florida, with her husband, Chris. *The Other Side of Everything* is her first novel.

THE OTHER SIDE OF EVERYTHING

LAUREN DOYLE OWENS

This reading group guide for The Other Side of Everything *includes an introduction, discussion questions, ideas for enhancing your book club, and a Q&A with author Lauren Doyle Owens. The suggested questions are intended to help your reading group find new and interesting angles and topics for your discussion. We hope that these ideas will enrich your conversation and increase your enjoyment of the book.*

INTRODUCTION

IN THIS SUSPENSEFUL literary debut, three generations of neighbors in a Florida neighborhood find their lives intersecting in the aftermath of a murder.

Bernard White is a reclusive, curmudgeonly widower. When his neighbor is murdered, he emerges from his solitude to reconnect with his fellow octogenarians.

Amy Unger is an artist and cancer survivor who begins to paint imagined scenes from the murder. But when her paintings prove to be too realistic, her neighbors grow suspicious, and she soon finds herself catching the attention of the police.

And then there's Maddie Lowe, a teenage waitress whose mother recently abandoned the family. As Maddie struggles to maintain the appearance of normal teenage life, she finds herself drawn to the man the police say is the killer.

As they navigate their increasingly dangerous and tumultuous worlds, Bernard, Amy, and Maddie begin to uncover the connections between them—and the past and present—in a novel that ultimately proves the power of tragedy to spark renewal.

TOPICS & QUESTIONS FOR DISCUSSION

1. The author opens the novel with a gruesome scene. What details stood out to you and why?

2. What do you think about Amy's reaction to news about Adel's death? What does this tell you about her character?

3. Describe Bernard's general outlook. How does he view his past?

4. What kind of losses are Bernard, Amy, and Maddie dealing with? How does each character cope?

5. How did Amy's cancer affect her relationship with her husband? Who's to blame? How would you describe their final conversation before he left for San Juan?

6. During her cancer treatments, Amy avoided a certain activity. What did she do and what sparked her inspiration to begin again? Do you consider the source of her inspiration normal?

7. Bernard attends Adel's funeral, sees the women gathered there, and thinks, *"It always seemed . . . that they had a heavier burden to carry."* What does this line mean? Given what you know about Bernard, what does this thought say about him?

8. How would you describe Bernard's feelings for and actions toward Vera? Can you understand his reasoning? Do you think Vera feels the same about him as he does for her? Why or why not?

9. A police detective casually questions Maddie at The Smiling Pig. How would you describe what happens to Maddie's memory during that scene?

10. After watching Adel's house for so long, Amy decides to break in. What is she trying to find, and what does she actually see when she's there? What was your reaction to Amy's actions in that chapter?

11. Who are the "originals"? What do they devise at their neighborhood meeting, and do you believe this system will be effective?

12. Bernard stays with Maryanne. How does this arrangement begin to change Bernard? What does it make him think about?

13. What do you think about the party scene with Maddie and Nate? Why was it shown to us? How did that scene affect your impression of Nate?

14. Review the scene where Amy begins to paint her captor. How does her impression of this person change? How would you describe the captor?

ENHANCE YOUR BOOK CLUB

1. Think back to when you were Maddie's age. What were you like? Do you understand her actions with Nate? With Charlie?

2. The characters in *The Other Side of Everything* are haunted by their pasts and memories. What continues to haunt you and how do you cope with these feelings?

3. There are many types of transgressions in this novel. Are any forgivable? Which ones would you say are forgivable and which ones are unforgiveable?

4. In reaction to the murders in the neighborhood, Bernard begins to interact with his neighbors, who all seem to lead separate lives now. Try reconnecting with your neighbors and introduce yourself to new ones.

CONVERSATION WITH LAUREN DOYLE OWENS

Q: **You did a remarkable job setting up the neighborhood and letting us see all of its mundane activities. But you're also adept at infusing the setting with a sinister atmosphere. What led you to choose this type of setting?**

A: I had always wanted to tell a story set in a neighborhood, where people who have seemingly nothing in common have to come together in some way. The year 2008 was a devastating one for me personally and for our country at large. The housing crisis hit my neighborhood west of Fort Lauderdale, Florida, particularly hard. As I struggled to cope with my own losses, I started to look around and see loss everywhere. People were being foreclosed on and houses were being abandoned. The sinister details in the novel were lifted right from that time. I don't think there's a single detail from the novel that I didn't observe somewhere. I had the idea to set up a tripod and take pictures of the abandoned houses around here, but I didn't have the guts to go through with it. Instead, I sat at home and wrote about what I saw.

Q: **We'd love to know about your writing process behind this book. How long did it take for you to get the story on the page? When you began writing, did you know how the story would end?**

A: The novel took six years from start to finish. I was writing from points of view of the characters in 2009, and later that year, I flew to Austin to produce some artist interviews at Austin City Limits. I plotted the entire novel between the time it took to fly from Fort Lauderdale to Austin. The remaining five years were spent just trying to get the story right.

Q: **Do you find that there are themes that recur in your writing?**

A: Oh yes. I've struggled with depression and loneliness throughout my life, and I think that a lot of my work has been about what it's like to move through life as a depressed person. At the same time, more recent issues I've been grappling with in my personal life—including whether or not to have a child and what it means to be a mother—have colored my work. The challenge, I think, is writing about these things in a way that doesn't weigh down the story.

Q: **Your characters are of all different ages. Why did you choose these perspectives? Did you have a hard time writing from the perspective of a teenager? An octogenarian?**

A: There's a universality between people of different ages, and even different genders, that we forget. We, or maybe the media, put ourselves in different buckets—I'm a woman, I'm a millennial, I'm a Sagittarius—therefore I must think about things a certain way. Underneath all of that, though, I'm a human being, and human beings are remarkably similar. I really think that with a certain amount of empathy and imagination, anyone can put themselves in the lives of others. As a writer, I just have more practice.

Q: Memory comes up many times throughout the novel. What's your fascination with memory?

A: I think it's more of a fascination with the past than a fascination with memory. And not even the past so much as the factors that contributed to the worlds and the lives around us. I'm always wondering *How did we get here?* or *Why are we this way?* To answer that, you have to go back to the beginning, or *some* beginning. I have a very good memory, so I'm able to go back to see my own defining moments, and I guess being able to see them is helpful as a writer, because I can more easily imagine someone else's.

Q: What were your favorite moments in the novel?

A: To get home, I drive over the bridge where Maddie lost her virginity. That entire scene—the lights of the airplanes coming in for landing, the slow-moving canal, the force of the cars as they drove past—is something I relive, at least emotionally, each time I'm in the car driving home. It's almost as if, for me, the ghosts of Maddie and Nate are still under that bridge.

Q: What are your reading tastes? What are you reading right now? Do you have a writer you admire?

A: I read widely, but particularly love literary fiction and memoir. I just read *The Fact of a Body* by Alexandria Marzano-Lesnevich and it really blew me away.

Q: What do you think happens to the characters after the end of the book?

A: I like to think that the characters who come together at the end of the book stay together, that they form a kind of family, that they're able to be for each other what each one was missing at the beginning of the novel.

Q: What's next? Are you working on anything new?

A: I'm working on a novel about a trio of women who don't yet know that they are sisters. Their lives are very different from one another's, so it explores the choices that women make, and how they live with those choices.